Little Boys Come From The Stars

Translated from the French
by Joël Réjouis and Val Vinokurov

Little Boys
Come From
The
Stars

EMMANUEL
DONGALA

Farrar, Straus and Giroux • New York

Farrar, Straus and Giroux
19 Union Square West
New York 10003

Distributed in Canada by Douglas & McIntyre Ltd.
Printed in the United States of America
First published in 1998 by Le Serpent à Plumes, Paris,
as *Les petits garçons naissent aussi des étoiles*
First published in the United States by Farrar, Straus and Giroux
First American edition, 2001

Library of Congress Cataloging-in-Publication Data
Dongala, Emmanuel Boundzéki, 1941–
    [Petits garçons naissent aussi des étoiles. English]
    Little boys come from the stars : a novel / Emmanuel Dongala ;
translated from the French by Joël Réjouis and Val Vinokurov.
        p.   cm.
    ISBN 0-374-18496-8 (alk. paper)
    I. Réjouis, Joël. II. Vinokurov, Val. III. Title.
PQ3989.2.D6 P4813 2001
843'.914—dc21

                                                    00-045610

Designed by Thomas Frank

Little Boys
Come From
The Stars

I was almost never born.

I almost never got to chase after a ray of light trying to catch it, almost never discovered those strange regions where dreams come to life and play before scampering along to sleeping minds. I almost never felt Aledia's breast behind the lantana bushes that scratched us as we passed. Honestly, I was almost never born. Maman left the hospital with me still in her womb.

She always swore up and down that she didn't do it on purpose, forever repeating in her meek voice: How could I have imagined, Matapari my son, that, after the twins came out of my belly, there was a third child tucked away somewhere in there, in the depths of my gut? The doctor was the first to ask Maman to leave her hospital bed and go home, and Mama Kossa the midwife assured her that it was all over and that she could go; then Papa, at once proud and worried about having brought twins into the world (troublesome children, hard to raise), had also rushed her back home. That's how she went home, forgetting me in her belly.

From what my uncle Boula Boula told me, it was only two

whole days later, while sitting on a bamboo stool washing the twins' diapers, that Maman felt pains strangely similar to the ones she'd felt during labor. She ignored them as much and as long as she could, thinking it was a passing post-birth thing; she had no experience in these matters since this had been her first time giving birth. She left the diapers alone and lay down on the foam pad she had set over a mat on the living room floor. Nothing doing, she was still hurting. No doubt about it, these were the contractions of a delivery—though it seemed impossible. By the ancestors' memory, no one ever heard of a woman carrying more than two children. In a panic, she called for Mama Kossa, the official village midwife.

Mama Kossa arrived lively as ever, always in a hurry as if chased by the spirit of an ancestor who had died abruptly, displacing behind her huge volumes of air, which, momentarily imprisoned in the vast folds of her boubou, then escaped in big violent gusts worthy of a Category 5 tropical storm. And yet, like the eye of the storm, her face always stayed calm and serene with its jet black eyes whose shiny depths scared off owls, drove sorcerers to suicide, and protected newborns. She brought that mystical pouch she always had whenever she visited a woman about to give birth, a bag that contained everything: herbs, medicinal plants, liniments, disposable syringes, vials, powders, and even antibiotics, since she practiced both traditional and modern medicine. She knew how to prepare potions to drive off evil spirits, just as she knew how to set up an IV drip. On top of her indisputable knowledge, Mama Kossa had a certain prestige in the eyes of the locals that the other midwives didn't, because she came from far away. No one knew where exactly. She had settled here twenty or thirty years ago, and many thought she was from Oubangui-Chari, from one of those tribes along a northern branch of one of the tributaries of the mighty Congo, from one of those tribes that had mastered forces our people here had no idea about, tribes that had nothing to learn even from the Pygmies. And since no one knew exactly which tribe she came from, local sorcerers and fetish makers feared her, and woe to the evil eye that dared go after a child delivered by Mama Kossa!

And so she came like a whirlwind. She knelt, wiped Maman's sweaty forehead, and gave her a probing look. I have pains, Maman said, moaning. I feel like I'm going to give birth again. Nonsense, Mama Kossa firmly replied. Have you ever seen a woman carry three, four children like a litter of pups? But Maman continued to protest forcefully and writhe in pain. Suddenly, Mama Kossa thought again, felt Maman's lower abdomen, then brought her hand just above the belly button, spread her palm, and began to concentrate. At that moment, I must have given a nice kick to make my presence felt, because according to witnesses (since I was still tucked away in the folds of my mother's womb), Mama Kossa's legendary calm face became a hurricane: Incredible! . . . she's going into labor . . . Never saw such a thing . . . Holà Maria, run quick, fetch wood, and make a big fire to heat up a big bucket of water . . . Mabiala, you run to the hospital, go tell the doctor that the teacher's wife is having a third child . . . No no, he won't believe you, he'll send you packing, tell him instead that Mama Kossa is with a woman whose water's broken and who may give birth on the road if we go to the hospital . . . She was digging in her bag as she was talking, pulling out compresses, flasks, needles. Yengo, run and get her husband, quick, tell him that his wife, the mother of his twins, needs her husband straightaway.

You have to figure luck was not on my side, because I had picked the wrong day to set my eyes on this world. It was the fifteenth of August: not only was this date important in itself as our national holiday, but it was August 15, 1980, the twentieth anniversary of our Independence, which made the holiday more than exceptional.

It was my uncle who helped me understand the importance of this day of rejoicing in a country where everything was an excuse to party. He explained to me that our country had once been occupied by white people, who had arrived here by accident on ships whose sails had been pushed by the tropical winds toward the African coast. The white people then began systematically scouring our coastland and even our inland regions, stealing people and selling them as slaves; that's why there are blacks in the United States today, and why Cassius Clay, alias Muhammad Ali, was born in Louisville, Kentucky, and not in Poto-Poto, a neighborhood in Brazzaville. Then there were missionaries who came to chase our ancestors out of their graves, out of the groves and rivers, and out of the huts they inhabited, to replace them with Jesus Christ, the Bible, and the cross; and the armed men who came along with them and installed themselves. In these parts, they were French. They ruled over us, ran the country, exploited us, taught us their language, sent us to their schools, and gave us new ancestors called Gauls. That's why we still speak French, love French food, and still like to spend our vacations in France, even if these days it is easier to get a visa to the moon than to that country.

These French so exploited us that twenty years ago we revolted against this exploitation called colonialism and became independent, that is, masters of our destiny. But since we couldn't get rid of everything they'd brought with them, things we'd lived with for a century, we made our ancestors come back while keeping Jesus, the Bible, and the cross; we kept their language along with ours, as well as their clothing, red wine, Brie, and baguettes. It was as if we were reborn from two roots.

Unfortunately, the three or four leaders who took over from

the French kept obeying these same French and other whites, having sold out to what my uncle called imperialism and neocolonialism. That's why the young military men overthrew these leaders in a series of coups d'état, killed them off, and took over. But these army men weren't any better, and so other army men plotted and overthrew them, and so on and so forth, until this day of my unexpected birth on the twentieth anniversary of the day that one of these military men (again, according to my uncle, who told me all these things) set up a "revolutionary" system based on something called scientific socialism, with Uncle Boula Boula serving for a time as one of its most important officials. He didn't tell me what that meant exactly but explained enough to indicate that this was something completely new, a definitive break with slavery, colonialism, neocolonialism, imperialism. They changed our country's name, anthem, and flag, and our models became countries called Communist. A star, hammer, and hoe were put on the flag turned crimson. "People's" was added to the name of every state institution, including the National Library. Folks couldn't pray, read, sing, think, or travel without the prior approval of the Chief of State, by virtue of the surveillance agencies he controlled. In short, red became the new fetish: people were to die for the red flag, one had to be red in order to be thought competent at work; the national soccer team, as well as the public squares and high schools, were afflicted with red.

So it was the twentieth red anniversary that was being celebrated, when I, a forgotten child, was struggling heroically to leave my mother's belly.

Our house, it must be said, was pretty far from the official district buildings, especially the town hall, where the festivities took place, so Yengo arrived there out of breath, his feet dirty and a bit swollen, since he'd chosen to run off without his plastic sandals. Although there was a huge crowd, Papa wasn't hard to find.

He was standing on a carpeted platform reading an important message. Now that I'm fifteen and telling you the story of my birthday the way Uncle Boula Boula told it, you can't imagine the importance a teacher had in the village back then; he was second only to the chief of police, who was the political red eyes and ears of the government. But as for competence, knowledge, prestige—these things belonged to the teacher. My father even told me that his father still remembered the name of his first elementary school teacher. That's why my father stood on this red platform decorated with the portrait of the President wearing his captain's stripes. My father, tie tightly knotted, in dark jacket and pants, surrounded by dignitaries, was reading the opening speech. Yengo didn't know how to proceed: how was he to get through this crowd, and then how was he supposed to convince the people in charge of protocol that he had an important message to deliver to this no less important teacher?

Luckily, Uncle Boula Boula appeared as if by magic next to Yengo. He wondered why this poor boy was in such a state. After talking to the boy, he realized it was an emergency and made his way toward Papa, who had just finished his speech and was bowing his head before the applause. Uncle Boula Boula, sensing the time was right, began whispering in the right ear of my father's bowed head: everyone saw Papa's eyes open wide in astonishment, and then he collapsed little by little, in slow motion, as in a movie or an instant replay, his hands grabbing at the portrait of the Captain on the way down. The crowd kept clapping as he tumbled and as the heavy ebony frame that held the presidential portrait fell on his skull with a thud. So Papa fainted, knocked out cold by the Chief of State and maybe somewhat by the news of my birth.

2

I was already born, wiped, washed, and wrapped when Papa hopped off the back of Mr. Konaté's truck, which typically carried sacks of cassava, planting stock, chickens, lambs, and sometimes pigs, but never human passengers. But for such an emergency—his wife had brought three children into the world at once—Papa had to be present as soon as possible no matter the means of transportation. Though he was incontestably the most educated man in the village, he was not the most powerful; anyway, wasn't it easier for a politician to get a state funeral than a scholar? All Papa's intelligence and scientific know-how weren't enough to get open the police chief's car, covered in the colors of state and driven by a chauffeur wearing a soldier's cap and epaulets. The only other car in running condition belonged to the medical assistant, who played at general practitioner and whom everyone called doctor, a car that, ever since the automakers did away with cranks, refused to start without a great push from two or three men. Still and yet contrary to what Mama Kossa used to say, the ancients were partly on my side that day, because at that very delicate moment when my father needed a ride to get to his wife, the West African merchant's truck suddenly came roaring along—the very same truck that ran almost exclusively during the dry season, when the roads weren't too swampy, the same truck that would cover you with sand and laterite dust as it passed.

Mr. Konaté knew only one holiday, which came at the end of Ramadan: Aid El Fitr, the day of Abraham's sacrifice, a holiday we called Tabaski. Mr. Konaté would park all his trucks, close up his shops and bars, and put on a great feast for all his employees, even though some embraced Islam only for the sake of that particular holiday. Mr. Konaté was a Muslim because, so I was told, it was the Arabs who, in their frantic race against the whites, arrived first in his part of Africa, where they enslaved and colonized. That is why we find blacks in the Gulf emirates and why in Algeria some think that blacks are still slaves. Truth be told, many people converted only to become rich like Mr. Konaté and had changed their names to Ibrahima, Mamadou, or Djibril. Since his riches enabled him to go to Mecca each year, rumor had it that he was an imam and was as powerful as the Ayatollah Khomeini.

My uncle, a practical man, stood on the side of the road that ran across the village; he could tell there was a truck approaching by the red fog of the laterite dust that hung over the distant plains. With an air of authority, he stepped into the middle of the road: the truck braked so suddenly that it lurched like an elephant, and had my uncle not thrown himself in the ditch by the road (forgetting his dignity and ceremonial attire), he would have been squashed by this crazed machine. As it bounced and settled back onto four wheels, the truck launched two bunches of bananas, three chickens, and a pig, much to the delight of the children, who proceeded to chase the animals after snatching up a few ripe bananas, thinking it was all part of the festivities.

Before the dust had settled, an angry man stepped out of the cab, vociferating, fists in the air, coming toward my uncle, who had already gotten back on his feet, his beautiful white suit as well as his hair, lashes, and eyebrows covered in a rusty laterite dust, a hue typical of our soil during the dry season. The man caught on quickly, for as soon as he saw my uncle's hunched ex-boxer torso, he relaxed his fists, faked a resigned smile, and said: "Be careful, sir, it's dangerous to stand in the middle of the road like that."

Everyone instantly recognized the man: it was Mr. Konaté himself, dressed on this day of my birth in a suit as grotesque as we Central Africans imagined them to be in West Africa. A big, blue, well-embroidered cotton robe; some beige slippers; a skull-cap on his head; and a little talisman in a small leather bag around his neck. But now the new accessory was a bump on his forehead caused by a violent encounter with the dashboard.

"Konaté! Your head's all swollen!"

"Boula Boula! So you're the one I almost ran over, *wallai*?"

"No time to talk, Konaté. The school principal's wife just gave birth to a third child. Such a thing is so strange that he must go to her straightaway."

"Three children? He's got three children? By Allah, what's so strange about that? I have twelve children myself, and my third wife—I married her three months ago—is pregnant already."

"No, not three children, a third child, dammit!"

"So if he's had a third child, add it up, he's got three children!"

"Enough, you can't understand, you're a Muslim."

Meanwhile my papa headed toward the truck in a haze, led by Yengo, who wanted to install him in the front cab in a manner proper to his station, but feeling a bit woozy, Papa insisted on lying down. Mr. Konaté, who also knew him—for who at that time did not know my papa, the village schoolmaster who had replaced the whites and was teaching reading, writing, and arithmetic to all the little children?—obliged. The vehicle's flatbed was lowered to unload two bags of grated ret manioc (still oozing), three bunches of bananas, and a goat: that made enough room for my papa to lie down and have Yengo sit next to him. Uncle Boula Boula squeezed into the cab with Mr. Konaté and the driver, and the truck took off, leaving the police prefect and the other notables to their speeches and festivities.

My papa climbed off the truck in better shape, but his suit was wrinkled, covered by wet, smelly patches of grated ret manioc drippings, and soiled by goat and chicken droppings. Being a man who knew how to handle life's bizarre twists, he walked bravely toward destiny and was the first to enter the living room that held Maman, Mama Kossa, and other women who'd heard about what happened. My uncle and Mr. Konaté followed him in. In spite of all he'd been told, it was as if up to that point Papa had yet to realize that he had a third child, for when he finally saw me in the flesh, wiped cleaned and squirming in Mama Kossa's arms, he took a quick glance and immediately kissed my two elders (by forty-eight hours), who were asleep in the same cradle, before asking for a chair and falling back in a daze, when he should have affectionately taken me in his arms, newborn angel that I was. My uncle, on the other hand, smiled and waved at me with his fingertips as if I could see him. Mr. Konaté, intrigued by what was happening, for he had yet to understand the reason for all this fuss about the birth of a child, dug around in the pockets of his big boubou, searching for God knows what.

Mama Kossa was getting ready to explain the strange phenomenon they'd all just witnessed, when the noise of two motorcycles followed by a car was heard at the front of the house. Doors were opened and slammed shut, and there was the prefect of police entering the living room, followed by his bodyguard and the two helmeted motorcyclists: the prefect wanted to be sure not to miss the great event live so that he could give a detailed firsthand account to the minister of the interior and to State Security, a report in which he would confirm that a woman delivered three children in a single pregnancy under his political and administrative jurisdiction.

Years later (I think I must have been a little over ten years old), when I was told what Mama Kossa said about me that day to this eminent delegation (never before seen at the birth of a child), I couldn't believe it. So when sometimes, in life, things happen to me that I understand and others cannot, I can't help but think, in spite of myself, that she wasn't completely wrong.

She lifted me and shook me, annoyed and furious because, even though I was breathing normally, I had yet to let out a baby's cry, which was supposed to indicate the child's initial connection to the chain of the living. I think that among the hundreds of infants she had helped bring from the other world into ours, I was an enigma she could not resolve. Though she scratched the soles of my feet, patted both cheeks, pinched my buttocks and earlobes, I stubbornly kept my silence. "This child should not have been born," she groaned, "as a matter of fact, he wasn't even in his mother's belly before—there were only the twins." The medical assistant whom everyone called doctor and who was the first to ask Maman to leave her hospital bed indicated his agreement with great nods of his head. "It was only when his mother went home that he, surely an ancestor who hadn't time enough to settle a score in his lifetime, floated through the woods and over the waters and crept into the sanctuary left empty by the twins and settled there. He will always be a troublesome child, I tell you, for no spirit returns to the world innocently. Still, little one, you're dealing with Mama Kossa here!" She pinched me once more and pulled my earlobes, still with the goal of making me cry, but got no results. "I shall make you talk, I shall protect you from people, and I shall protect people from you."

She laid me on a piece of white oilskin, using it as a crib liner, opened her famous pouch, pulled out two or three herbs still fresh, crushed them, and rolled them into a mango leaf funnel. She picked me up again, blew into my ears: "Child of surprises, you shall hear sounds and words others will not." She took the mango leaf, now an eyedropper, and put a green drop of the leaf's juice on each eyelid: "Spirit-child of the waters and woods, you shall see wonders that others will not." One drop in each nostril: "Ancestor-child who has come back among us, you shall smell sighs and fragrances others will not, you shall sense events others won't even guess." She took my two brothers from their cradle, laid us against one another, three little creatures, of which the third (me, that is) should not have been there. Speaking to me in particular, Mama Kossa said, "And now, scream, cry!" I remained obstinately silent, eyes closed. "Rub his cheeks with crushed cola nuts and mangrove coal," proposed old Kengué, who had once been a midwife. "No," replied Mama Dziki, "put a piece of wild pepper on his tongue and then see if he doesn't cry." They also proposed pricking me with the needle of a sterilized syringe, making me inhale fresh peppermint and soursop perfume, rubbing my feet with elephant dung, and wetting my buttocks with buffalo urine.

Mr. Konaté, whom they also called Imam, for it was said that no one since the Prophet had gone to Mecca as many times as he, signaled to Mama Kossa. He pulled a book out of his pocket, a small Koran. That was in fact what he had been pawing for in his pocket all the while, and what my uncle, who told me everything I know about my birth, had mistaken for a talisman. He flipped through it rapidly, found a chapter, and began to read a verse in a singsong Arabic spiced with a strong Dioula or Hausa accent that no one understood. He then copied out the verse in pretty arabesques full of dots, detours, and loops, weaving from right to left, rolled the page into a thin scroll, and asked Mama Kossa to slide it into my left palm. She did so, and at that very moment there was Father Boniface, the Catholic priest of our district.

Since the Church had authorized the priest to go around in civilian clothes, Father Boniface exhibited his faith only by a fat ebony cross that hung loosely around his neck, always visible on his chest

whatever his getup; he threw it over his back only when he ped-
aled standing up, leaning on his bicycle, which, they say, came
straight from Rome. He loved cycling and, in a land where everyone dreamed only of cars, endured much by virtue of his strange
passion for this contraption. What struck the gathering as the
priest entered the living room was that he was in his liturgical attire with its lacy surplice, rosary and missal in hand, as if he had
come to administer last rites though I was just starting out. In any
case, he was blown in like someone who had the Devil on his tail.

My father must have truly been dazed, because for the first
time in his life he saw a priest without bristling. He'd inherited
that instinctive reaction, which could range from the most harmless joke to open incitement, from his own father, who had also
been a schoolteacher, one formed during French rule in the secular and republican spirit, and for whom public schooling, with its
morals and its sense of civic duty, was an act of faith. He had not
hesitated to chase away a white priest who had taken over his
classroom in order to say Mass there. But that's a long story I'll
tell you some other time.

Father Boniface, too, heard that a trinity of children had seen
the light of day at the village schoolmaster's house; surely such a
strange happening could not have come from the Lord. Thinking that my papa was still at the great banquet commemorating
the twentieth anniversary of our Independence, he had dressed
quickly, pocketed the instruments necessary for his service, and
mounted his bicycle. When he came on a gust of wind into the living room, his attention was drawn directly to the three creatures
lying cheek by jowl on the white oilskin. He greeted all those
present, whom he hadn't really noticed anyway; with his sprinkler
in hand, he was ready to splash the suspect creature, meaning me.
Unfortunately, unable to detect at first glance which one of the
three was me, he began to splash one of my brothers. The latter,
undoubtedly upset by getting wet, began to cry, and Father Boniface smiled, thinking that there was the accursed child and that his

cries were the manifestation of the Devil panicking in the presence of a man of God. But my other brother too began to cry so the other wouldn't feel too lonely, since that's how twins are, doing everything in tandem. Father Boniface then panicked: he had been told there was only one suspicious little runt, and now he found himself facing two and at once began splashing all three of us frantically while jabbering in Latin. *"Vade retro Satana,"* he shouted in finale.

Mr. Konaté, amused, bent my uncle's ear and said to him: "He's got to be kidding if he thinks he can cast away Satan with a few drops of water! Doesn't he know the Koran says Abraham used stones to cast away the devil who tried to tempt him?" But before my uncle had time to see whether the bump on Mr. Konaté's forehead had gone down enough so he could answer, Papa woke up and in his stentorian voice bellowed at the priest: *"Vade retro* yourself!" Startled, Father Boniface backed away and finally discovered this standing delegation, since only my father was seated and Maman supine. Mama Kossa, seeing things getting out of her control, tried taking them back in hand. She took the two crying twins in her arms and began singing one of her Oubanguinian lullabies, while I stubbornly kept quiet.

No one knew if it was Papa's voice or the priest's holy water, or if the drops Mama Kossa drizzled into my nasal passages had produced their effect: suddenly I sneezed twice and opened my eyes. I must have taken notice of the horrors of the world then, because finally, for the first time, I let loose with my beautiful and much-awaited voice. The effect must have been remarkable, because Maman and Papa rose right away, one from his chair, the other from her sofa; the bodyguards instinctively snapped to attention so suddenly that one of them accidentally squeezed his trigger and let off a resounding shot, piercing the ceiling and the corrugated roof; Mama Kossa squeezed the twins, who had suddenly gone quiet, a little tighter in her arms, while the police chief found himself brutally tackled to the ground by his eager bodyguard and the priest and Uncle Boula Boula found themselves lying on the floor. Mr. Konaté took off his skullcap and placed it on his Koran, which he had been clutching since the priest's arrival as if to preserve himself from the cross of the infidel.

I had cried, I had made my entry into the world of the living, I had taken my place in the long chain of the ancestors and descendants of my tribe; I was no longer a little runt, no longer a soul that had gotten lost in the waters or in the woods while searching for human existence.

And so I, who should not have been born, had as my witnesses Mama Kossa, the most famous midwife of the region, who, it was said, was a Yakoma from Oubangui-Chari; Papa, principal of our school; my uncle, about whom I still have much to say; Mr. Konaté, the richest merchant of our region, who, given the circumstances, could be regarded as a diplomatic representative since he came from abroad, and who, ardent marabou that he was, had slipped a verse from the Koran into my left palm; a Catholic priest, who had sprayed me with holy water; a chief of police who represented the President of the Republic on this day of the twentieth anniversary of our nation's Independence; and that's not counting a bodyguard, two motorcyclists, some anonymous women there to help or to pity Maman, a police car and driver with a fancy cap and assorted colors, two American motorcycles, a bicycle from Rome, and a one-gun salute. As you can see, the only thing missing was a bugler playing the national anthem. And given all these things, how could Mama Kossa keep saying all the years that I was a child who shouldn't have been born at all because I wasn't in Maman's belly the day she came to the hospital to deliver my two twin brothers?

3

My father was nine years old, younger than I am today, when men first walked on the moon. It is even said— but I admit that it's difficult to believe, even though I got this from my uncle—that when Papa was born you couldn't follow the World Cup or the Olympics live and Coca-Cola had yet to spread the selling of soft drinks to our village. Even Michael Jackson had yet to become famous, there were no music videos on television, and rap and ragamuffin were still unknown . . . If all this was really true, I wonder how men managed to fill up the twenty-four hours of the day, three hundred and sixty-five days a year.

The year of his birth, the white people who had occupied our country left and the country got its independence and became a republic, complete with a flag, an anthem, and ministers cruising about in Mercedes on our laterite roads.

Grandfather was decorated twice that same year, first by the French on the final Fourteenth of July that they celebrated in our country as its chiefs, and a second time a month later, August 15,

Independence Day, by the first president of our liberated country—both times for the same reason: he had chased off a priest
who had dared hold a Mass at the school. Grandfather had not
been among the witnesses of my birth, and not because he was already too old and they were afraid to disturb him—it seems to me
that he'd seen so much throughout his long life that, unlike the
others, he would not have been troubled by the circumstances of
my birth—but, sad to say, rather because he was regarded as dou-
bly rejected in the dustbin of history. Hero that he had been, he
now saw himself being called a reactionary and a collaborationist
by the new revolutionary Marxist-Leninist government that was
running the country the day I was born. The reason? He had been
decorated by the French colonial power and then by the "neocolonial" power of our first republic.

He was one of the first Africans to have received his certificate
of indigenous studies and to have continued his education until
he became a schoolteacher. He was from that breed of teachers
formed under the French colonization for whom public schooling,
secular and republican, as I've said, was a true article of faith. The
future of the world was in schooling, and nothing, neither religion
nor philosophy, not even the ways of the ancestors, was to inter-
fere. Papa, in his turn, pushed this principle so far that, twenty
years later, around the time I was born, when he became the principal of the regional school, the stepping-stone for entry exams to
secondary and technical school, his big project was to recruit Pygmies from the depths of the equatorial forest and sign them up for
public school, believing that if he didn't do it Father Boniface and
the other priests and pastors would lead them off to become pros-
elytes. But let's get back to Grandpa.

One Sunday, while passing in front of his school, Grandfather
noticed an unusual crowd, and, coming closer, he saw a bearded
white priest celebrating Mass. Seized by anger, he didn't waste a
second chasing off the intruder and kicking out all the faithful
who had come to violate these grounds of republican and secular

education. Back then, the priests still wore the long robes called soutanes and spoke only Latin, even to our parents in the most remote villages. Maybe that's why they did not understand ordinary language. And so, when my grandfather told him, "Monsieur, in the name of the secular republic, I ask you to put an end to your show and leave these premises, which are under my authority," it seemed as if the use of the word *show* to describe his religious ceremony was what most vexed the priest. Yet as Papa would later explain to me, Grandfather didn't mean any malice by it. He had learned that word quite a while ago when, by an exceptional favor, the Lemba high priests had authorized the colonial governor to assist in a nonsecret part of their sacred ceremony, so vital for the life, health, and balance of the whole clan. At the end, the governor had put his white pith helmet back on and told Grandfather, the young schoolteacher who was accompanying him: "Not a bad show." And so, for Grandpa, all religious ceremony was a show. But this priest, unable to bear that his be called a show, got upset and declared that Grandfather was an agent of the Devil, picked up the instruments of his office, and left, followed out by the children of the choir, among whom was Father Boniface.

The undying superstition in our country at the time was that you never let a priest with whom you just had a dispute leave your house without pulling on the cord of his soutane, since otherwise he'd carry away your soul along with him, and then either it would be the end of your life or you'd have the Devil on your tail till the end of your days. That was the thought that suddenly occurred to Grandfather. And as soon as he saw the cord of the black soutane heading for the door, swaying defiantly on the waddling hips of its wearer, he ran up, pushed aside two choir children (who fell against the faithful, burning them with the melted wax of their candles), and then pulled with all his might and fury. The cord, instead of coming loose in one piece, tore off a nice patch of soutane. The priest turned around, shocked, and when he saw his torn clothes and his exposed underwear, he viciously brought his big cross down on Grandfather's skull. Grandpa screamed in pain and threw an uppercut at his aggressor's bearded chin. Luckily for him, he was being held back, for his fist did not miss the cleric's chin by much.

The matter went very far, because, as expected, the Church filed a complaint with the district commandant. The latter, torn between justice (which was on the side of Grandfather and his respect for the laws of the Republic, which called for public schools to remain secular) and his feeling of racial solidarity with his compatriot, finally sided with the priest, who nonetheless never again had the courage to come and say his Mass at the schoolhouse.

You didn't know Grandpa if you thought he would stop there—he who had always openly bragged about having a grandfather, real or imaginary, who fought the Portuguese in the Battle of Emboli of October 25, 1665, a battle in which the victorious Portuguese beheaded the king of the Kongo and looted the kingdom. He wrote a letter of protest to the head of the school board, another white man, who was the boss of all the region's schoolteachers.

Unfortunately, the boss was a friend of the district commandant, who housed him during his school inspections. He blamed Grandfather and threatened to fire him if he forgot his place again. This response had the opposite of the intended effect. Grandfather became furious and wrote an indignant letter to the school board chief's superior, the school inspector for this French overseas territory, who returned his letter accompanied by another in which he gave Grandfather hell, accusing him of ignoring the chain of command and affixing another reprimand to his record in addition to suspending his salary for six months. Everybody around Grandfather got scared and told him to calm down, to leave it alone not only because he wouldn't gain anything in his crusade against a priest and a white administrator, and not only because of the salary, but because he was risking the prestigious role of the native schoolteacher. Nothing doing—in a burst of arrogance, Grandfather now added another name to the list of his direct ancestors: Kimpa Vita, better known as Dona Beatrice of the Kongo, a young heretical woman who had singlehandedly raised an army against the Portuguese and had for a time restored the kingdom. He took his finest quill, dipped it in a well of violet ink, and, hand on the blotter, wrote directly to the highest academic authority in French Equatorial Africa, Mr. André Davesne, Inspector General. I remember his name because he had written a book, *Tales of the Bush and the Forest,* which my father still piously kept, for, he told me, it was thanks to this book not only that he had learned to read and write but that Grandfather was able to save his honor.

He wrote:

Monsieur Inspector General of Schools
for French Equatorial Africa,

I, Tezzo dia Mayéla, native teacher at the Béla school, appeal to your goodwill in the matter of an obvious injustice of which I have been the victim. This wrong is not worthy of our motherland, in which justice should be the natural complement of the triptych Liberty, Equality, Fraternity. For having defended the separation between our secular republican school system and the Church by chasing away a bearded, soutane-wearing papist accompanied by choir children, who had invaded the school to put on the show of a Sunday Mass there, I have been thrice punished and reprimanded and by an administrative authority no higher than the district commandant, the head of the school board, and the territorial school inspector. My faith has been shaken and I doubt that France, our motherland, can offer its indigenous citizens any protection whatsoever. Enclosed are the letters of reprimand sent to me.

I urge you to consider my case.
Yours bitterly and respectfully . . .

He folded the letter and the enclosures, slipped them into a thick paper envelope, and licked its edges covered with Senegalese gum before sealing it.

There was only one courier run a week, and even back then this was carried out by a truck belonging to Mr. Konaté, who had just moved to the region and was starting out in the trading business; between bunches of bananas, bags of manioc, chickens and pigs on one side, and on the other side mattresses and other furniture of families on the move, he transported free of charge the only bag of mail that contained all the correspondence of the village. He had an old Dodge truck he'd bought back for a pittance from an American missionary for the Jehovah's Witnesses whom the French authorities had deported for preaching antipatriotic doctrines, in particular the refusal to salute the national flag. So we were never sure at what exact time that old bucket would arrive, even if tradition would have it come on Thursdays at 2 p.m. and leave the next morning at 8 a.m. For twenty weeks straight, Grandfather showed up in front of the small post office, blending with the crowd that awaited the old Dodge, without receiving any answer to his letter of protest. He finally got weary, understood that an African will never get justice from a European, sulked conspicuously on Bastille Day, and refused to remove his hat each time he came across the commandant. His loathing for the bearded white priest who had invaded his school turned into a loathing for everything the priest and the Church represented; and that was the spirit in which he raised my papa, his eldest son. One must admit that this loathing demanded no particular effort, since it was a natural tendency, this latent anticlericalism underlying the public education ideology of his time.

The matter was buried and forgotten when, six months before the fifteenth of August, the announced date of our country's Independence, the new and last white commandant of our district sent his chauffeur to pick up Grandfather. This was an event, since, at

this time when the parties were fighting to replace the white colo-
nizer, Grandfather might be nominated district chief or even—
and why not?—commandant to replace the white one. By the time
he found his tie, smoothed out his coat, which had been stored
in a suitcase containing sweet-smelling crystal white mothballs,
dusted his only pair of leather shoes and his felt hat, without
which he never went out, a crowd had gathered in front of the
commandant's office to observe his arrival. He sat on the right side
of the backseat of the commandant's car since that was the trend
now among all the politicians who were to govern the state in six
months. The commandant received him in person on his porch,
shook his hand warmly before the gathered crowd, and led him inside. Grandfather was intrigued by this sudden consideration from
an administration that had wrongly and shamelessly penalized
him, but for the crowd there was no doubt he was going to be the
next territorial governor.

Once they were seated, after some solicitous remarks, the
commandant held out a letter from the *commissaire de la République
française*, the representative of the President of the French Republic in equatorial Africa. There was also a letter from Inspector
General André Davesne, addressed to "Dear friend," and indicat-
ing to him that he was the very type of African that France had always dreamed would be achieved at the end of its historic work of
civilization—an independent and freethinking man. He praised
him for defending the public school, and all blame was withdrawn
from his record; he was even promoted two ranks and his salary
was reinstated with back pay. As for the high commissioner, he
confirmed to Grandfather that French justice was color-blind, that
all French citizens were equal in the eyes of the law, and that, in
view of his highly courageous if not heroic act, an official acclama-
tion would be included in his dossier. By this time, Grandfather
did not doubt that he was entering into legend or that he was at
least becoming a historical figure: on the one hand, even French
officialdom proudly mentioned him in its speeches and official

documents, took him as an example of benign colonization, of the magnanimity and fairness of France in Africa; so he was to be decorated on the last Bastille Day of their reign by the last high commissioner of the French Republic in the country. On the other hand, the new leaders, after obtaining a bloodless independence, and thereby in need of heroic acts, took Grandfather as the archetype of the obstinate and impassioned struggle of the African people against colonialism and obscurantism. And so he was also decorated on the very day of Independence, on the Place des Héros, by our new President.

In any case, less than ten years later, when a revolutionary regime was imposed by the military that had carried out the last coup d'état against the military that had carried out the coup d'état against the military that had overthrown our first president because he was a lackey of imperialism—by then the events that made my grandfather a national hero were no longer heroic. If my grandfather had been decorated by the French, they said, it was because he was mentally colonized and had internalized the culture of the masters and had reacted as programmed, like a good nigger. And if Grandfather had been decorated by our first republic on Independence Day, that was because it was a neocolonial, lying dog of a government in the service of imperialism and receiving orders from abroad.

I saw Grandfather for the first time when I was already eight years old, when my papa and I spent a month in the village where he had gone to retire. He was already very old but still read through thick glasses. In his vast brick house, he had created a study, where he kept his most important memories.

There were big books, old encyclopedias, and old French catalogs from the fifties, notably those of Manufrance-St.-Etienne-Loire and from La Redoute à Roubaix, from which he had placed orders many times. I was immediately struck by the big cardboard map hanging on the wall, which he certainly must have used to teach the children of Papa's generation. The surface of the planet was cut out in a puzzle whose fragments formed a multicolored patchwork; a legend at the bottom of the map attributed an empire to each color. And so there was a French empire, a British empire (dominions and colonies), a Spanish empire, a Portuguese empire, an Italian empire, a Belgian empire, a Dutch empire, and mandates of the League of Nations. I began looking for my own country right away, and I found it bathed in the color of the French Empire, which covered a large portion of central and western Africa. I saw that my country didn't exist as such but was part of a mass called French Equatorial Africa, while the other mass was called French West Africa. And there were on this African map many countries I had never heard of: Oubangui-Chari, Anglo-Egyptian Sudan, Upper Volta, the Gold Coast, Rhodesia, Tanganyika . . . Since I already knew how to read pretty well by the age of eight, I read names of places that sounded strange and at the same time magnificent to my ears, wonderfully rolling off the tongue: Rawalpindi, Chandernagor, Curaçao, Sulawesi, Chittagong, Nizhni Novgorod . . . In Africa, I savored Timbuktu, Gaberones, Kalahari, Bahr al-Ghazal, Kilimanjaro, and . . . Ouagadougou! What a wonderful name! Ouagadougou! I repeated the name twice, so loud the second time that Papa heard and came near.

"Ah, Michel, you're looking at your grandfather's old colonial map from before World War II?"

"Yes, Papa. And was there also a Congolese empire or a Senegalese empire in Europe? In France?"

He smiled. "No, my child, for historical reasons too long and too complicated to explain to you, colonization happened in only one direction, north to south. All these countries became independent, at least formally; many have now changed their names to mark this break with the colonial past."

"Did they also change Ouagadougou?" I asked, with apprehension.

"Uh, well, Upper Volta no longer exists, but Ouagadougou is still there."

"Ah." I was relieved. "Papa I would like to go to Ouagadougou."

Papa laughed and said to me: "When you grow up, you can travel the world. You can go all the way to Ushuaia if you want. I see you're fascinated by this old map of the world. I shall give you a current map one of these days."

I was happy, and I thanked him for the promise as I followed him outside, all the while casting anxious glances at the statuettes and carved masks Grandfather had collected in a corner of the room, objects that frightened me as much as they attracted me, in particular a small figure spiked with nails that had a mirror on its stomach.

This was also the first time Grandfather had even seen me, and he was happy; he took me in his arms and put me on his knees. "Ah, so you're my little Matapari. They didn't call you Batsimba or Milandou because your birth is an enigma, right?" He laughed. "But the world is full of enigmas, for everything profound is not revealed upon first sight; the universe is masked as it winds its course, and men, after eating, dancing, and making love, spend the rest of their time trying to decipher what is hidden behind the appearance of things. That is why they write books and why those who don't know how to write seek answers from the forests, listen to the animals, dig the earth, or watch the stars. You must know everything, my child, the books of man and the book of the universe. Learn, learn without pause from the wise." I did not quite understand what he meant and stared into the eyes of my father, who stood beside him, content just to nod approvingly.

They once asked me to accompany them on one of their numerous peregrinations, which I can still vividly recall. They had awakened me very late at night or else very early in the morning, at five o'clock. While I was still staggering in my sleep and rubbing my eyes, Grandfather said to me in a voice filled with mystery, "Come see the birth of a new day with us."

We started walking while the night was still pitch black, moonless, and speckled with stars. Grandfather was out front with a torch; I was in the middle, trotting along on my little legs as fast as I could to keep pace with his giant steps; and Papa rounded off the procession. We were out about half an hour, I think, and the sky paled little by little. It was only when we arrived that I realized we had reached the peak of the highest mountain that dominated the village. The climb had been rough; many times I slipped on the dew-wet grass, and many times Papa picked me back up with a firm hand while Grandfather teased me. But my efforts yielded a true reward. It was the first time in my short life I felt so close to the sky, and I looked around me: the vast plain that spread out all the way to the great impassive river slowly and majestically snaking its way to infinity. And that's when I saw it! First, it was like an eyelid opening on the world, preceded by golden rays embracing this eastern part of the sky; then, little by little, as if wrenching itself out the depths of the earth, we saw all of it, egg yolk yellow at first, then brighter and brighter until there it was, blinding, master of the world. The sun! That great organizer of our life, our seasons, our harvest. I saw him being born; I now knew where he came from. I had been initiated into one of the world's mysteries, the birth of a new day. I had deciphered a page of the universe, just like Grandfather said.

We went back down the mountain as it was getting quite hot; I was sweating profusely and had become very thirsty. Grandfather made me drink fresh water collected from ravenala leaves, and we ate fresh wild fruit. We were now in the little forest bordering the village; Papa and I followed Grandfather, who showed no signs of fatigue despite his advanced age, on the narrow path that led us all the way to the source of the river where the village drew its drinkable water. Squatting, I drank this pure water that came from the earth's insides, that sprang up through the rock fissures to pour down on the white sand that carpeted the riverbed. Grandfather explained a few things to Papa at length, and then, with me still trotting behind, we left the forest for the savanna, and crossed a small grove that seemed important to them. We finally arrived at the village at dusk, but our hike didn't stop there; once more, we visited the tombs of the elders of our clan. The moon was already perfectly white and round when we finally returned to the village. I was exhausted.

An aunt forced me to wash with water (full of strange herbs) that she had heated on a wood fire in a large bucket placed on three rocks. I thought I was big enough to wash myself, but she insisted, rubbing my body with a plantlike sponge and my feet with a pumice stone, then dabbing me with some lotion in a flask to protect me, she said. From what? I asked. From the snakes along my path and from life's accidents. They gave me food. I wanted bread, but they didn't have any for there was no bakery in the village. I was really worn out, and since there wasn't a television, I couldn't watch the music videos from the last *Top Africa* or better yet *X-OR*, the new Japanese cartoon series that had replaced *Goldorak*, to find out whether Gordan—at that very moment the chief of Cerex wanted to kill him—didn't transform into the fourth dimension after disintegrating his rival with his laser gun. So I decided to go to sleep instead, letting the adults continue their conversation by the fire. I saluted Grandfather, that hero who had dared take a swing at a priest, and who was decorated twice, banished by the military, yet despite all seemed to be enjoying a pleasant retirement, always cheerfully reading the books of man and trying to decipher the book of the universe behind its masks. "Matapàri," he said to me, "the day I am buried, you must be there."

4

Matapari! Problems, worries, nuisance! Matapari! Such was the nickname they attached to my family name. Of course, names no longer meant anything for, since colonization, we no longer named somebody for a particular reason but instead, boy or girl, we simply inherited our father's name; only first names allowed for fantasy. That is how many girls now bore names previously reserved for men and many specifically female names gradually disappeared from our patrimony. As for me, while my papa had given me the proper name of Michel, I got stuck with this ominous nickname, Matapari!

Matapari here, Matapari there. Some used the diminutive Tapari, while children taunted me, yelling loudly whenever they saw me: "Guess who's coming from Pareee? Matapareee! Matapareee!" And I ended up believing I really was different.

As for worries, it is said that I created those for my family and myself as soon as I attained freedom of movement. First, it was my left arm. I was sucking so much on my left thumb that Maman noticed I was left-handed. This was confirmed as I was growing up.

By age four or five, I did everything with that arm: greeting people, lifting things, throwing rocks, roughhousing with my friends, or serving a volleyball. For Maman, this was a source of panic. One of her grandfathers who was left-handed—the only one in the whole history of her family—ended up being buried beneath the nsanda tree for having refused the test of the *nkasa*, mandatory in their tribe, that white and bitter hemlock that instantly felled sorcerers and spared innocents. To refuse this test was to admit one's sorcery. Maman feared I was the reincarnation of that ancestor, especially given the fact that Mama Kossa had confirmed that I was not in my mother's belly at the hospital along with the twins and that, being the spirit of an ancestor who'd died violently and so took to homeless drifting, I had taken advantage of the spot left empty by my brothers to settle in, tired of floating about in the early morning air of the forest and over the waters like the morning fog that clings to the groves of the mountain slopes. Since she called herself a Christian—with a Bible always at her bedside—she did not fail to consult Father Boniface.

Choosing an hour when he was sure Papa would be at the school, Father Boniface came to the house on the bike he had brought back from Rome, where he had spent six months at the Vatican; he said that this bike was once owned by a certain Fausto Coppi. Since no one in our district had heard of Fausto Coppi—a saint? a magician? a sorcerer? a friend of the Pope?—no one dared touch it, not even the older boys, whose favorite game was to snatch bikes while the grown-ups chatted and do stunts to amaze us younger kids—look! no hands . . . no feet . . . sitting on the frame . . . on the handlebars—before quietly returning them. But nobody dared touch that bike. Father Boniface didn't believe in our animist customs, he said, but he did believe in the Devil and the Lord. He explained to Maman the origin of my defect: no, it was not an ancestor returning, it was simply due to an incident on the day of my birth. Maman did not recall any incidents besides the priest's holy water causing all three of the children to cry and then Papa's *"vade retro* yourself" in response to the priest's *"vade retro Satana."* "But no," he insisted, "before that." Since Maman still couldn't figure it out, he revealed the source of my sinister left-handedness: it was because on the day of my birth, Mr. Konaté had slipped a verse from the Koran into my tiny left hand. And how could one remedy that? With Christian prayer!

Unfortunately, Maman and her family weren't content to rely on mere prayers to save the arm of their child, so they also used physical restraints. They tied a big rock and a heavy piece of wood on my left arm to immobilize it so that I would use only the right arm. This bothered me whenever I played with friends, and I would often lose my balance. Curiously, I would be fitted with these prostheses only when Papa wasn't around, and they were taken off as the time of his return approached. Things got worse when Papa left for the capital for reasons related to his work.

On a day when they had completely attached my arm to my body after noticing that I often found a way to rid myself of the stones and boards and return to my activities with my left arm, we won a game of marbles we were playing in the courtyard. We celebrated, mocking our adversaries. A fight followed. I could fight with only one fist, and at my first punch I lost my balance and fell. Our adversaries jumped me, and I got seriously messed up: a swollen eye, split lip, a nose that became the size of a banana, and ripped shorts. Maman and the women visiting her heard my cries, and our aggressors scattered like sparrows. Maman was terrified. The yelling women carried me, freed my arm, washed me, changed my clothes, and treated me. "Matapari," they were all saying at once, "you can't keep still, you're always looking for fights, always putting yourself in hopeless situations. Look at your brothers: can't you keep still for an instant like them?"

And I looked at my twin brothers. They resembled each other perfectly, the same T-shirt with Batman in midflight, same shorts, same shoes, and the same little Texas Rangers baseball caps. They were clean and well-behaved and looked at me with a distant air as if I weren't their brother but a usurping stranger. No one took up my defense, no one recognized that if I had been beaten, it was because I literally had one arm tied behind my back. I was so miserable that I didn't even want to get better; I would lie on my little bed and refuse to eat. That's when I got a fever.

I was shivering so much under my covers that it amazed me to feel my body burning. I sank deeper and deeper into my fever and into my slumber, and I began retracing the hike I had taken with Grandfather in his village. Then, because of the clarity drops Mama Kossa had put in my eyes, nose, ears, and mouth the day of my birth, I began seeing and doing things I had never seen or done before. I first began floating through the groves and the forests all the way to those places in the mountains where the springs gush forth and where Mamiwata, mother of the waters, often hides. Oh, the beautiful purity of water at the source! It seemed to sing. I continued climbing the mountain and reached the summit at dawn: again I saw the performance of the sun springing from the depths of the earth to shine upon the world. For a long while, everything around me was all light and gold. Ah, if only I could live off light! I stayed there fascinated for so long that I came back down only with the sun, which, shedding its golden crown, became great and red as a heart and returned to shine upon the dark land of the ancestors. Once more, I drank water from the source.

Unfortunately, thanks to the night, I got lost on my way back and found myself in a strange realm full of dreams preparing to fly off to sleeping minds. There were lovely ones, there were amusing ones as well as ugly, scary dreams. I saw a dream in which a lion was chasing a man and catching up with him. This dream was destined for Mr. Louzolo, our great hunter, the one who had killed a buffalo last week. I caught that dream by the tail, and since I wanted two of the same, I succeeded in copying it and sent a couple to my brothers to give them a good fright. I diverted another dream that was heading for the sleeping mind of Ma Lolo, the young and beautiful wife of Mr. Bidié, the richest merchant of our village and the only man who owned a tango accordion in our country; he was not as wealthy as Mr. Konaté, but he was rich nonetheless. It was a dream in which Ma Lolo was wearing the nightgown she had wanted ever since she came to the house to flip through the women's magazines that Papa bought for Maman from time to time. It was a long silk gown cut very low and translucent enough for her breasts to show through; she was quite beautiful in it. I was sorry for making Mr. Bidié miss out on such a lovely dream, but since I knew that Father Boniface wasn't married and there was a rumor that priests didn't like any women except for nuns, I sent the dream to him instead, three nights in a row.

I discovered that animals, too, had dreams; I saw an astonishing dream that was about to flow into the slumber of a hind: it was a lion fleeing from a herd of hinds. I watched the dream of an orangutan, but, not being too careful, I was sucked along with the dream into the animal's sleep, made prisoner, and I couldn't get out. I began groaning like an ape, gobbling bananas, and, from a simple lefty, I had become quadridextrous, leaping from tree to tree. I struggled for a long, long while before liberating myself from the dreamland of this big ape, a realm that no longer pleased me. Run, run, get away! I felt a coolness on my forehead, I opened my eyes and saw a string of shadows around me just like when I was born: I recognized Papa, the medical assistant we called doctor, a few of Maman's relatives and friends, and my uncle. There was also a table with disposable syringes, medicine vials, bottles of aspirin, a sort of yellowish syrup in a flask, as well an IV suspended above my bed. Everyone seemed worried and relieved at the same time. I was hungry and asked to eat something. I drank some water and gobbled up a whole bowl of Quaker oatmeal.

I learned later on that I had suffered a serious case of malaria, lasting three or four days. Papa had been called back home. I received intravenous and intramuscular injections, I was fed drop by drop through an IV, I was massaged, Maman had prayed with Father Boniface first, then by herself when Papa had returned, since the priest considered himself *in partibus* in the heathenous zone that our house became whenever Papa was around. Our doctor, the medical assistant, had panicked on the last day of my illness and had asked Papa to find a way to evacuate me to a district hospital or even one in the capital, as I began groaning like an orangutan, moving my jaws, and waving my arms and legs as if to grab hold of something in the air. The doctor had dropped the words "acute episode" to impress everyone. But luckily the fever had gone back down after the last IV, and a little while later I opened my eyes and asked for food.

I recovered pretty quickly. All the same, I had the impression that my brothers were perhaps scared to be left alone with me and held on to Papa's arm, or Maman's or somebody else's, a gleam of fear in their eyes every time they were told to go kiss their little brother or even when I simply approached them. Maman told me that, on the second day of my illness, my brothers who loved me so much were so pained at the sight of me being sick that they both had the same nightmare (something that often happens with twins)—a nightmare in which a great lion had chased them, caught them, and, at the very moment he was about to take a bite out of them, they started screaming in unison; they had also seen me in the dream siccing the lion on them. "It will pass," said Maman to reassure them—or to reassure me.

Since no one dared tell my father how I had gotten sick—that is, the fact that my left arm had been tied down so that I would become right-handed—I didn't tell him either. To this day he has never found out that his son was born left-handed. But the illness did have a positive side to it, especially the part when I was trapped for a while in the dreams of an orangutan, because when I finally escaped these dreams, I was perfectly ambidextrous.

Before my birth, there had never been triplets in our region or even, as Mama Kossa claimed, in our entire country. It seemed to me that this was something altogether unheard of. With me, however, a new phenomenon was born, one that became more and more frequent, for in the space of the decade after my coming to the world, Mama Kossa would help deliver four sets of triplets and one set of quadruplets (of which unfortunately none survived)—it was as if once a taboo was transgressed, there was no going back.

So up until my birth, people knew only of twins. They were celebrated, they were feared, they were worshipped, and their mothers had a certain name and status among the women. They were capricious children, of course, but their whims had been mastered long ago; they were perfectly integrated into our cultures, and if they were raised according to tradition, they were a source of good fortune, wealth, and happiness. The firstborn twin was always named Banzouzi and the second Batsimba. And when

the mother gave birth a few years later, the child was called Milandou, "the one who came after." Accordingly, I was neither Banzouzi nor Batsimba, and evidently not Milandou. So who was I?
What should I be called? That's how I was stuck with "Matapari,
problem child."

Today, thanks to my father, the birth of triplets or even
quadruplets no longer causes such a stir in our village life, except
maybe in that family which, having prepared only one set of baby
clothes, ends up with three or four children. Thanks to Papa,
triplets found their perfectly natural places in the already resolved
problems of life. For, after his initial shock at the annunciation of
my birth, he wanted to understand what lay behind this phenomenon, and, waving off the explanations of Mama Kossa, Mr.
Konaté, and Father Boniface, he immersed himself in books. He
wrote to the BBC listeners' mail; he consulted professors of
genetics and biology at our national university and spoke with gy-
necologists; he sacrificed ten months of salary to buy the dozen
volumes of *Encyclopedia Universalis*. He would repeat to anyone
who would listen the scientific explanations about female hyper-
fertility, simultaneous fertilization of eggs, about identical and
fraternal twins, as well as bizarre terminology such as triplets who
were monozygotic, dizygotic, or trizygotic. There was only one
mystery he could not resolve: the forty-eight-hour lapse between
my two ziggy-wiggy brothers and me.

Papa's quest definitely changed the course of his life. He devoted his body and soul to the pursuit of knowledge. He sub-
scribed to *Sciences et Vie*, to the French edition of *Scientific
American*, to *La Recherche*, to a philosophy journal, and registered
for correspondence courses at the university. He didn't stop there,
for when he noticed that many interesting articles were written in
English, he ordered a textbook and teach-yourself language tapes.

Compared with Papa's obvious knowledge, Father Boniface
impressed me less and less, even though Maman continued to dis-

play absolute trust in him. As a matter of fact, in the tradition of both my father and my grandfather, I no longer resisted making jokes at the priest's expense.

One afternoon during my convalescence, while Papa was at the school, Father Boniface visited me. "We prayed a great deal for you, my child. We truly snatched you from the claws of evil, for you were possessed. You tossed and turned, you screamed, you snapped your jaws like a demon."

I didn't know where he had gotten this information, which seemed to convince Maman, who was nodding her head in approval. Personally, I had a rather nice recollection of those days when, as people said, I was delirious playing around with dreams, a period to which, if given another occasion, I would voluntarily return. But soon Ma Lolo, whom I affectionately called Auntie Lolo, the wife of the old merchant Bidié, came along. I don't know what got into Father Boniface, but he got agitated without hardly even looking our visitor in the eyes when she held out her hand. She sat down and for the hundredth time began flipping through the eternal magazines where she admired all the negligees and nicely primped ruffles. Father Boniface watched her furtively, carefully avoiding eye contact, then despite Maman's protestations suddenly got up to leave without finishing the session of exorcism and benediction he had promised to make us undergo. He mumbled that he had extreme unction to administer and hopped on the Roman bike he had gotten from Fausto Coppi, and started pedaling away, standing, his ebony cross dangling on his chest.

Auntie Lolo was as beautiful as I had seen her in my vision, and I remembered that I had sent that dream to Father Boniface, three nights in a row. I started laughing then but tried not to laugh too loud so as to avoid Maman's attention, so I choked a bit and got the opposite result—a coughing fit mixed with laughter. Maman got scared, thought I was delirious again, and began regretting out loud that the Father had gone without sanctifying us.

Finally I managed to control myself and stopped laughing and crying, to her great relief.

A week later, completely healed, I was coming home from school, folders and books in my school bag strapped on my back, and I came upon the priest. He braked beside me and put a foot down in the dust. "Matapari, everything all right?"

"Yes, Father."

"You have to come see me even if your unbelieving father doesn't want to recognize the love that Jesus bears witness to, a love for his sake and yours. For without Him, I don't know what would have happened to you during your illness. In fact, at your age, you should already be baptized. Your father doesn't want it, he says that the choice is yours when you come of age. It's a shame; he doesn't realize how he keeps you from heaven's door."

"Yes, Father."

"Yes Father what? Yes, you're going to be baptized or yes about something else? Be grateful to God for having saved you. Go on, take care, I'm in a hurry."

He got back on his bike and started pedaling. Not knowing what had gotten into me, I called out to him: "Still dreaming about Auntie Lolo?"

He braked so hard that the back wheel of his bicycle bucked like a horse and he fell over the handlebars. His missal and rosary flew off. He hit the ground so hard that a cut opened on his forehead in the middle of a big fresh lump. Blood leaked onto his habit. I didn't know if I should come to his aid, and when I decided to take a step toward him, he had regained consciousness and looked up at me fearfully, trembling, shaking his finger. "Get away, get away, you're possessed by the Devil, child of the Evil One you are. How did you read my soul . . . how do you know I dreamed of . . . of . . . Get thee away! Lord protect me!"

I got scared because I thought he was going mad, and I took off at full speed.

Ever since that incident, it seemed to me that Father Boniface was more afraid of me than of Papa. In any case, he gave up on our house: he never came back, despite my mother's numerous invitations. We learned, without understanding, that Father Boniface was in penitence, that he no longer received any followers and had written to his superiors requesting a transfer to another diocese.

6

While Papa read books and instructed the children, Mr. Konaté and Ma Lolo's husband, old Bidié, were merchants and sold things to people, Father Boniface was a Christian advertising Jesus Christ, and Mama Kossa helped women bring their children into the world, I never knew what Uncle Boula Boula's profession was exactly. He had arrived in these parts three years after my papa had been assigned here. This isn't where my father was from originally; he was from the Boko district, where my grandfather retired. Anyway, Uncle Boula Boula arrived here because, some said, he had fled the capital to hide, and still others said, because he was wanted. He was older than Papa and Maman.

He was tall, pumped up, and had a very hairy chest. In fact Boula Boula was actually a nickname he was given in his boxing days because he had once dislocated the jaw of an adversary with a right uppercut and immediately set it back in place with a left uppercut. To this day I still see him lifting weights, and I am sure he could outbox Rambo. When he got angry, his whole body would vibrate: this was a result of the kaman, a talisman he was given in his youth that gave one the strength of buffalo. It was made from assorted powders, herbs, and the ashes of a wildcat's claws, not to mention the right hand of an ape to add cleverness and dexterity to feline grace and power, all of it well mixed and applied to incisions done on the wrists of the happy beneficiary. So Uncle would vibrate under the spell of the kaman, and if he didn't have an adversary before him, he would start smashing bottles on his forehead and grinding up the broken glass without harming himself the least bit, or he'd smash cinder blocks with his head. One day I'll have to ask him to perform a kaman incision on me so I can beat up my older twin brothers.

Nevertheless, he was not a quarrelsome person. On the contrary, he was charming, generous, and even quite intelligent, in a way different from Papa's. His great generosity of spirit led him to set up a business that did well for a while, until cunning and jealous minds accused him of fraud. Thinking that all of his peers were swindlers and that his own bright ideas ought to be shared with the people instead, he created a company called the Office of Free Ideas, or OFI. Though he didn't know how to use a computer, he bought a secondhand Japanese model to lend a bit of class and credibility to the business. Has anyone ever seen a business without a computer at the end of this twentieth century? Often, to impress a client, he would turn on the color monitor, start typing on the keyboard, and set off the dot matrix printer so that its staccato noise might reinforce his self-confidence before his interlocutor.

The idea of the company was simple. A person who had a problem would come and consult the office, which would provide him with answers free of charge. A few bad mouths maintained that OFI was just a cover for my uncle's more questionable activities, but I am sure they said so not only out of jealousy but also because they ignored the fact that in our modern world fortune smiled only on men with innovative ideas like Uncle Boula Boula.

One day I asked him how a for-profit company could sustain itself from this concept, and he told me that it worked because his approach was based on transparency: he was paid only if the solution worked, and, since his answers always worked, he had nothing to worry about.

He had, as a matter of fact, pulled off an advertising coup with the Vietnam War. I should mention that, long before my birth, the Americans, with their helicopters, bombers stuffed with radar and air-to-surface, surface-to-surface, and surface-to-air missiles, napalm bombs, and chemical defoliants, were for who knows what reason fighting the Vietnamese, who had only rifles, Kalaschnikovs, and rocket launchers. But for all their technology, the Americans still couldn't win. So one week after he had opened his office and tapped a few keys on his computer keyboard, his dot matrix printer—which he always refused to trade in for a laser one because the latter made less noise—printed out a solution, which he immediately shared with his friends. Like every good solution, it was simple: the Americans had only to declare that they had won the war and leave Vietnam triumphantly like winners. What does world opinion matter anyway? After all, an opinion can be given and taken back.

You can imagine how surprised he was when he learned a few days later that an American senator had made the exact same proposition! There was no doubt about it, this senator had stolen my uncle's idea! And how could this senator have been made aware of an idea that came from a little advice office in a little town in a little country in tropical Africa, lost in the middle of nowhere? By the local American ambassador, of course, a spy like the rest of them, hooked up with the latest newly invented technology, the fax and electronic mail. And so, with some pride, Uncle amended his logo: "Office of Free Ideas: the advice office that gave America the solution to the Vietnam War."

"Everyone would come to consult me," he told me, "from the unfaithful husband to the university professor who wanted to be-

come a government minister." But there were jealous people
everywhere, folks who would get nasty when it came to other people's success. "It was the thieves' strike that did me in," he con-
fided to me one day when I asked him why he had fled the capital.
"I don't like thieves, but I also hate injustice. One morning, I
learned from a radio news report that a former government minister, the big boss of our country's only party who, as everybody
knew, had embezzled twenty million francs from a charitable
Scandinavian organization that was supposed to reform our country's health care system, had been released after a show trial. It was
scandalous! I knew he was a big thief because he had refused me a
deal on office supplies only to give it to a brother of his mistress,
even though I had the lower bid. So I was very angry when I heard
about his release. Going to the market that morning, I witnessed
an awful scene: a kid fifteen or sixteen years old had just been sav-
agely beaten and would have probably been killed if the police
hadn't happened to walk by. He had been caught in a flagrant act
of theft of a few fingers of bananas hardly worth a few pennies!
The police threw the kid in their van, and I don't know if they left
for the hospital or the morgue. I was disgusted. That's when my
advice office came upon the appropriate answer to this two-tiered
system of justice: a strike!

"So I proposed to all the thieves that they go on strike for a
week. Imagine, Matapari, a city where nothing would be stolen
anymore! You can roam the streets with millions of francs without
a care; you can leave your car anywhere with the key in the igni-
tion and find it there when you come back; put your clothes out to
dry for the night and find them hanging there the next morning;
the public treasury would have no need for safes for its gold bul-
lion! There wouldn't be any more work for security companies, no
more new orders for the manufacturers of wrought-iron security
gates, and insurance companies would lose half their clients. But
most of all, the police and national guard would have to fire three-
fourths of their forces and the rest would only be needed to direct

traffic and help children and old ladies cross the street. Imagine
the annoyance of the politicians who would no longer collect their
ten percent kickbacks from government contracts. Imagine, Matapari! This was more than a revolution, it was an earthquake, a
cataclysm worthy of the apocalypse, that I had set off! There was
panic. Naturally, one didn't have to wait too long for the higher
powers to react.

"The secret police accused me of disturbing state security.
The tax agencies came to check on my accounts in a most meticu-
lous manner, and used the pretext of a few undeclared pennies to
accuse me of fiscal impropriety. Finally they induced a client to
press charges against me, as if my office was fraudulent when the
solution I'd given him had worked like a charm! He had come to
see me because he suspected the wife of his best friend of being
unfaithful. He asked me to find the damned lover. I gave him the
solution: his friend should put a tap on his own phone! What did
they discover? He himself was the cuckold! The wife of his best
friend was just a go-between who arranged rendezvous for his own
wife. Imagine his shock. Since he was shattered and incapable of
facing this unpleasant reality and, what's more, since he was the
head of the narcotics task force, he pretended he'd discovered suspicious plants in the small nursery where I was experimenting
with natural fibers from sisal, hemp, jute. He accused me of trafficking . . . drug trafficking! So with all this pressure, and because
I wanted to keep my peace of mind, I had to close up shop. I
wasn't chased from the capital, nor did I flee, I simply decided to
retreat here to have some peace. If anyone tells you I did time in
prison, that's not true, I was just arbitrarily locked up for three
months."

I must say that it was really from Uncle Boula Boula that I
learned things about everyday life. It was he who, by the way,
shared with me the events that took place during my birth, which
I've already told you about. In spite of this, I can't tell you exactly
what work he actually did here to get by; he went to the capital

from time to time, but he often hung around the village. In fact, if I feel close to him it is also because there is a secret pact that has bound us ever since I was six—ever since that day when, wanting to test my courage before Ma Lolo, he realized I was just a coward. I made him swear never to reveal this story to my twin brothers; I would die of shame if they learned that despite all my swagger I was just a wimp. Until this very day he has kept his word. Here's the story.

It happened one morning during the dry season. School was closed, the students had gone home for summer vacation, and Papa had gone to the university in the capital for the yearly lab sessions that complemented his correspondence courses. It was the season when men and women would light peat fires to prepare the topsoil for the next rainy season; so there was no one around in our neighborhood. Maman was gone with my two twin brothers, Banzouzi and Batsimba, and since I didn't want to go with them, I stayed by myself and played in the courtyard with my marbles. I got thirsty, as often happens, and I went inside my uncle's house to drink some water. It was at that moment that I heard Uncle Boula Boula's loud voice. "The neighborhood sure is quiet, everyone's gone and no one will be back before evening."

"And why are you the only man hanging around when everyone else is in the fields?"

That's when I recognized the voice of Auntie Lolo, the wife of old Bidié, who had a store on the street corner where we sometimes went to buy soap and Coca-Cola or a can of corned beef or sardines when we had nothing else to eat. He was so old compared with his wife that for a long time I thought she was his daughter. We kids liked him a lot because he had an accordion that he called a bandoneon; he told us that he was the only person who owned one in the whole country. He would tell us that, long ago, he had been a kitchen boy in Europe and that he had met an Argentinean who recruited him into an orchestra; and for our amusement, he would play us snatches of tango, waltz, bolero, paso doble, and a few others I forget. That morning I'd seen him take Mr. Konaté's truck to go stock up I know not where. The two voices got closer to the door. I was afraid of being seen by my uncle, so I ran to his room and hid under the bed.

"Lolo, can't you see it's a little chilly this dry season? Come do a little exercise with me, we'll warm ourselves up nicely."

"You're shameless, I'm going to tell my husband."

Me, I didn't see what was so shameful about doing a little exercise, for often, when he wasn't deep in his books, Papa would tell us: Come along, children, let's go do some exercise, and one-two, one-two, we would get in a single file, Papa in his blue jogging suit, my two brothers in identical sweat suits, I in a sweatshirt, shorts, and Nikes. Then we would kick around a soccer ball like Maradona, even though Papa would chew our ears about some Pelé or other, who, he'd say, was the greatest soccer player of all time and compared with whom Maradona was only perhaps a good second. We would always finish off our exercise sessions with a Latin phrase he read in his books; he'd say, "My trinity"—that was what he called us—*mens sana in corpore sano.*"

"You don't know what you're missing with your old geezer of a husband—come on, let's get down to the rhythm, we're going to shine our rumps."

I then understood that he wanted to dance with Auntie. I didn't tell you, not only was Uncle built for boxing but his physique also made him a great dancer; you had to see him wriggle his butt on a dance floor, especially when he moved his rear end to the rhythm of a rumba or an Afro-Cuban salsa. But I didn't see why he wanted to dance so badly now, since I couldn't hear any music.

Auntie Lolo was saying no, no, but from under the bed, where I was scared to breathe for fear of getting caught, I couldn't see her make any effort to resist when Uncle pulled her to him; they came into the room, to my great surprise, for one usually chatted with visitors in the living room and not in the bedroom, and both

installed themselves on the bed. All of a sudden they were lying
down. The bed sagged. I feared it would cave in on me. Then I
heard them tossing and turning and making sucking noises, with
Auntie Lolo's "no, no I don't want to" getting weaker and weaker
and my uncle's "yes, yes, that's it, good," getting stronger. Then a
pair of pants landed next to me, followed by a blouse, then a shirt,
and then the rain of clothes grew stronger, a loincloth, a bra, and
two pairs of underwear, a man's and a woman's. That was when I
really got scared. The bed began to bounce up and down, left to
right, a flurry of painful oh's and ah's issued from Uncle's side,
while Auntie's no, noes, had become yes, yeses, with the *s* breathed
out slowly and at great length. I was scared, very scared, I didn't
know what was happening. Were they fighting? Were they hurting each other? I was completely panicked when I suddenly heard
my uncle let out a plaintive cry followed by Auntie's groans, and
then the bed abruptly stopped trembling. Had he strangled old
Bidié's wife, the very one who often came to flip through Maman's
fashion magazines?

After a while the groans stopped and my uncle started snoring. I was still so scared at having been a witness to a crime that to
better conceal myself I picked up the shirt, loincloth, blouse, bra,
and underwear and put them on top of me. They stayed still so
long that despite my uncle's heavy breathing—he was snoring like
a MiG-23 getting ready for takeoff—I thought that they were
dead and I had been an accessory to a real-life crime. I was especially worried that if they gave the investigation to a James Bond
or a Kojak, they would find out that I was under the bed and
therefore a witness. My body was becoming stiff from keeping
still. I took my fate in my two hands and decided to take a look. At
the very moment I was about to poke out my little head to peek at
what was going on and ultimately flee, Auntie Lolo reached out to
grab her clothes strewn on the floor in haste, as she addressed my
uncle. "Let's not hang around, we've got to go."

Her palm, which she had opened to grasp her clothes, patted

the part of the floor where the clothes had supposedly fallen and, finding nothing, she directed her arm under the bed, her palm still open; her hand touched the fuzzy hair on my little skull, then recoiled sharply as if bitten by a snake, hesitated a moment, then felt again, and suddenly she let out a cry of terror: "A devil, a devil, there's a demon hiding under the bed!"

She jumped from the bed, naked, terror-stricken, and ran toward the door. Uncle leapt, also naked, caught her in midstride, threw her back on the mattress, and, before he got a chance to lean over and look, I bolted from under the bed like a jack-in-the-box and took off like the savanna gazelle, scattering their clothes all the way to the outside door of the living room; in the blink of an eye I saw Auntie Lolo, who was lying on her stomach trying to conceal her nakedness.

I was trying to hide behind a lantana bush when my uncle caught me. He gave me two good slaps, and I started to cry; he pulled me out from the thorny bushes roughly, inflicting a thousand scratches on me. "Matapari, naughty kid"—I was getting a good spanking at this point—"tell me, have you been under the bed long?"

"Yes, yes," I said in tears, "before you came in the bedroom."

These simple words of truth seemed to plunge him into a state of panic. "Oh God! Shit, shit, shit! Matapari, tell me, you've seen everything, eh? no? Maybe you didn't see anything, all right?"

"I . . . I . . . I seen you two laying on the bed," I said, my voice choked with sobs and hiccups. "I heard Auntie Lolo say 'no, no,' then 'yes, yes,' then I seen all your clothes fall on the floor and all of a sudden the bed started shaking and I got scared it would collapse on me."

"No . . . no . . . Aaaah!" he moaned mysteriously as he shook me strongly.

"I got especially scared when you cried out and when Auntie groaned. I thought you killed her."

"Stop. That's not true, and those weren't clothes falling . . . uh
. . . the bed wasn't shaking, it was me beating on the mattress to
chase away the bedbugs and—"

"But I saw Auntie Lolo naked and she was—"

"Uh . . . I mean . . . you know, the bedbugs . . . they like
women . . . they stick to their bodies and . . . and . . . you have to
undress them completely to—"

"I saw you naked like her too and—"

"Stop!" he yelled, holding me by the throat, nearly strangling
me.

He was looking left and right like a hunted beast. What was
happening? I was just telling the truth. Then he abruptly let go of
me and started laughing. "Ha ha ha! We got you good, Matapari!"
He gave me a friendly pat on the back. "You see, we saw you come
in the house and hide under the bed, and we said to each other:
'We're going to scare little Matapari.' So we came in the room,
and we started shaking the bed and screaming as if we were fighting and then we played dead. It worked, you got scared, you fell
for it, and we had a good laugh. I ran after you because, since I
like you, I was disappointed to see that you were less brave than
the twins. Tough love, you know. That's why I beat you up a little.
You see, we played the same trick on them. But they knew right
away that we were joking and we had a good laugh together. Well,
I'm going to tell your embarrassing little story to Banzouzi and
Batsimba; they'll have fun teasing you and—"

"No, Uncle, please, I'm begging you, don't tell them; I would
be very ashamed. I'll kill myself if you do it."

"But, my child, you know I like you more than all the others.
Well, I promise never to tell this story on the condition, of course,
that you never tell it either, never—"

"I promise! I swear, Uncle. Thank you so much."

"If you ever tell this story, then not only will the twins know
about it but the sorcerers could learn it too, and, my poor child, I

will be unable to protect you, and they'll sic their owls on you at night and gouge your eyes out."

Of all nocturnal birds, the owl was the one I feared most. I knew it was the bird sorcerers used to transmit their mysterious messages to one another, but they could also send owls to land and hoot on the roof of anyone they wanted to jinx.

"What's more, don't forget, if you repeat this story, I won't incise you with the kaman and then, even in the smallest little fight, your brothers will grind you to dust like manioc flour in a mortar."

"Oh, of course, I'd never, Uncle."

"You are brave, little one," he continued, satisfied. "What do you want, cake, some candy?"

"I want a Coke."

Ever since that episode we have been very close, and he still pays lots of attention to me. As for Auntie Lolo, she always rushes toward me, pets me, and gives me many small gifts, and offers me biscuits, fruit juice, or soda every time I come into their store; she's even nicer and more attentive when old Bidié is at the counter.

Now that I've told it to you, please, don't repeat it, because if you do Uncle Boula Boula will hear about it and will break his silence and won't incise me with the kaman that will make me strong as a buffalo. He will reveal to the whole world that I am just a girlie compared with my twin brothers, and I would die of shame if this story of my cowardliness reached them. You won't repeat it, right? Promise?

7

I got better, my scars had healed, and I was now ambidextrous to the great joy of my mother, who thought that since my right hand had become useful again, the left one would automatically become impotent. In any case, I could sense that the warning Father Boniface had instilled in her regarding me from the very beginning hadn't completely left her mind and that, in one way or another, she felt it her duty to protect my brothers from me. Even though I was a child as normal as my two elders, my unexpected birth, so out of the ordinary, continued to give her real concerns. She was not raising us as a single group but as two, one consisting of a pair, the twins, the other of one individual, me. And so, when she bought pants, for example, she picked out two of the same color for them and one of another color for me. I don't want you to think she didn't love me. She loved all of us, but in a manner more complicated than Papa's.

Papa, he loved us all the same way. He often took us out to play sports, but to be honest, he spent most of his time reading the encyclopedia and all the journals he was always receiving. He would often get excited by what he was reading, his eyes glowing triumphantly whenever he would discover "a truth unknown until now because of the limits of our present-day knowledge" or "a truth concealed by certain people for ideological reasons," as he would say. He would then call us over to explain it to us, but this rarely interested my twin brothers, who by far preferred watching videos or TV, so I alone would often stay with him and listen, impressed, reading the books of man and the book of the universe, in the words of my grandfather.

One day when I entered his small study crammed with books, pencils, and scattered papers, he was kneeling on all fours over a big open atlas observing the earth's surface in fascination. Over on one side, on a sheet of paper, he had drawn twenty-four lines, which all met at one point: the North Pole, he told me.

"Come and look, Michel." He was the only one who called me Michel, the first name he had given me at birth, while all the others called me Matapari. "These lines here are called longitudes." He pointed to one and traced with the point of his pencil all the way up to where all of them met. "The time is the same along this entire line, from the south all the way up north. Now look. Look at this point where all the lines of longitude meet"—he indicated the exact point with the tip of his pencil—"this is the degree zero of the globe, the origin and terminus of all the lines of longitude." I listened to him, intrigued, since I didn't see what he was getting at.

"Tell me, what time is it when you are exactly at the pole?"

The answer was obvious to me: "Whatever time my watch says," I answered.

"But the time on your watch depends on your longitude! When it is noon in Brazzaville, it is 11 p.m. in Anchorage, Alaska! Now here, at the degree zero, here you find the origin and terminus of all the hours of the globe. No, you cannot ask for the time at the North Pole, my child. Here all time is the same, one hour is a day and one day is three hundred and sixty-five days, in other words, a year. Wow!" he exclaimed. "Have you ever thought about that?"

It was interesting, I admit, but I didn't see what there was to get so excited about. It wasn't worth a *Robocop* episode I had just seen on TV. But Papa's like that. He'll get excited about an idea, a word, a phrase in a book! Enthusiastically calling all his children to talk to them about it, then forgetting all about them and diving once more into his reading.

Maman's love was, as I said, more complicated. It was more difficult for her to manage because she wanted to save our souls. And my soul gave her many worries, especially after I saved my brother Banzouzi from certain death.

One day I had lost all the marbles I had at a game of loser-wins with my friends. To keep playing, I had replaced them with seeds from a plant that thrived in a humid corner of Maman's manioc field; when they matured, these seeds were bigger than corn kernels, hard and shiny like pearls on the outside, their color varying from an ashy gray to black. I had a pocketful when I got home. That's when Father Boniface came along. He apparently knew these seeds, since he took them in his hand and said to Maman: "Well now, these here are Christ's tears. Some call them Job's tears, but I prefer calling them Christ's tears. It was from one of the tears the Lord shed on Golgotha that this plant was born. These seeds make excellent rosaries. You just need to make a hole, string them, and add a cross. Christ, who loves the poor, will gladly accept this humble instrument of prayer until the arrival of the real rosary you ordered."

For once, Father Boniface was right—each seed was shaped like a big tear. I nevertheless thought that they would make a better necklace than a rosary. Unfortunately, Maman and many of the other women of her village found the priest's idea to be a stroke of genius and carried it out right away. But with the arrival of the real rosary, which she had ordered from the devotional objects salesmen in the capital, she gave up the homemade one in favor of the manufactured beads made of black plastic. This happened quite a while ago. The homemade rosary had by now disappeared and we had forgotten all about it until when, no one knows how, one of those seeds found itself snugly lodged up the nose of my brother Banzouzi.

Everyone panicked. We quickly took him to the little clinic that served as our hospital, where our "doctor" was in residence and where my brothers were born. Maman was crying. I wanted to tell Banzouzi not to breathe too hard, for fear that the seed that blocked one of his nostrils would go down all the way to his lung and kill him, or else take root and yield a bunch of other seeds that would certainly choke him eventually, but they wouldn't let me talk to him. The doctor arrived with a bunch of scalpels and other instruments whose names I don't know, alcohol, and antiseptic oil. They entered the operating room. I stayed outside with Batsimba, and we could hear Banzouzi's cries, the doctor's swearing, and Maman's "don't cry," "don't move," "Lord help us."

Our village was quite small, so news and rumors got around fast. They must have reached Father Boniface, since I saw him arrive. It was my first time seeing him in a long while, in fact since the day I had provoked his fall from his friend Fausto Coppi's bike. He came into the waiting room, his big ebony cross dangling on his chest, tossed off a "hello, children" without looking at me, and then went to caress Batsimba's head. At the moment he was about to sit down, the door swung open and the doctor came out, his face drenched in sweat. Father Boniface jumped back up on his feet.

"Ah, Father," said the doctor, "glad to see you. It's serious, very serious. He urgently needs an operation performed by an ENT specialist. I tried removing the seed, but it sank in deeper; I also fear the risk of infection. We have to hurry. I'm going to see if we can evacuate him to the capital as soon as possible. You can come in."

Father Boniface went inside; Maman must have been happy to

see him, since he no longer came to the house on account of Papa and me. I don't know what they said to each other, but after a while Maman came out and asked Batsimba to go and be near his brother, who was asking for him. I also got up to go in, for he was my brother too and I wanted him to be in good health and standing on two feet so I could regularly beat him up with my fists after Uncle Boula Boula incised me with the kaman. "But no, you see, Matapari, your brother Banzouzi is doing very badly; Father Boniface thinks that your presence could do him ill and your brother could die from choking if he saw you or if you touched him. Batsimba is his twin, and you know that twins do everything together, that is why it is important he be near Banzouzi. But don't worry, we all love you; anyway we'll let you in when he is better."

I was miserable, but to avoid upsetting Maman, since I knew she always believed whatever Father Boniface said, I did not protest, didn't even cry, and I calmly stayed by myself in the waiting room. Anyway, I knew that my two older brothers, twins between themselves and triplets along with me, always had a certain mistrust of me. Was it because of that lion that had chased them in their nightmare during my sickness, or was it simply because of all the stories Mama Kossa and the others kept telling about my birth before Papa reestablished the scientific truth? And just then, speaking of Papa, there he was: "Michel, what disaster is this? Where are the others?"

I pointed to the operating room.

"Come with me."

"Father Boniface doesn't want me to . . ."

"Boni . . . who? Come on!"

He took me by the hand with authority and burst into the patient's room. Batsimba was holding Banzouzi's hands, Maman had hers clasped, her head bowed and covered with a kerchief while Father Boniface recited a prayer. Papa didn't even say hello. "Boniface, what is this bullshit about some God's tear up my kid's nose?"

The prayer was immediately cut short. Everybody looked at Papa. Banzouzi's eyes caught mine, but he didn't die, contrary to what Father Boniface thought.

"Where's the doctor?" Papa yelled, after noting Banzouzi's painfully sibilant respiration through one nostril.

"He went to see if he could be evacuated to the capital," said Maman.

"It's serious," the priest managed to articulate, gazing at me worriedly.

We all remained silent around Banzouzi, waiting for the doctor. I looked at my brother; he was in bad shape. Each time his wheezing stopped for an instant, Maman would stop breathing too and make an awful face until his wheezing resumed. The patient's forehead glistened with sweat and, in a sudden rush of tenderness, I held out my left hand to wipe his forehead. Then events unfolded rather quickly.

"Don't touch him, you'll kill him!" yelled Father Boniface, who, his eyes horrified, had leaned forward to hold back my hand. My mother let out a cry of panic. My father understood nothing of what was going on. Meanwhile, my hand was quicker than that of the priest, who wanted to hold it back, and at the moment he felt my palm on his forehead, Banzouzi got really scared, his eyes widened, he hiccuped, curled up, backing away; he almost choked and then let out a powerful sneeze. The seed stuck in his nostril was propelled like a champagne cork, ricocheting against the eye of Father Boniface, who was still leaning forward, before falling on Banzouzi's mattress.

"Lord Jesus!" the priest cried out in pain and starting rubbing his eye.

"Hallelujah, a miracle!" Maman exclaimed.

"What a happy coincidence, this sneeze," my father said enthusiastically.

Banzouzi was now breathing comfortably, happy to have his nostrils clear, and he and Batsimba both looked at me in surprise.

"My eye, he gouged out my eye!"

Like a Good Samaritan, my father went and took a look. In fact, the priest's eye hadn't been gouged out at all, though it was pretty red and runny.

"It's nothing," said my father, "merely irritation and a lot of tears. Christ's tears, are they not?"

The priest got upset and quit the room and Maman's life too. We never saw him again. Then the doctor arrived, preoccupied, with a stretcher and two men and started talking to my father, who hadn't been there earlier. The doctor had managed to talk by phone to a qualified ENT instructor at the University-Hospital Center in the capital. He had told him that it was serious, that the child risked infection if the foreign body wasn't removed within forty-eight hours, and that the consequences could be fatal. He had then seen the prefect, who, after some hesitation, had agreed to let his patrol car, a brand-new Japanese 4 × 4, serve as an ambulance for the schoolmaster's son. It was only when he finished talking that he noticed Banzouzi breathing normally. He couldn't believe it. He thought he was dreaming.

"It's a miracle," said Maman.

"Not at all," said Papa. "The sneeze was unanticipated and, I would even add, unpredictable. It's a coincidence. Isn't it said that a coincidence can work wonders?" he continued in a playful voice. "It is a coincidence when a random radioactive core particle decays within a given and quantifiable system. The quantum leap of an electron is a coincidence. It's a coincidence that a sneeze could eject a seed from a child's left nasal passage!"

Maman's spiritual problems grew worse from then on. She was lost. She no longer knew if I was the child of the Devil as Father Boniface kept saying or if I was an instrument of God. I had saved my brother's life simply by placing my left hand on his forehead, while the modern medicine practiced by our doctor's scalpels had failed; and I had managed this against the opinion of a Catholic priest who had completed an internship in Rome in the Pope's stable. There was too much evidence in my favor. She finally took my side—I was her child after all—and she decided that I was indeed an instrument of the Lord.

It was in that period that politics erupted into our lives.

8

I don't know what had gotten into him, but the President of the Republic, the very same who had knocked out my papa with his heavy portrait the day I was born, decided to come celebrate the fourteenth year of his rule in the county seat of our little district. This was my opportunity to see him in the flesh. He had representatives from the one-and-only Party to scout ahead and prepare the visit and explain to us the historic significance of this decision. In effect, for our Beloved Beacon, the revolution was to begin in the countryside and would be largely for the benefit of the rural masses instead of the rapacious bourgeoisie of the cities; that is why he had chosen our little village, in advance of the grand spectacle of the fifteenth anniversary to be celebrated in the capital the following year.

Before I go on, I ought to let you in on all the ways our President is called, so that we don't have to come back to that: Supreme Guide, Man of the Masses, the Man of Concrete Action, the Popular Leader, Peacemaker, Friend of the Youth, the People's Man, the Providential Guide, the Founding President, the Man-

Always-Proven-Right-by-History. I'm sure I'm forgetting some, since the radio and the Party's agitprop section invented a new one each week, but I promise to note them each time they come to mind.

In honor of this high-level delegation, the prefect had declared a day off, with pay. I was very pleased because that meant a holiday for us, and I planned on playing soccer with my friends, then going to Ma Lolo's to get her to give me a Coca-Cola, and finally going to watch some music videos at Uncle Boula Boula's. Unfortunately, it was not a real day off, since we were forced to stand under the hot sun and listen to the speeches of those guys sent by the Popular Leader, the Man of the Masses and Concrete Action. Anyway, besides the officials, one could also notice the presence of the men and women who sold things at the market for a living. Those were the people who were referred to as the masses. Only Papa was sulking during the ceremony because, said he, the students should not be recruited into a party, especially one that was unopposed and revolutionary. He had stayed home reading, certainly unraveling yet another enigma in the great book of the universe.

But what struck me most during the visit of these ambassadors of the Man-Always-Proven-Right-by-History was Uncle Boula Boula's activism. He never told me he was a Party member, and yet, presto, there he was with a medallion in his buttonhole, a big red thing that looked like a beer bottle cap engraved with the Party insignia. He fussed over the chief of the delegation like a real mother hen. He served him as chauffeur, guided him to where he was supposed to stand during the ceremonies, and always arranged himself so that he wouldn't be too far away from him. Unable to personally house this illustrious guest, who was also a member of the Political Bureau of Party Organization and Propaganda—the prefect took it upon himself to provide lodging—Uncle had nevertheless succeeded in inviting the guest to dine at his house one night.

I'll remember this dinner for a long time: there was an appetizer, hors d'oeuvres, two main courses (Uncle had slaughtered a lamb and three chickens), crushed manioc leaves, which we call *saka saka*, accompanied by salted fish, salad, red wine, mangoes, pineapples, . . . and apples! How did he manage to get some in our little village, since these fruits did not grow here in equatorial Africa? I wouldn't know, but I ate two and hid two others to bring back to my brothers to impress them. Uncle, who was unmarried and therefore needed help for his cook, had asked me to be there. I shuttled from kitchen to table with clean plates and utensils, and from table to kitchen with dirty dishes and glasses. Each time, I took the opportunity to drain the dregs out of the guests' glasses.

Uncle discussed things he had never told me about. It was only then that I understood how modest my uncle Boula Boula had been, since he had concealed from me all these things he was now telling this high political official, for example, the fact that he had done serious university studies. "Following a stay in France, a bourgeois and capitalist country where I lived quite comfortably, I decided to give it all up for a stay in the German Democratic Republic. I learned a great deal there, Comrade P.B. Member." The members of the party called each other "comrade," and saying "mister" to someone was tasteless. "Above all, I learned that a revolutionary party must be explained and defended; so I enrolled at the Karl Marx Hochschule, where, after three years of arduous study, I obtained a doctorate."

"That's impressive! You're a doctor in what?" asked the comrade P.B. member.

"Doctor of Agitation and Propaganda!"

"Excellent! I too received a habilitatus from the GDR, Workers Militia Section. We have an opening for a doctor of agitation at the Party. The Party needs qualified Red men like yourself in its ranks, especially when they have been trained in Democratic Germany. It is in fact the Stasi that trains most of our State Security staff, though a number of them have been trained by the Securitat in Bucharest. I will most certainly speak with the President about you."

My uncle quivered with pleasure like a live fish thrown in a hot frying pan. In any case, one thing did puzzle me: As far as I know, Uncle, as well as Papa, had never traveled overseas!

"Some cognac or Marie Brizard?"

"Cognac," answered the important member of the P.B.

"And you, Comrade Prefect?"

"Marie Brizard."

I had never seen all these drinks with their strangely shaped bottles at my uncle's. He was so happy that he did not notice me sitting in a chair in a corner of the living room eavesdropping, until he asked me to take away the glasses and go get the champagne that was in the freezer. I gathered the glasses on a platter and went in the kitchen.

I found a well-dressed young lady sitting by the kitchen table, a lady I vaguely knew. It even seems to me that I had seen her once or twice with Uncle Boula Boula, but I'm not completely sure. I found her as pretty as Auntie Lolo in the nightgown from that dream I sent to Father Boniface. I thought she wanted to see my uncle, and I asked her name so I could announce her. The cook interrupted and chewed me out for my curiosity, but I persisted until she revealed that Uncle Boula Boula knew that the lady was here, and that it was he himself who had sent for her to help the honorable comrade do his room. "But it's night," I said, "you don't clean up at night!" "Shut up!" she replied brusquely, "you're only a child, don't meddle in grown-ups' business."

I shut up and told myself that Uncle Boula Boula should have thought about getting the room of the comrade member of the Political Bureau of our one-and-only revolutionary Party cleaned up earlier, instead of having this poor lady sweeping at night. In fact, she seemed like a novice, for she did not even know how to dress for the job. Instead of old clothes and gloves to handle the water bucket, broom, and mop, she was dressed as if she were go-

ing to a party: a tight little dress that hardly got past her knees and
held back her breasts with great difficulty; her hair was very well
done with brown extensions sewn into her own hair, framing a
heavily made-up face. I'm telling you, she was as pretty as Auntie
Lolo. Having cast off her high heels under the chair, she downed
big gulps of beer that the cook had served her to help her while
away the time. I only wished that she would not sweep the leaves
in which we had wrapped manioc or spread salt on the floor: Maman had told me that doing any of these things at night could
awaken sorcerers and other evil spirits.

So I left the lady to her long wait, and I put the glasses, whose
last dregs I had drained without the cook's knowledge, on the
kitchen table. In this manner, I drank a bit of martini (sugary, bit-
tersweet, and pleasant), cognac (dry and rough on the taste buds),
whiskey (I coughed, I thought there was a fire in my throat),
Marie Brizard (sweet, with the smell and taste of anise), and red
wine. My head started spinning, and I could barely walk a straight
line. I got the champagne bottle my uncle had asked me to bring
out of the freezer, but, as I turned, I hit my knee against the table
and the pain made me trip and as I tried to catch myself I knocked
over the tray of glasses, which shattered in a great tintinnabula-
tion, as the bottle of champagne, the only one my uncle had to offer his guest, slipped out of my hands and glided gracefully before
noisily exploding on the concrete floor, while I, carried by my momentum, flew into the dining room. The detonation of the champagne bottle gave everyone a start, and I barely escaped death
since the bodyguards of both the prefect and the illustrious comrade already had their weapons pointed at me, thinking this was a
bombing. My uncle was upset: he had lost the champagne bottle
that was supposed to have crowned the evening and made him an
important and deserving host. He gave me two good slaps, and I
started yelling and ran home in tears. It was the first time I had
seen him get so upset since that day he scared me with Auntie
Lolo: come to think of it now, I think he really must hold a doc-

torate in agitation, the way he had shaken the bed that day with
Auntie Lolo, and all just for the pleasure of giving me a good
fright.

Everyone was already in bed when I arrived home, except for
Papa. I was already thinking of an explanation for my tears (I
didn't want him to know I had broken the champagne bottle destined for the glass of the member of the Political Bureau from the
capital), but he asked me nothing as he opened the door. I don't
even think he noticed I'd been crying, though right away I noticed
that gleam of excitement he had in his eyes when, as he would say,
he was on the verge of discovering a hidden truth. "Michel, with
Antarctica, it's clear. Scott, Amundsen, no doubt, Amundsen was
the first. But the Arctic, the North Pole, there's something un-
clear, fuzzy."

He dragged me into his study, and I saw that he was once
again embroiled in the earth's poles and longitudes. On the table
and on the floor there were encyclopedias, books on the search for
the Pole, magazines with titles like *National Geographic* and *Ebony*
featuring pictures of dogs, sleds, and of a black man and a white
man snugly muffled up in their coats, standing around a United
States flag stuck in the ice.

"Peary's account is vague. What happened when, feet frozen,
exhausted, he sent his chief navigator ahead, and what happened
when the latter stepped onto point zero of the ninety-degree latitude north, thereby claiming the title of the first man to have
reached it?"

I admit that I didn't understand much of what he was saying,
and I didn't know any of the people he had named. All I knew was
that the earth had a North Pole and a South Pole, the two resem-
bling each other like twin sisters, almost identical except that one
was just a frozen ocean while the other was a continent; it was cold
like we couldn't even imagine here on the banks of the great
Congo River, a bone-shattering cold, and when you peed outside,
your piss froze before it hit the ground; and also there were six or

seven months of night nonstop and six or seven months of day. Oh
yes, Papa had also explained to me that there wasn't any earthly
time over there since it was the meeting place of all the lines of
longitude. But I had eaten too much, sipped too many potent
dregs, and had had a good cry; so I was tired. I could not restrain
myself from yawning and immediately wished Papa a good night.
I went to my room to go to sleep, all the while trying not to wake
up my two brothers, who were already snoring. I hoped they were
dreaming of apples, so that tomorrow I could impress them by offering them some.

9

The next morning, I was awakened by an insistent honking in front of our house. I got up and dressed right
away, while my two brothers, twins between themselves
and triplets with me, snored on. I wondered who could be so rude
to the point of rousing people at the crack of dawn. When I got to
the door, Maman was already there, pulling on the bolts and turning the key in the knob. Meanwhile, the honking turned into
knocks on the door. There was Uncle Boula Boula standing at the
door when Maman finally opened it. He was in a suit and tie despite the early hour; he was still wearing the famous red Party
medallion that I'd already noticed yesterday on his lapel. Farther
off, parked on the clay road, a Japanese jeep stood erect, high on
its four all-terrain wheels, the famous "four-wheel drive" that we
abbreviated to a mere "4 × 4 FWD."

Maman, stunned, addressed her brother sharply: "What's going on, Boula Boula? Has the Lord announced the end of the
world for you to be making such a racket?"

That's it, I said to myself when I saw my uncle, he's come to denounce me to Maman for the champagne bottle I blew up. It was probably really the prefect's bottle and he was surely looking to be reimbursed. How much could a champagne bottle cost? Where were Maman and Papa to get the money to reimburse him? There I was, head bowed, nowhere to run.

"Great news, little sister! I am going to be nominated to a high position in the Party. I am going to the capital this very moment with the comrade member of the Political Bureau, who was willing to do me the honor of taking a minute to meet my family, meaning you. Don't you disappoint him now, I've said so many good things about you and your husband."

I let out a sigh of relief. He was not here because of me. Maman, on the other hand, was still perplexed. She pointed her finger at the red medallion: "What sect have you gotten yourself into? Tell me the truth, which heathen sect does this medallion belong to? The Mahikari or the Order of the Solar Temple?"

"Are you kidding? This is a Party medallion!"

"The Party? But since when are you a member of the Party?"

"Shush!" Uncle put his fingers over his two pouting lips, casting worried glances at the fat sedan idling on its fat all-terrain wheels. "Don't talk so loud, he can hear us. Old Bidié's wife lent me her husband's medallion. The merchant is too old, and for the sake of our district's good image, there was a need for the presence of a young and dynamic member of our Party. If the comrade from the P.B. asks about this, you have to say that I'm one of the oldest Party members in our whole region. Understood?"

"What, you want to teach your sister how to lie? Don't you know that, according to the Ten Commandments, lying is a sin? You've never been a member of the Party!"

"Well, I am now."

"But why?"

"I'll explain it to you later. You'll see that it's very important and it will enable me to solve a whole lot of problems. Come, don't keep the comrade waiting, I'm going to present to him my sister and her husband. Matapari, go get your papa and be quick about it."

They headed toward the car. Nimble as a squirrel, I went to call Papa and, just as nimbly, I returned to let my uncle know that the mission was accomplished. My zeal was not innocent, I wanted to make up for my folly of last evening, to get back into his good graces and earn my kaman.

Meanwhile he was saying to the comrade: "This is my younger sister, a great militant with the Party's Women's Revolutionary Union, an organization that unfortunately has yet to have a cell in our district."

The comrade listened to him, nodding his head approvingly, eyes hidden behind dark glasses. Despite this camouflage, I could see very well that he had not passed a restful night, for he had bags under his eyes and his face was drawn. His quarters must have been so large that the poor girl I had seen last night had to take such a long time cleaning up that the poor fellow must have gone to bed quite late, probably around four in the morning, and that's hardly two hours of sleep! He clumsily tried concealing a yawn that Uncle didn't even notice, so busy was he overwhelming him with words: "That is, in fact, my next objective, to establish the first cell of this union in our district, because it is urgent that we encourage our women, so often left behind, to stand up for the revolution incarnated by our Party and its Guide, Comrade—"

"Lord Jesus," Maman began, without waiting for the end of her brother's sentence.

"Ahem!" My uncle coughed noisily to conceal Christ's name from the ears of the important individual: all members of the Party had to be Marxist and atheist, most of all the representative of the Women's Revolutionary Union. It would be a catastrophe if the member of the P.B. came to discover that Maman, presented as such, was in fact injecting herself with the opiate of the masses.

Uncle suddenly remembered that Maman always wore a cross and, panicking, he looked at her neck: whew, much to his relief, Maman didn't have it on. Then, Papa arrived.

He strode up, tightening the string of his pajama pants. Though he sure wasn't happy to have been awakened so suddenly and forced to go out on the street in his domestic attire, he was alert and had a relaxed face, as if he had had a long, restful night, though I had seen light filtering out of his room until quite late.

As soon as he saw him, my uncle started singing his praises. "Comrade member of the Political Bureau, the person walking toward us is my brother-in-law, the director of our regional school. A true scholar who has read Marx, Engels, Lenin, and all the Russian revolutionary literature. Ask him any question about *Das Kapital* or Lenin's NEP, or anything you want about the Revolution, he will answer you, he will even show you the page if you want. If he wasn't present at the ceremony you presided over, it was not for lack of revolutionary enthusiasm, but simply because he had a bout of malaria. It is vital for us to have as our children's educator a man so versed in the dialectic, since—"

"Good morning. What's going on, Boula Boula? Have you solved Fermat's last theorem that you're dragging me out of bed at such an early hour?"

Carried away by his dithyramb, Uncle didn't realize that Papa was already right behind him. So he was cut short and hesitated answering Papa's question. But he wasn't the only one: the comrade from the Political Bureau, who wasn't supposed to show his ignorance before a rank-and-file militant, hesitated too: he was wondering if Fermat's theorem wasn't something developed by Marx in *Das Kapital* or a theoretical question posed by Lenin to justify the Revolution (as for me, I knew neither Marx, Lenin, nor Mr. Fermat).

Uncle tried to remedy the situation: "Uh . . . Comrade, I present to you my brother-in-law, director of the regional school."

"A pleasure," said he.

"Likewise," said Papa in his turn, "and who might you be?"

Uncle Boula Boula sat on burning embers. For the important guest, it was unthinkable that someone in this village not know who he was, he who had made the heart of our town beat like a tom-tom, he who had mobilized the whole village over the past three days, he—the Party's Number Two, second only to the President of the Republic! Matapari's devil of a father! You're going to get me in deep shit when I was this close to getting what I wanted!

"Oh yes," stammered my uncle, "excuse him, Comrade, he's had a bout of malaria for the past three days, so he was not aware of your arrival and didn't know that the Party had sent ahead a scout to prepare for the visit of the Supreme Guide of the Revolution, the Comrade President of the Republic."

Uncle was very slick, since his speech was also filling Papa in, and he followed up right away so that his brother-in-law would not protest against the allegation that he'd just had a bout of malaria: "But anyhow, this is a serious man, and I'm sure that, despite his absence from our ceremonies, he was with us in spirit."

"Very happy to meet you," said the important member of the Political Bureau. "It is rare to see an entire family totally devoted to the revolutionary cause. Just like your brother-in-law, who will certainly share a high level of responsibility in the preparation of the President's trip, you would be of great help to us. Soon we are to open a school in the capital for our delegates; I've been told that you know the Russian revolutionary literature very well—"

"Ah," said Papa, forgetting his rude awakening and the fact that he was in pajamas. "Pushkin!"—his eyes gleamed with excitement—"it is from him, from this grandson of Africa, that the true revolution of Russian literature dates. *Eugene Onegin!* Some say that this unclassifiable novel so embraces the Russian language that it is untranslatable."

Apparently, the representative of the Man of the Masses and Concrete Action had never heard of Pushkin, African descendant. Since Papa had read many more books than he had, he wasn't sure if this Pushkin was one of Lenin's revolutionary associates or one of those bourgeois intellectuals that he had steadfastly fought against. He therefore tried to bring the discussion back to solid ground, the infallible Lenin, in other words: "The great Lenin wrote that—"

"Lenin! Are you kidding? You dare put Lenin on the same level as Pushkin?"

"That's right," my uncle hurriedly interrupted. Uncle knew about Papa's straight talk when it came to a subject he held dear, and thus feared that the scholar would say something that did not conform to the Party creed. "Of course not, Lenin is another thing altogether, incomparable and inexhaustible. But we shouldn't keep the comrade any longer, we have a long road ahead. Goodbye, everyone. I'll probably be back in a week." He was already in his seat, slammed the door, and signaled to the chauffeur to get moving. The comrade smiled at Maman, waved imperceptibly at Papa and me (let's not forget that he and I were already old acquaintances since we'd dined and drunk together at my uncle's last night—well, almost). The car took off with the might of its four-wheel drive before disappearing in the laterite dust, auburn beneath the yellowish rays of the rising sun.

Papa turned toward his wife and said: "I still don't understand why Boula Boula came to wake us up so early."

"It was to announce that he has gotten into the Party."

"Boula Boula, a Marxist-Leninist? Don't make me laugh. Are you sure that your brother isn't up to something fishy with all this?"

Maman shrugged her shoulders and headed for the house. Papa tousled my hair affectionately, and I began to trot along beside him as he again tightened the string of his pajamas around his waist. But I think that I was most happy because Uncle had kept quiet about the champagne incident. I went into our room whistling and noticed that my brothers, twins between themselves and triplets with me, were still sleeping; they shared a big bed while I slept alone in another, much smaller bed. I opened the French windows wide to let as much light as possible fall on their eyes, but they still would not wake up. So I pulled out their big cotton-stuffed bolster and swatted them with it, shouting, "Wake up, lazybones, it's noon already!" They started and looked at me with dread, but my smile reassured them.

"I have a surprise for you. I brought you back some fruit from Europe that I stole last night at Uncle Boula Boula's. Guess what it is."

"Mangoes," said Banzouzi.

"No, mangoes are tropical fruits!"

"Papayas or soursops," Batsimba corrected.

"No, idiots! I'll tell you: apples!"

"Apples?" they chimed in a perfect duet, in their eyes a glint of doubt mingled with desire.

"Yes, apples," I declared, offering one to each with the generous, sweeping gesture of a great comrade.

10

My uncle had changed after the fifteen days he spent in the capital. He had returned in a 4 × 4 FWD Pajero with tinted windows, wearing a suit as new as the medallion with the portrait of the President of the Republic that now hung on his left lapel, against his heart. He had also come back with a new title as long as the Congo-Ocean Railroad: Executive President of Vital Works for the Fourteenth Anniversary of the Revolution Celebrated Exclusively outside the Capital. The acronym of this new title, EPOVWFARCEC, was so long itself that it was abbreviated to FARCE, which, you can imagine, led everyone to joke and tease my uncle, whom they all now called Comrade FARCE. I fought many times with (and got thrashed by) imps who teased me about this, and I'll be glad when Uncle gives me the kaman so I can defend his honor so often ridiculed in my presence.

I understood the importance of this new title only when he came to the house with propositions for Papa. First, he was being driven by a chauffeur, which showed he had become as important as the prefect; then, he was accompanied by a man who followed him everywhere, opened car doors for him, carried his briefcase and other accessories such as his hat, raincoat, or umbrella when he had one. As far as I was concerned, that showed he was even more important than the prefect. He came by the house as early as the morning after his return, with a case of twelve champagne bottles carried by his henchman and labeled Moët & Chandon.

He was happy, even jolly; he embraced Papa and held him in a vigorous bear hug. "So, brother-in-law, how's it going? How's my sister? Put down the carton and go wait for us in the car," he said to his factotum.

The man obeyed right away.

"What the hell is he doing with this majordomo?" asked Papa.

"This is my orderly and bodyguard."

"So, you are more important than the regional prefect, who merely has a chauffeur?"

"But, my dear, the Party runs the State and, besides, I am the personal representative of the President of the Republic. I think you still don't understand, brother-in-law. I have become the most important individual in this village, this district, this prefecture. Everything has to go through me, especially the major work that has to be done to mark the great ceremony that's just on the horizon. I have absolute power. You want to supply cement, bricks, boards for a new building in town? You need my signature! You want to supply stacks of paper, pens, and furniture for some offices? My signature! Your business wants to participate in the construction of the stadium where the ceremonies will take place? My signature! And a signature is expensive!"

"So then you are a sort of godfather?"

"Well, well, brother-in-law, always these outrageous comments about the Party and the esteemed representatives of the people. I also wanted to tell you that I've gone into business."

"Who lent you the money?"

"Are you doing this on purpose, or are you really that naïve?"

He got out of his briefcase three pieces of stationery with different headings and logos. The first sheet was entitled "Δ-Contact: Bureau of Management and Computer Studies"; the second read, "ACC: African Construction Company. All contracting, from draft to finished work."

"You'll notice," he said, "that the name here is in English; it sounds American and seems more professional," he concluded, putting the sheet down. "As for the third, I'd like to open a shop, Boula Boula Sports—BBS, but I'm worried about using my own name. In fact, in view of the responsibilities I'm assuming, it's not the best idea for me to manage these businesses directly; I should stay in the shadows. I would like you to run Δ-Contact. It is a mathematical symbol, sounds precise, and it suits you as a teacher. You know that the President of the Republic is going to mark the fourteenth anniversary of his coming into power here and will also hold a session of the Party Central Committee: reams and reams of paper will be darkened not only by all the accounts taken and the motions of support and gratitude to the leader, but also by the many journalists who will come from all over the world. A specialized office is therefore needed to offer them all the necessary services, from simple paper to telephones and faxing, and Δ-Contact will be that office."

"Very interesting," said Papa.

"I'm not finished," he went on. "As for the ACC, I don't yet know who I can trust with it. You know as well as I that the whole grandiose ceremony has to take place in a stadium. Since the time of the Romans and the Greeks, the fights of the gladiators, the circuses, not to mention the Olympic Games and the Soccer World Cup, everything takes place in a stadium. And so, we are going to build a thirty-thousand-seat stadium for the occasion. So you can understand the necessity for a high-powered construction company . . .

"And as for Boula Boula Sports, the occasion will call for sporting events, and one needs jerseys, cleats, balls . . ."

"That's it," Uncle said with conviction, as if Papa's intelligence was finally waking up and rising to his own level. "But I was just thinking, I should create a fourth company, a restaurant, since all the people who will pour into our city have to eat, drink, and dance. Ah yes," he said, happy to have fallen upon this new idea, "for this one the name must be French; it should evoke Paris since it seems like French cuisine has a good reputation around the world. La Tour Palmée, no, Le Maxim's Tropical, no, not evocative enough. Well, I'll think about it later."

"You still haven't told me how you're going to finance this."

"But that's obvious, since all contracts must go through me. And since I am not actually compelled to create these companies, it's enough to create them on paper and make subcontracts."

"You're a crook, Boula Boula," Papa said without hesitation.

I was afraid that Uncle would take this badly and leave the house, slamming the door behind him, but not at all; on the contrary, he smiled and attributed Papa's notions about accounting to his naïveté, since, as was often said, my father had read so many books that he sometimes forgot the harsh reality of the real world.

"Well, as for you, you're a Candide, and that's worse than being naïve," he replied. "Do you think that the politicians who fight and kill each other for power do it all for the one love of the Party? The Party? Do you think that they vie to be in the Political Bureau just out of love for the people? It's to eat, old man! To eat! I succeeded, and now I want my piece of the cake. And not all for myself like some selfish person but for my loved ones too. I'm naming you director of the Δ-Contact, and I'm naming my sister, your wife, head of the restaurant."

Papa starting laughing. "Have you heard of nepotism?"

"Uh, no. What kind of business is that?"

Papa didn't answer and kept silent for a good while. My uncle stared at him, impatient. "Well?" he pressed.

"You know what you ought to do to rehabilitate yourself a little? Build a library with all the money the Party is going to waste on this event."

"Is there a profit in it?"

"Oh yes, and how!"

"How much and in how long?"

"In ten years, fifteen, maybe a generation."

"I think you're messing with me again, aren't you? I give up, too bad for you. Stay poor, you and your wife, I'm leaving."

Uncle was finally upset. Not as much as when he had discovered me under the bed in which he and Ma Lolo were amusing themselves at scaring me, but upset nonetheless. He scooped up his papers, dropping the Δ-Contact stationery, which I picked right up to give back to him. He clicked shut his briefcase and called for his orderly. He affectionately but forcefully passed his fingers through my hair, and left forgetting to shake Papa's hand and to take back the case of champagne.

11

Ultimately, Papa was wrong and Uncle Boula Boula had won his bet. The major work soon began. My most vivid memory of it was the field trip Papa had organized for all the middle school students, at the very beginning, when they started clearing the forest to make way for the stadium. "Children, come attend the massacre," he had said. As director, he had decided to close school for the whole morning to permit us to attend a lesson about the majesty of nature with our botany teacher. I admit that I was distressed by what we saw. When we arrived, they had already opened a trench of several hundred yards through the forest; the bloody laterite color of the ground made it look like an artery. The powerful bulldozers continued to advance, mangling the branches, and with the sharp edges of their shovels wounding the trunks of the smaller trees that gushed white sap as they broke, and then moving along crushing everything under their studded tracks. When the bulldozer came upon one of those hundred-year-old trees that it could neither break, crush, nor uproot, they would switch over to a gas-powered chain saw; they started the motor and, inch by painful inch, the murderous chain of the screeching saw penetrated the live flesh of the sapwood. Once the mass was slit like someone's neck, the equatorial giant came crashing down with the racket of prehistoric beasts, destroying everything in its path, a violent cataclysm in this peacefully balanced environment: legions of squawking birds took flight, terrified screaming monkeys leaped away from tree to tree, vine to vine, night butterflies and other hidden insects suddenly exposed to the sunlight panicked and went berserk, as did the phosphorescent ferns that would be killed by the sun . . . The fallen tree was quickly sawed to pieces and the logs hoisted up by huge cranes that deposited them onto truck beds. What a sight!

Disgusted, Papa went and left us alone with our botany teacher, who asked us to follow him a hundred yards into the forest. He began explaining to us the importance of the jungle. How the humid tropical forest contained more than half of the living species on Earth and helped maintain the ecological balance of the planet. How there wasn't any other natural environment in the world as precious and irreplaceable; how even a limited atomic war would be less of a catastrophe to the planet than the disappearance of these forests.

He then explained to us that the richness of the tropical forests' vegetation and its apparently inexhaustible fertility were deceptive, since in reality they relied on poor soil, acidic and practically without humus; when the trees are uprooted, the soil soon dries up and turns to desert. Imagine the catastrophe that awaits us when you figure that, each year, twenty-five million trees disappear because of the desires of men. And yet, he added, people can live in harmony with the forests, as we see with the Pygmies of Central Africa, the Yanomami Indians of the Amazon, and the Papuans of New Guinea, all of whom have been living within them for millenia.

But I was most fascinated by his account of the forest's life cy-

cle. For trees as for people, life was a continuous struggle. And for
the plants, the struggle for life was a struggle for light. When a
tree dies and falls or when it is broken by a tornado, the light suddenly rushes into the new opening in the thick overhead canopy:
the other trees then begin a furious race toward the light, toward
the yellow ball of energy that is the sun—such is the biological
strategy of the trunk reaching skyward. Soon, when these trees at-
tain full height in their turn, the gash will close up naturally, leaving a lovely green scar, a tight new archway of trees.

It was after this massacre that our town endowed itself with a
grand twenty-five-thousand-seat stadium; a new multilevel building with a superb meeting hall had risen from the ground and
housed, among other things, offices for Δ-Contact and the African
Construction Company. Uncle had two offices to himself, one in
which he took care of Party business, and another in which he
took care of his own. A hotel had been built, containing a restaurant, Aux Agapes Tropicales, as well as a nightclub. Finally, a palace had been constructed to accommodate the President during
the three days of the ceremony, a palace that would afterwards be
occupied by the local Party chief, that is, my uncle. A town had
emerged from nothing, a town with its own airport and satellite
dishes beaming in CNN, the BBC World Service, and other international channels live. The population had tripled and now included many foreign families like Aledia's.

Uncle had bought a new Mercedes and had transformed his
house into a veritable mansion. Like every important business-
man, he opened bank accounts in France and Switzerland. And
not only had he made Ma Lolo his secretary but he had also appointed her head of the Women's Revolutionary Union. Old Bidié
had timidly protested, saying he would have no one left to help
him run his store, but Uncle, out of the goodness of his heart,
found Bidié a young employee paid for by the Party. The old man
refused, declaring that he'd always lived honestly by his own work

and didn't see why he should now accept being supported by some Party, especially the one-and-only Party. Uncle was dumbfounded. Since he had been appointed FARCE, it was the first time that someone, apart from Papa maybe, had defied him. So instead of coming up with an argument for the old man, he simply proposed to give him the honor of opening the festivities with a rousing accordion interpretation of the Internationale before the Chief of the State, the leader of our Revolution, and his thousands of guests from all over the world. No one could refuse such an honor! But old Bidié refused: "My bandoneon will never let forth even one note of your Internationale," he shot back at my shattered uncle.

As for Auntie Lolo, she had changed; she now had a bunch of wigs, new pairs of shoes, and she'd ordered all the nice clothes she had always dreamed of in Maman's magazines. She had given up the cheap Nigerian products that one could buy at the market and straightened her hair and made herself up only with authentic products from America; by steadily treating her epidermis with lightening products, she had made the dark chocolate brown of her skin so yellow that I feared she would become completely transparent. She and Uncle had completed a very important Party mission in Paris, London, and New York, and were awaiting campaigns scheduled for Tokyo and Hong Kong.

There was no doubt that, with six months till the festivities, six months till the arrival of the Man of the Masses, the Man of Concrete Action, the Popular-Leader-Always Proven Right by History, Uncle Boula Boula was the most important person in town, maybe even in the country—apart from the other person I just mentioned, obviously. I even asked myself if he wasn't going to be appointed prefect, and I was sure that the man currently holding the position must have been crocodile green with envy of my uncle. Yet to my surprise, there they were, the two of them, in Uncle's Mercedes, stopping in front of our house.

I was playing soccer a ways off when I saw them pull up. Since I was sweating and I did not have a towel, I wiped myself with the palm of my hand and blew my nose real hard with my two fingers to clear the snot; then I wiped my hand on the butt of my shorts to make sure it was clean before I held it out to them.

"Is Papa here?" asked Uncle after shaking it.

"Yes, he's in his study reading."

"Marx maybe," said the smiling prefect to my uncle.

"Surely," said my uncle smiling back. "We are a noted revolutionary family."

"Come," I said. "Come in, I'll go get him. Maman is not here."

The moment I held out my hand to open the door, it opened by itself and Papa appeared, with that spark in his eyes that I knew so well by now, that spark of discovery: "Matt Henson, it's Matt Henson!" he said to me.

The two visitors looked at him, disconcerted, evidently understanding nothing of what Papa was yelling about. I thought it was some kind of fit, for I was told that with people who read a lot, like geniuses, from time to time the circuits of their brains become like rush-hour traffic jams, so they might behave strangely. Papa himself once told me that a great genius named Einstein had a brain so jammed that he couldn't remember his own phone number.

But, noticing that I wasn't alone, Papa addressed the other two as well. "I think I've succeeded in putting the missing pieces of the puzzle into place. You see, deep inside of himself Peary felt that if he didn't succeed this time, he never would, and he was only forty-five minutes away by sled from his celebrated North Pole, from the ninety-degree North latitude that he was trying to reach for the eighth time. He had to place as many variables as possible on his side; he had already suffered much from the rigors of the climate and was incapable of walking because of frozen toes that had just been amputated. So in order to avoid any unwelcome surprises, he sent ahead his faithful scout Matt Henson, in whom he had full confidence. Matt Henson was black—we now say African American, I think—and he had participated in the seven previous missions. You have to admit that he was an extraordinary being: a navigator, of course, with all the science that involves, but he could also repair a sled and was an excellent harness dog driver and igloo maker. He spoke Eskimo and thus served as an interpreter; he also had very good rapport with the people of Greenland, since he had a child with an Eskimo woman.

"Thus, on April 6, 1909, Henson was the first to reach this most coveted tip of our planet. He symbolically positioned himself on a block of ice at the exact spot—you will recall that it is not a continent but a frozen ocean—when he saw the white fellow coming. Since Peary had great difficulty walking by that point, Henson helped him up to the same spot beside him. The two then planted the flag of the United States. They called the Eskimos over and took the family pictures that were diffused throughout the entire world. So Matt Henson really was the first man to have stepped onto the North Pole. He then graciously agreed to let Peary return forty-eight hours ahead of him to announce the news to the world," Papa concluded with a grin.

The prefect and Boula Boula were completely lost. In their suits and ties they were sweating in the densely humid tropical air and threw mutually worried glances at each other, asking themselves if, despite the dignity of their high political office, it wasn't time to skedaddle before the teacher's mild madness turned into frothing lunacy. But I had understood. Papa had simply unraveled the enigma he had talked to me about the day when I had, alas, fled Uncle Boula Boula's house after breaking the champagne bottle, and found Papa entangled in longitudes and time zones. Spellbound by his discovery, he was impatient to share it with me. Thus I came to the rescue of my father's mental health, put in doubt by these two notables, by asking a relevant question and thereby showing that what he was saying was in fact logical and that I knew exactly what he was talking about.

"Ah, so that's the answer! But in the final account, Papa, what does it change if it was Matt Henson instead of Peary that was the first man to reach the North Pole?"

"It doesn't change anything as far as science is concerned, but it is important for history because Matt Henson was a black African American and because, for ideological reasons, the West has generally long refused to recognize these people's rightful role in human history. I bet you won't find Henson's name in your dictionary, while you'd certainly find Peary's. And this tells you that Peary holds the right to the title and the merit of the discovery of the North Pole, since after all it was he who had conceived the project, found the funds, directed and realized it. But again, it does not change the material and objective fact that it was Matt Henson who first set foot on the North Pole."

Point made, he finally turned his attention to the visitors: "To what do I owe the honor of your visit, gentlemen? Come, enter, excuse me for letting you stand outside twiddling your thumbs."

Good God, Papa! Usually, when you dealt with a representative of the Party and the State, as we say, you were quick to fulfill their desires; the least procrastination could cost you your career or even your life. Such was the power of the Single Party at that time: it saw all, it controlled all, and it was always right even when it was wrong. But Papa, he made things move at his pace, and I always wondered how long that would last.

They followed Papa inside the house and made themselves comfortable. Papa yelled at my older brothers, who, as usual, were watching TV, to lower the volume. He asked me to serve his two guests something to drink.

Uncle, who felt at home, spoke first. "Brother-in-law, you know the esteem in which our prefect holds you. It is in fact at his insistence that the comrade member of the Political Bureau repre-senting the Guide of the Revolution was willing to meet you during his stay in our fair town." The prefect nodded in approval. "In fact, the comrade member of the P.B. told me that he very much appreciated the conversation you had together."

"Boula Boula," said Papa, "I know you did not come just to shower me with roses. Stop rambling and tell me what you want, and if I can I will do it with pleasure."

"In effect," said the prefect, who snatched the words out of Uncle's mouth, "we came to ask you to help us write the speech I am to give during the visit of the Chief of our Revolution. We could not find anyone as qualified as you. I would like something lyrical for the occasion, something powerful! First, a few words of praise for the Guide who made a little paradise out of this country, who brought back our peace of heart and peace of mind, the Steersman who skillfully navigated our Revolution through the storms and turbulence created by capitalist troublemakers and reactionaries, the Man of the Masses, the Man of the Concrete Action, the Man whom only Destiny—"

"But you are writing your speech yourself," Papa interrupted. "You don't need me for that!"

The prefect, carried away by his own lyricism, was surprised by Papa's untimely interruption.

Uncle Boula Boula quickly intervened: "These are only general ideas. It is up to you, a teacher and great reader of revolutionary texts, to polish them."

"Frankly, Boula Boula, do you want to know what I really think? I was born the year of Independence, meaning I didn't really know colonization or the struggle for Independence. But I read a lot about this period, and I've talked about it a lot with my father. Do you really think that we've endured all this sorrow, all this suffering, for the sake of freedom, so that we could be here on our knees twenty-five years later, dumbly reciting with a wooden tongue, without an ounce of originality, singing the praises of some captain who came to power by force?"

"Don't say that!" Uncle Boula Boula interrupted, horrified, as if he wanted to shove these words of sacrilege back down the throat they came out of. "Don't you know that men have lost their lives for less? Lucky for you Comrade Prefect knows that you don't mean what you just said and, as we say, your words have overtaken your thinking."

"Rest assured," said the prefect in a conciliatory tone, "I have not heard those last words you just uttered. As we say, the village chief sees no evil. Come, let's forget about it, I'm only asking for a token gesture: write up this text for us. In fact, it won't be the first time you've participated in our celebrations; remember the ceremonies for the twentieth anniversary of our Independence, that memorable day when your third child was born?"

I was proud to hear that my birth had left its indelible print and had become a reference in the annals of the Republic.

"But you just put it so well," Papa nearly yelled, "the anniversary of our Independence and not the anniversary of an armed man coming to power!"

"So you refuse!" said the prefect, annoyed and already getting up. "I shall mull over all the consequences of your refusal and, trust me, don't underestimate the power of the Party," he threatened as he left, followed by Uncle, who was glaring wrathfully at Papa.

"By the way, Boula Boula," yelled Papa, "you forgot your case of champagne again. Me, I prefer palm wine."

The orderly opened the car doors and both settled into the backseat of the Mercedes, which quickly drove off.

I thought Papa would grow fearful and regret his refusal to collaborate. But he was no more distressed than if you had told him I missed an episode of *Dona Beija*, the series that had replaced *Dallas* on TV and was causing quite an uproar. He said to me: "Your uncle is funny. He really thinks I have time to waste when I have a whole library waiting for me. You know, Michel, I am truly happy for Matt Henson."

12

The event was a great success. Never had our small town known such affluence as during those three days when it became the de facto capital of the country. Ambassadors; foreign radio and television journalists; businessmen seeking new markets; Zairean gold diggers hailing from as far as Kasai or Katanga; Lebanese Shiites, like Aledia's family, searching for a new Beirut, came to make their fortune here by opening general stores; West African merchants negotiated Dutch textiles; military men and secret agents came to protect the precious life of the President of the Republic; and finally, the Prince of Peace himself, Friend of the Youth, escorted by his entire Political Bureau and the Central Committee, not to mention the Party's mass organizations—the Women's Revolutionary Union, the Union of Socialist and Revolutionary Youth, the Artists and Writers Union, the Peasants Revolutionary Union, and the United Confederation of Workers. I hope I didn't leave anybody out. All these beautiful people had invaded our modest village.

Three days of ceremonies, parades, sporting events, great

feasts, and great speeches filled the stadium Uncle built. Good thing it was the dry season; otherwise the rain would have put out the flames of our revelry. Maman was the only one who was disappointed. She had proposed to open the ceremonies for this fourteenth anniversary of our beloved President's coming to power with a public prayer at the stadium to place the event under the protection of Jesus and the Holy Spirit, but the organizers, her brother chief among them, had rejected this idea, arguing that our Revolution, modeled after the Soviet Union's, was Marxist, Leninist, and atheist, and consequently considered religion the opiate of the masses. Since Maman didn't know what opium was—neither did I, I'll admit—Uncle explained to her that opium was like palm wine: it put you in a state of inebriation and made you forget your worries here on Earth.

I experienced this ceremony up close, since I had been among those picked to do the gymnastic tributes, so I was in the first row when the Chief of State launched his magisterial attack against imperialism. He was in top form. The country was his. Its men, women, children, its animals obeyed every twitch of his finger and every blink of his eye, and not a leaf on a tree could move without him being aware of it.

"We will have no more colonialism," he proclaimed in an imposing voice.

"No more!" we replied with the same conviction, fists in the air.

"No more capitalism!"

"No more!"

"Down with imperialism, neocolonialism!"

"No more!"

"Long live the Revolution!"

"Viva, viva, viva, defend the cause!"

"Thank you," he said.

Delirious applause came from the stands, echoed by successive waves all the way to the back of the stadium before flowing again toward the front, like the waves the spectators make with their banners at soccer games.

"Well," he resumed with satisfaction. "Now that we have overthrown imperialism and its pawns . . ."

I never found out what we were going to do having overthrown imperialism and its lapdogs, because all of a sudden, hailing from I don't know where, a rather stocky man appeared before us and stood by the podium, solidly planted on his legs, barechested, a loincloth slipped like a G-string between his thighs and wrapped tightly around his waist. He wore a talisman around his right arm, his huge biceps pumped up like a basketball. A red bandanna was on his head, while his face was covered with geometric patterns painted in kaolin white and clay red. Finally, he held a bow with an arrow cocked in one hand, while the other arrows filled a quiver on his back. He reminded me of the pictures of black warriors in the books about explorers Papa owned. They say it was with such arrows and lances that they had dared fight against the colonizers, who had actual automatic rifles. No wonder they lost. It was also the first time I had seen real arrows, I who was used to rifles and machine guns, to Rambo's rocket launchers and to the light sabers in *Star Wars*. Anyway, there he was, fierce and determined. The President's bodyguards immediately surrounded their boss, but the fellow didn't care, for he had already begun to speak:

"Comrade President, my name is Etumba. I come from the village of Entsouari, and it took me two days to get here by foot. We suffer a lot in the villages. There isn't any health care, there isn't any medicine, and each day our children die of malaria, AIDS, and diarrhea. We are hungry. We don't have any money to buy sugar, salt, soap, and clothes. We are not lazy, but we don't work because we are discouraged. There aren't any roads left to get our products to market, and it's already been three years that our harvest of groundnuts, coffee, walnuts, and corn has been rotting in the granaries, covered with mildew. We're suffering too much, Comrade President, we're suffering too much, we can't anymore! This is no kind of life."

He had succeeded in capturing the huge crowd's attention, and they were growing noisier and noisier. But even we, the students who were making such a ruckus, quieted down when we heard this sincere voice so charged with emotion. He continued speaking into the microphone that crackled and every now and then howled with feedback because he spoke a little too close.

"Each time we ask what we did to God and our ancestors to be condemned to live such a curse, the people from the Party you send us always reply: 'This is all the fault of imperialism and its pawns.' Imperialism is the cause of our malaria and our AIDS. It is imperialism that lets people grow fat off our backs and that keeps the money in the city. Imperialism makes our groundnuts and our fish rot in our granaries and gourds, imperialism, always imperialism! So, when I learned that you were coming here for the ceremonies and that this imperialism always tailed you wherever you went to try to stop you, I, Etumba, acknowledged as the bravest man of the village, the most skilled of its warriors and hunters, I came to defy this bandit of imperialism! Let him come so we can fight to the death, so I can defeat him once and for all! And then we will live happy on this land blessed by our ancestors."

He planted his two slightly spread feet firmly on the ground, flexed his biceps and the muscles of his bare chest, stretched the cord that held the arrow, and, his face still fierce and determined, called out to his adversary: "Mr. Imperialism, come out and fight me if you've got a pair of well-hung balls! I'm waiting!"

Mr. Imperialism never showed up for this epic combat. On the contrary, the crowd, caught like a hind in a floodlight up to this point, began to grow agitated. Some applauded, others laughed, and I was simply puzzled. I looked at the podium, where the President was smiling like all the other members of the Political Bureau around him. He said something to his protocol officer, who had Etumba brought up onto the stand. He warmly shook his hand, to the amused cheers of the crowd. That's how we struck terror and defeated imperialism, colonialism, and neocolonialism in our country.

The great success of the event was also a great personal success for Uncle Boula Boula, who was no longer FARCE. The President was so impressed that he promoted him to the Party's Central Committee and sent for him to come to the capital. That is how he left us. Six months later, we learned that he had been elevated to the Political Bureau, and that not only had he become the number two in the government but he had also been entrusted with the planning for the fifteenth anniversary of the Revolution, that is, the anniversary of the coup d'état carried out by our Supreme Guide on a date that coincided so happily with the thirtieth anniversary of our Independence and, even more happily, with my tenth birthday. Auntie Lolo also got a promotion; she became national president of the Women's Revolutionary Union, which meant that she, too, left us to go settle in the capital, promising to return twice a month to visit the old husband she was abandoning.

13

Ah, the thirtieth anniversary of our Independence! I turned ten years old that day, and I can tell you that Uncle had truly outdone himself. The parade he had organized in the capital lasted over four hours and followed a historic speech by the Chief of State that lasted an hour and forty-five minutes. The parade started off with a procession of the city's young unemployed idlers; they had been picked up in a raid the week before, were dressed up in blue, given crew cuts and clean shaves, and then compelled to march behind a long red banner with yellow letters that read: "Despite the imperialism and neocolonialism that has confined us to unemployment and misery, we firmly support our Revolution and its Guide." Next came the women from the market, various merchants, high school and university students; then there were the officials and different groups representing the professions, such as firemen, nurses, doctors, all walking behind huge portraits of the Supreme Leader of the Revolution.

We had all gathered around the TV, watching the broadcast live and in color. Maman was sitting in the living room with us, and all of us would scream, "There's Uncle!" each time the camera panned over to her brother sitting in the second row of the stand, his butt firmly planted in his padded armchair, one leg on top of the other like a big shot. He had gained weight and was a bit pot-bellied, which was a sign of wealth and abundance for someone like him, who was not too long ago as skinny as a Sahel cow. In the first row sat the Man of the People himself, flanked by some fifteen invited heads of state along with their legal wives. It was fascinating to see all the high-ranking government officials marching like children in uniforms embroidered with the Leader's likeness. How fantastic it was to see the fighter jets doing aerial acrobatics and passing overhead at full speed followed by a startling *boom*.

The journalists commenting on the event were ecstatic and uttered their breathless descriptions at an astonishing pace: "Just look at these tanks the automatic rifles the soldiers before the arrival of our Supreme All-Powerful Guide all of this would have only been a fifteen-minute procession but thanks to him it's already been an hour that this military parade has been going on, and yes"—his colleague took over—"never in this citizen's memory have we seen a parade of such popular success now we have color TV's air-conditioned cars all-terrain 4 × 4's the latest MiG fighters and all of this thanks to this man whose immortal name is acclaimed all around the world . . ."

Papa came into the living room drenched in sweat, back from his jog. He alone had not been interested in the televised broadcast. He had woken us up early that morning yelling: "Happy birthday, children, you are ten years old today and are entering adolescence. Come get your gifts." I was the happiest of all for when I opened the big box that was meant for me, I found a globe. It was round and spun on its own slightly tilted axis. Right away I looked for Ouagadougou, found it, and was pleased with myself. Papa then left for his jog, and I'll admit that we were so glued to the TV screen that we wolfed down the cake Maman had prepared for the occasion in the wink of an eye.

As soon as Papa came through the door, Banzouzi yelled to him that we had seen Uncle Boula Boula. "If you wait a little," Batsimba immediately continued, "they're going to show him again." The physical exercise must have worn him out, for Papa slumped in the armchair next to me and also began watching. Another panoramic shot. "Uncle, Uncle," we cried out in a chorus. Face shots of the leaders with their dames. "Now will you look at that nice kabob of dictators, not one of them has any legacy other than guns," Papa commented. Back to the tanks, machine guns, MiGs, and helicopters. "How many roads, schools, and hospitals buried!" Papa sighed again. He got up and went to take a shower.

After the parade, the TV continued its news report with a live broadcast of the dedication of the Leader's secondary residence, located some thirty miles from the capital, before all the dignitaries, with Uncle Boula Boula in the front row. The imposing villa was built of Carrara marble imported from Italy on cargo planes; it was set in the middle of a garden designed by a Chinese landscape architect. While we admired the lamps and chandeliers, the lanes of bonsai in a country known for its gigantic trees, Papa, on the other hand, almost transfixed, was admiring one of the living room walls, to which the camera had returned after a long pan over the whole place. Suddenly, I became interested too.

It was a wall completely covered with mirror fragments, concave, convex, all irregular shapes, and juxtaposed in an indeterminate fashion in which no design could be discerned, in such a way that if you stood before it you would lose your sense of orientation and perspective; all these mirror fragments reflected an incoherent world in which your body was dismantled and where you felt you were losing your mind.

"Curious," said Papa, "that resembles one of Escher's mosaics."

As a matter of fact, it did resemble an engraving by the Dutch artist whose work Papa had shown me in a huge book he had brought back from the capital after his last retraining internship:

Gödel, Escher, Bach: An Eternal Golden Braid. With this book, Papa had explained and entertained us with the concepts of the paradox, the loops of a system of self-reference, and optical illusion.

I can't resist sharing my favorite paradox with you, the one about the liar. Suppose I am Congolese and I tell you: "All Congolese are liars"; since I'm Congolese, I must be lying, so then all Congolese aren't liars; but if all Congolese aren't liars, then what I say is true, meaning that all Congolese are liars after all, therefore I'm lying . . . and so on ad infinitum. On the other hand, I fully appreciated the loops of the system of self-reference only when I saw the engravings and lithographs, in particular the lithograph called *Drawing Hands,* which depicted two hands drawing themselves, the first drawing the second, which was drawing the first, and so on in an infinite loop. As for optical illusions, this wall of mirrors was a perfect example. Uncle stood before it, shifting around, making faces, performing acrobatic contortions. Everybody laughed wholeheartedly at the images reflected in the wall of mirrors, the impossible and illogical images of a shattered and incoherent world. The Guide of the Revolution seemed just as pleased, deeply nodding at the explanations given by an Asian woman (the decorator?) standing at his side.

Uncle's show didn't stop there, because that night he once more inflicted upon us the rebroadcast of the speech of the Friend of the Youth, the Prince of Peace, but this time it had commentary, as if the speaker had not been clear enough. The journalists would take one of the President's sentences, say what the President was going to say, let you listen to what the President was saying, and then conclude by telling you what the President had just said. They did it sentence by sentence, and at the end rebroadcast the speech again *in extenso.* They then repeated the exercise in the various vernacular languages of the country. I was drunk from TV and the President's face, and at the moment I was getting up to go to bed, the rebroadcast was suddenly interrupted and an announcer appeared and said: "Dear viewers, stay tuned to your small screen. A very important announcement will be read to you in a moment on the occasion of this historic day."

I sat back down right away, and we called: "Papa, an important announcement!" He groaned in his study, where he was listening to music, and came out in his pajamas, slumped back down on the couch, and, just like the rest of us, listened for the announcement, which wasn't a long time coming. We saw Uncle Boula Boula appear, his Party medallion gleaming on his lapel and a full-length portrait of the President displayed prominently behind him.

"Maman, Maman!" cried the two twins, "come see Uncle."

"Again?" said Maman, who came into the living room just as her brother had begun to speak:

"Comrade compatriots and Party militants. As in the life of a man, so too the life of a nation consists of unforgettable moments. Such a moment came in October 1917 for the great nation known as the Soviet Union, date of the great socialist revolution that shook the planet and from which the world still draws inspiration today. So too in our country, this fifteenth of August, the thirtieth anniversary of our Independence, but, most important, the fifteenth anniversary of our Revolution, must be marked by an indelible seal. That is why the Central Committee of our Party has decided the following in a special session:

"1. To appoint to the rank of Marshal for Life, the highest military rank of our country, our Comrade President, who, despite his untold service to the Nation and the Revolution, has for more than fifteen years remained a simple captain out of his exemplary modesty.

"2. To start a mandatory subscription, a ten percent deduction from the salaries of all workers over a brief twelve-month period, to permit us to rent a flight either on the European Ariane rocket, or the American space shuttle *Challenger*, or on a Soviet Mir spaceship, and to launch into geosynchronous orbit 22,250 miles above our equator a giant bust of our new marshal, a bust made of gold-plated fiberglass. Day and night, this bust, fixed above our heads, will be our faithful sentinel at the zenith of the firmament, so that every child of our nation, gazing upon this new star sparkling among the constellations of the celestial canopy, will point to it and say: 'Our Supreme Guide watches over us!' "

End of speech. Uncle had delivered it in a firm voice, without hesitation, like a true leader. I was proud of him, as were my two brothers. Maman said nothing; was she silently thanking the Lord for having given her such a worthy brother? I looked at Papa. He had a smirk on his lips. I awaited the words of praise that he was at long last going to pronounce regarding Uncle. He got up with a slight sigh and said to Maman: "Human bullshit knows no limits, especially when it slips the gentle bonds of Earth."

14

At twelve, I was older than when I was ten. Don't laugh, I'm not just stating a fact as flat as our school blackboard; what I mean is that, personally, I had not felt any difference between being six, eight, or ten years old, but at twelve I really felt like another person. I felt taller, I had become stronger, and my biceps were as big—well, not quite but almost as big—as the ones of that guy who wanted to kill imperialism with his arrows and assagais on the twenty-ninth anniversary of Independence. Now I would often gaze at my own body in admiration: at thirteen, I discovered little strands of hair sprinkled on my lower belly and in my armpits. A little while later, they had become so long and so bushy that they formed a veritable rug over my pubic area, as dense as the dry paspalum with which Grandfather stuffed his mattress when he had no cotton.

When we took a bath, I proudly exhibited my new rug to my older brothers, whose fuzz had barely started stirring under the skin; and I would make them jealous by telling them that soon I would have a boxer's chest as hairy as Uncle Boula Boula's. Sometimes at night, before going to sleep, I'd tickle the hair around my willy, making it swell and grow big and hard as a banana—well almost as big. The first time I noticed this phenomenon, I was afraid that my virile member would remain rigid forever like a stick and that I wouldn't be able to put it back in my underwear. But I was scared for nothing, for I very soon discovered that when it became rigid like that, it was enough to massage it, delicately and at length, with the palm of the hand; it then let out a whitish substance, thick and sticky like okra juice, and soon became soft again. Even my voice had become transformed, losing the whiny falsetto I so hated.

I shouldn't boast, but at thirteen I was a tall fellow, beside whom my two older brothers looked puny, to the point that some wondered if we had really come out of the same belly. I no longer felt like I needed Uncle Boula Boula's kaman if I took a notion to give them a good beating. And I had become a great athlete, the one who would lead the school team to the championship, a victory that earned me my first kiss from Aledia!

We were in the last minute of play, the trophy was as good as gone if we didn't score a goal. As usual I was playing left forward. Suddenly, I received a nice midfield pass from our sweeper. I jumped up, cushioned the ball with my chest, then blocked it with my right foot. I had barely gotten moving when two opposing defenders were at me. I feinted to the right and pushed the ball to the left; the first opponent went for it and fell away to the right, and I slid the ball between the legs of the second one and found myself all alone facing the goalie in the penalty zone. I could read the panic in the goalie's eyes, for he knew I was as good with my right foot as with my left. But before I had time to lift my heel to lob a nice kick past him, I was viciously tackled from behind by one of the returning defenders. I collapsed nose-first on the grass. The referee whistled vigorously and took out a red card while calling for a penalty kick. Our fans were hysterical. There was some contention on the field and even a few surreptitious punches the referee did not see, but at last the ball was placed. Naturally, I was asked to convert the penalty kick. I positioned myself, taking a moment to savor the goalie's anxiety, and then kicked it to the right. He lurched left. Goal! Final whistle. I was smothered, picked up, and carried off on somebody's shoulders. I was Pelé, I was Maradona. We had won the cup. The cup that would earn me my first kiss from Aledia.

The cup had been presented by Aledia's father, one of the Lebanese who had settled here around the fourteenth anniversary of our Revolution, when Uncle Boula Boula had transformed our little village into an international city complete with airport, hotels, telephones, and fax, not to mention a multimedia conference center. But that was already three or four years ago and nothing was left of it! The airport had operated for one season, and by now the grass had invaded the runway and only a coughing, crackling little twin-engine prop dared venture there every now and then. The bush had reclaimed the gigantic stadium, whose walls and foundations had been splintered by brambles, not to mention the Indian fig tree's robust tentacles; the sections of the stairs and the wooden stands that had not yet been turned to dust by the patient labor of termites had rotted from the combined effects of sun and rain. As for the nightclub, the hotel, the restaurant, if they had any patrons left, they were certainly ghostly ones who shared the place with the roaches, mosquitoes, and bats at night. All that money spent, all that time and effort! The energy of an entire nation had been mobilized for three months straight for the sake of a ceremony that lasted a few days, and once the party was over, the equatorial forest rushed to take back the land it had momentarily ceded to men.

And so, out of all the folks who besieged our town—ambassadors, journalists, Zairean adventurers, West African merchants—only Mr. Hussein El Faisal Al Moustapha Husseini Morabitoune had stayed, all the others having left our village for better horizons. He now had a monopoly over the entire little market of the area and had pushed the competition into bank-ruptcy. Mr. Konaté and his truck were history. The brave Muslim witness of my birth had finished by giving up; he had packed and left for his native Senegal or Mali to live out the remainder of his days. This did not change anything as far as we were concerned, since the Lebanese guy also had trucks that moved goods and since he continued to sell us Coca-Cola, videos, and new canned foods that came from as far away as China and Korea.

As for old Bidié, besides losing Auntie Lolo—who had now dedicated herself, body and soul, to the Party and to the revolu-tionary duties assigned to her by her boss Uncle Boula Boula—Bidié also found himself on the rocks, but he wouldn't go down without a fight. He went toe-to-toe before screaming for a time-out. So when the new canned foods arrived from China and Korea, he spread the rumor that they contained dog and cat meat—for didn't the Chinese eat dogs?—animals taboo in our ali-mentary culture. Mr. Hussein El Faisal Al Moustapha Husseini Morabitoune smiled and organized a party, much like the one in honor of our championship victory, where he had the can labels read out loud by anonymously picked students, Bidié's own nephew among them: "puerco, pork meat, corned beef, pilchards, sardines in oil, baked beans . . . " No mention of dog meat.

The Lebanese grocer's sales shot back up, and, as long as Hus-sein El Faisal Al Moustapha Husseini Morabitoune's stores were well-stocked, old Bidié would lack customers. So old Bidié in-vented another story. He said that in the 1950s there lived in the capital of Belgian Congo a white man, a Portuguese who had a magic flashlight. Each time he encountered a black man, he would shine the light at his eyes and the person would become dazed and start grunting and walking on all fours. All the white man had to do was catch and fatten him up. Hair grew all over the poor cap-tive's body, his skin became thick as hide, and he became a pig. He ended up as sausages, blood pudding, lard and baked beans, and other canned pork products.

The Portuguese merchants who had arrived during the age of Angola and run all the stores in our villages had all gone home and had been replaced by the Lebanese. So, Hussein El Faisal Al Moustapha Husseini Morabitoune was no less than the reincarnation of that white man with the magic flashlight. His cans of puerco, pork meat, or lard and baked beans were nothing more than the flesh of black people transformed into pork. In fact, was it any surprise that he himself, a Muslim, never ate this meat while having others eat it?

I must tell you that old Bidié's argument carried weight. Soon, people from Grandfather's and even Papa's generation confirmed the story about this white man who ravaged Kinshasa and was nicknamed *moundélé ngoulou*, "the white man who changed men into pigs." The warning then spread regarding all of Mr. Hussein El Faisal Al Moustapha Husseini Morabitoune's food cans, though we'd grab the few cans of the same brand that were sold at old Bidié's. In fact, we were now afraid to cross paths with the Lebanese at night for fear of being caught in his bewitched flashlight.

Since in our country rumors run faster than a thief chased by a dog, this news reached the capital, where Mr. Hussein El Faisal Al Moustapha Husseini Morabitoune had stores as well, and his business went into a tailspin. So the good man, feeling his honor impugned, no longer smiled so much and seized the occasion of the National Culinary Fair to have his revenge and definitively put old Bidié out of the food business.

I don't know who had the idea to organize this fair, but it was said that in Africa, particularly in our country, we produced nothing, that we imported almost all of our basic consumer products— cars, videos, Coca-Cola, and corn flour—though our country had great agricultural potential. If we imported so much food, it was because of our own laziness: throw a groundnut or tomato seed out the window and it'll grow by itself! To counter this ruinous trade imbalance, it would be necessary to consume domestic prod-

ucts. That's why the minister of agriculture had organized this
Culinary Fair.

By fortunate coincidence, my father just happened to be going
to the capital to receive from the university diplomas that marked
the end of his long correspondence studies. He wanted to be
present since the graduation ceremony was to be presided over by
a great physicist from the Third World, the Nobel laureate Abdus
Salam of Pakistan. He was coming to our country as special guest
of the government to participate in the First Congress of African
Scientists, and the university had taken the opportunity to involve
him in their conferment of academic stripes. I asked Papa if I
could come with him, and he willingly agreed, which, to my great
disappointment, did not at all bother my two elder brothers.

So we took the opportunity to go visit the fair, and I admit
that I had not known that our country was so rich in fruits and
vegetables until I discovered the main exposition hall: mangoes,
papayas, soursops, litchis, avocados, tangerines, safous, pineapples,
guavas, tamarinds, and I'm leaving out a few, were laid out as far as
the eye could see. Same for the vegetables. Who needed apples
and pears after seeing all this?

Mr. Hussein El Faisal Al Moustapha Husseini Morabitoune,
the great economic operator who still had faith in Africa despite
this continent's dreary situation, was invited by state television to
inaugurate an agricultural competition for the occasion of the fair.
He began his presentation by singing the praises of the Chief of
State and of the government's number two (meaning Uncle) for
their farsightedness and their national spirit. He congratulated
them for their decision to launch a reappraisal of local food pro-
duction. But, as everyone knew and had been reminded by the
Comrade Revolutionary Leader himself, continued Hussein El
Faisal Al Moustapha Husseini Morabitoune, Africa's problem was
that it had a deficiency in essential nutrients, such as proteins and
vitamins; therefore it was vital that local recipes integrate the sup-
plementary nutritional richness of the developed world by way of

imported products such as canned goods. That was why he was inaugurating this "competition for the best local recipe made from
canned foods."

When Papa heard this, he got angry. "Once again, someone
minding only his pockets! Instead of encouraging the peasants to
consume fresh products, he manipulates people with pseudo-
science so that they will buy canned foods with uncertain expira-
tion dates. We have to shut down this merchant of deception, this
swindler, creator of false needs. Michel, we're going to take part in
this competition!"

No sooner said than done. Papa temporarily forgot why he
had come to the capital, meaning the conferment of his stripes,
rented space at the exposition, and began exploring every market
in town for the products he was going to present. He hired a few
cooks to prepare what he'd gathered, and when the competition
opened our stand was ready. A large sign was hung out front; it
had green letters on a white background, magnificently traced
with a whole lot of loops and upstrokes as only the teachers of
Papa's generation knew how to do so well. The slogan read:

> *For protein, vitamins, and virility,*
> *eat insects!*

Meanwhile, toward the back, a banner traced in revolutionary red
with the same beautiful writing had the following injunctions:

> *Avoid canned foods, eat fresh products!*

I must tell you that, in my humble opinion, our exhibit was
the most original: we had caterpillars (the two edible species
found here); field crickets; cicadas gathered at the beginning of
the rainy season; green grasshoppers and plain crickets; winged
termites captured as they swarmed, which lost their wings when
you touched them; fat, greasy, white palmiste worms; and others

whose names I admit I do not know. Who needed frog's legs or limp snail flesh after you saw all this?

Uncle Boula Boula and Mr. Hussein El Faisal Al Moustapha Husseini Morabitoune nearly keeled over when they found themselves before our stand. Uncle was inaugurating the exposition in the company of the minister of agriculture, the Lebanese grocer who was the contest promoter, and various other top brass of our One Party. After the minister's speech, which, in the space of ten minutes, had cited the name of the Chief of State fifteen times and that of Uncle—who was more and more being presented as a worthy successor to our Great Guide—ten times, Uncle was presented with a pair of scissors on a little red pillow with which he cut the green ribbon that symbolized the agricultural show. We applauded him at the same time as he was applauding himself, as they do in Lenin's country, our model. He had then put small pieces of the ribbon in the upper vest pockets of both the minister and the Lebanese, and we clapped some more. Then they began their tour, under the vigilant eyes of the armed bodyguards who watched over Uncle's precious life. And that's when they found themselves in front of our stand.

Uncle opened his mouth in shock, but no sound came out, as I cried: "Uncle, Uncle!" real loud and proud to let everyone know that this important person, this number two who had inaugurated the exposition, was none other than my uncle, my mother's big brother; Mr. Hussein El Faisal Al Moustapha Husseini Morabitoune grimaced, then blushed as he read Papa's banner, while Papa went on and on: "You see, this is just a sample of the edible insects of our country; they are neglected sources of protein and vitamins, and they're delicious"—he throws a fat grilled and salted palmiste worm in his mouth, chews it up, savors it, and sucks it down, while I grab a handful of caterpillars boiled to a pulp in salty water, season them, and chase them down with a gulp of ginger drink made that very morning—"taste some, Political Bureau Comrade, try a grasshopper, Mr. Minister, or perhaps our Lebanese friend would like a handful of termites?" (The minister and the Lebanese contorted their faces in disgust.) "Beware of canned foods," Papa kept pattering, "first of all they're expensive, and often the ones sold to you have expired and then you risk botulism. Eat vegetables from your own fields, eat the fruits of your native land, mangoes, papayas, tangerines, oranges, and I could go on, but one shouldn't leave out our edible insects, rich in nutrients . . ." Papa went on and on, the Lebanese blushed and blushed, while the minister of agriculture couldn't take it any longer and let out: "This is provocation, Comrade P.B. Member."

"Indeed," added another top Party official, "this is a sabotage of our revolutionary activity."

Uncle looked at them hesitantly, then finally, without a word, let himself be led away to another stand by his protocol officer.

Though the officials sulked, our exhibit won a true popular victory. People were glad to see the insects they knew so well scientifically recognized as healthy and nutritious food, the very insects that some of their compatriots considered food for savages when they began eating *hachis parmentier*, sausages, Camembert, and imported red wine. We were actually victims of our own success, as each visitor, imitating Papa and myself, did not resist sneaking a handful of termites over here, two or three worms to munch on over there, and then four caterpillars to snack on over there, to such an extent that before morning's end our stand was empty and we had to close up shop.

I was so happy! I told Papa: "Don't worry, Papa, it was supercool, we'll get first place."

We didn't get first place, or any place at all. That night, the television report about the exposition didn't show our stand and didn't even mention it. Instead, they showed Uncle Boula Boula beside a certain Mr. Hussein El Faisal Al Moustapha Husseini Morabitoune tasting a recipe consisting of *saka saka*—crushed manioc leaves—*au* canned corned beef, then a dish of crushed yam *au* canned pilchard, and finally red sorrel *au* canned sardines. But the main attraction was at another stand . . . Ma Lolo's!

Oh yes, she was here, more done up than ever, brown as a ripe red papaya, hair in a wig, dressed in an outfit adorned with gold jewelry around her neck and hanging off her ears. Auntie Lolo, still as lovely as I remembered her when she used to feverishly leaf through Maman's magazines ardently admiring the magnificent clothes. Auntie Lolo, still as splendid as in the dream I had sent to Father Boniface! There she was, smiling, surrounded by ten or so young women in aprons.

"Voilà," the journalist was saying, "what a shining example of humility, as well as militancy, for our people, to see the President of the Women's Revolutionary Union herself not hesitating to get her hands dirty to make what Senghor calls a 'cultural crossing,' 'a fusion of tradition and modernity,' 'Hellenic reason meets Negro emotion,' in other words, the traditional culinary art of the banana, the taro, the yam, and the cassava, merged with canned corned beef, pilchard, and pork, and—why not?—frog's legs and escargot." And the camera panned over the food cans stacked neatly one on top of the other. "Try our *saka saka au* slices of canned pork meat, Comrade P.B. Member," Auntie Lolo began, stuffing a spoonful in her red-lipped mouth before respectfully holding out the plate to Uncle. He had a taste, inclining his head like a connoisseur, and offered some to the minister of agriculture, who in turn tasted, while Mr. Hussein El Faisal Al Moustapha Husseini Morabitoune, a Muslim who couldn't eat pork, approved with great nods of the head. "So this is really pork from a can," said Uncle. "Yes, a can of *pork meat*," Auntie Lolo and the Lebanese replied in chorus. The camera zoomed in on the can so that one could perfectly make out the label. "Incredible," said Uncle. "One might think it was fresh meat!" Head shot of Hussein El Faisal Al Moustapha Husseini Morabitoune, who answered: "This is genuine meat from the best pigsties of Europe and from France in particular." "Were the baked beans made with it?" "Of course, Comrade P.B. Member." "Very good, very good, can we have another taste?" "But of course, Comrade Member." Auntie Lolo quickly obliged.

The other big surprise was a Special Grand Prize, concocted right after Uncle's inspection, which Auntie Lolo won forthwith. She got a nice little red convertible for it. Later, I discovered that the magnificent Oriental rug in Uncle's living room, on which I had unfortunately spilled some Mercurochrome—which made him furious—had likewise been offered by the Lebanese after the contest. Needless to say, after this Culinary Fair and the canned goods recipe contest, Mr. Hussein El Faisal Al Moustapha Husseini Morabitoune heard nothing about any old Bidié again . . .

If I spared no detail telling you the story of this Culinary Fair where Auntie Lolo won the jury's Special Grand Prize, it was only to show you the importance of Mr. Hussein El Faisal Al Moustapha Husseini Morabitoune, Aledia's father, the same one who had provided the beautiful loving cup that had been presented to my team when, climbing down off the shoulders of the crowd that had swept me off my feet after my magnificent and unstoppable penalty kick, I proudly took my position next to the players standing in a neat row before the podium, where the prefect was flanked by the Lebanese, the sponsor, and Papa, the school principal. That was when I really saw Aledia for the first time.

She was supposed to hand the cup to the prefect for him to present it to me. She came forward in a magnificent flowered dress, so light that the wind would lift it up every now and then and she'd try to plaster it back onto her thighs each time. Her long black hair was tightened in a knot behind the nape of her neck before blooming again to hang loosely down her back. She was smiling. She was beautiful, and at that very moment I think she was even prettier than Auntie Lolo. Yes, it was the first time in my life that I had found a woman prettier than Auntie Lolo. She delivered the cup to the prefect, who held it out to me as everyone cheered. I shook the hand of the prefect; I shook the hand of Papa who reminded me of his credo *mens sana in corpore sano* and smiled; I shook the hand of the Lebanese, who was still congratulating me, and just as I was about to get down from the stand, the prefect, who still had Aledia in front of him, asked her to kiss me under pressure from the crowd, which was yelling, "A kiss, give him a kiss!" She raised her lips to my cheek (I already mentioned that I was tall for my age, taller than my brothers) and . . . kissed me!

It was at precisely that instant of my life that I fell for Aledia.

I don't know what got into me. I quivered from the contact of her lips as if a bolt of electricity had gone through my body. I was on fire. My skin was all clammy. I was submerged in a garden of fragrant orange trees and incense as the breeze that blew through her hair and her face reached me. My whole body felt tingly; and my willy, to my great surprise, began to stiffen and I was afraid this would be noticed. I wanted to grab Aledia, engulf her in my arms, and press my body against the breasts that swelled beneath the bosom of her dress . . . Aledia!

I missed the first step coming down from the stand and found myself on the grass sooner than planned. I regained my footing without dropping the cup, after a number of quick little jerky steps. Everybody laughed and applauded, including Aledia. I had salvaged my cup and my dignity!

I couldn't stop thinking about Aledia afterwards. First, I tried to learn about her family. Her father was a Muslim like Mr. Konaté and, like him, did not drink alcohol—except maybe behind closed doors as I had once caught Mr. Konaté doing. But, people also explained to me, Hussein El Faisal Al Moustapha Husseini Morabitoune was not the same type of Muslim as Mr. Konaté, since he was a Shiite. All this was tangled enough until I learned that Muslims were fragmented into sects, such as the Shiites, the Sunnis, Sufis, et cetera, just as Christians were Catholics, Orthodox, or Protestants and then Protestants could still be

Kimbanguists, Evangelicals, Baptists and Anabaptists, Methodists, Pentecostals, Apostolics, et cetera.

Aledia! At thirteen, I lived for her alone. Each time I was sent on an errand, I made sure I would pass in front of the Lebanese store, hoping to catch a glimpse of my beloved. In fact, I had looked in Papa's thesaurus for words to call her: my chick, my doll, my mousmay, my girlfriend, my love. The last time I had seen her was when Maman had given me these nice jeans from America, authentic Levi's. I was so proud of them that I decided to go strutting about before her and openly declare my love. I put on my nicest shirt, the celebrated jeans, and my pair of black Reeboks. I combed my hair, I sprayed myself with the lavender cologne I had sneaked out of Papa's closet, and being well aware that the pimples sprinkled all over my face could foil my powers of seduction (oh, how I hated these pimples!), I courageously decided to make my declaration by generously offering her a can of Coca-Cola.

This was really my day, because Aledia was at the cash register by herself, with a worker unloading merchandise out of a cardboard box. A heat wave flooded my face when I saw her smiling at the other end of the counter. I swallowed twice before saying: "One Coke please," while putting down two hundreds and a fifty. She opened a big refrigerator (or a large icebox, I don't remember anymore), took out a can, came up . . . and she recognized me!

"Well, Matapari the champion, hello!"

Have you ever heard the beating of your own heart? I heard mine knocking like a tom-tom to an offbeat rhythm. There was her hand, held out toward me. Her perfume invaded me, the same fragrance from the stadium. I was drunk and knew not why, and instead of speaking as I had intended and declaring my love, declaring that even fresh water could not quench my burning throat and breast, I took her hand and brought it to my lips as I had seen it done in a French film . . . and at that very moment, her father appeared!

"*Oukh Roj!*" he said in Arabic. "*I'Th Hab!*"

He was so red that I thought his face had caught fire. "Out, dirty nigger! Get out and never set foot in here again!"

Then he went at Aledia in Arabic. I don't know how I got out of there. Papa had told me many times that the great genius Einstein had shown that nothing could move faster than light. I wonder if I didn't prove his theory wrong that day, for no one until this day has ever moved his tail so quick. To this day, Aledia's father, Sir Hussein El Faisal Al Moustapha Husseini Morabitoune, still owes me the two hundred and fifty francs that I left on his counter.

Some time afterwards he sent his daughter back to Lebanon. But I do not despair; I know that Aledia loves me since she gave me her hand to kiss that day. I will find you one day, my beloved, and I will take you away, far, far away. We will go to a town whose name has been in my dreams ever since I discovered it on my grandfather's map of the world when I was just eight years old. I've read books about it and seen pictures of it. It's on the border of Sahel; over there, there are no trees to hide the immensity of the sky. I promise, Aledia, I will go to Lebanon, I'll snatch you from the claws of Shia Islamic sharia, and we'll live happily ever after in Ouagadougou.

15

For many weeks after Aledia left, I cared for nothing but books. I haven't gotten around to telling you yet, but I've been reading stories from books since the age of seven, actually. I began with children's books, moved on to preteen ones, and I am proud to tell you that today I am capable of reading books written for adults. My middle school teacher even told Papa that I was a very precocious child. In fact, I spent my third grade in the fourth-grade class and then skipped fifth to go directly to sixth grade; I was told that if I continued to do so well, they would let me pass my first school certificate a year early.

I had already read *Robinson Crusoe*, *Treasure Island*, *The Dark Child*, *One Hundred Years of Solitude*, *The Wonderful Adventures of Nils Holgersson*, *Tom Sawyer* and *The Adventures of Huckleberry Finn*, Andersen's *Fairy Tales*, some stories from Bengal, *The Adventures of Pinocchio* and his nose that would grow each time he lied, and I'm leaving some out since I can't mention them all. But books became my true companions, my real friends, and my only refuge when Aledia my love was snatched from me by her devil of a father.

At first, I was so heartbroken that I began to relive everything I had experienced with Aledia, without distinguishing dreams from reality: the first kiss at the podium, her exotic perfume, her long black hair decorated with cattleya orchids, the sweet sensation that spread from below my stomach through my whole body the first time I had touched her breasts behind the lantana bushes that scratched us as we passed, the fatal kiss on the hand when her father caught us . . . Despite all these recollections, I was still so heartbroken that I wanted to wound myself, so that Papa, my brothers, and especially Uncle Boula Boula, who had Lebanese acquaintances, would notice the stigmata of my love for Aledia and this would compel them to intercede with the Honorable Hussein El Faisal Al Moustapha Husseini Morabitoune to convince him to go back on his decision and send for his daughter from Beirut even if it meant that Papa and Uncle had to pay for the return ticket and, for my part, I would have to forgive the debt he owed me, that is, the two hundred and fifty francs I had spent on a can of Coca-Cola that was never served to me. After a long search, I could not find a way to wound myself without too much pain, and then I thought it over and realized that it was dumb to harm myself. That mean old man should be punished instead. Finally I told myself, Forget it, Michel, avenge yourself on that Lebanese villain!

And so I decided to kill Mr. Hussein El Faisal Al Moustapha Husseini Morabitoune.

As all of you certainly know, the first step in killing someone is to become a tough guy. I decided to be a tough guy.

A tough guy doesn't let himself be pushed around. So when Maman or my brothers would call for me, I'd never answer the first time, always waiting for my name to be called two or three times before showing myself. Sometimes, when I knew it was time for supper and everyone was waiting for me before they could eat,

I deliberately prolonged my walk so that they would eat without me and I could eat my meal in solitude just as I bore my pain in solitude. This often irritated Maman, and I would get an earful from her: "Lord, what is happening to this child!" And Papa even slapped me around once or twice, a rare thing indeed. But contrary to what they undoubtedly thought, their exasperation enthralled me—a tough guy must be independent and free. I was still missing the one thing all tough guys sported in the movies (and I should tell you that I've seen a lot of movies, too), and that was the cigarette!

I managed to get myself a pack, not just any kind of cigarette but the ones smoked by the gruff men with thick beards, skin tarnished by the sun, riding bucking broncs at the rodeo, lasso in hand, or downing a glass of whiskey in one gulp before drawing six-shooters from their holsters in the all-out saloon brawl; not just any kind of cigarette, but the ones smoked by men who, eagle-eyed under their Stetsons, galloped across the plains of the Far West, their tanned leather boots well propped in their stirrups, bandannas around their necks flowing freely in the wind, faces peering toward the setting sun. Yep, I was lighting up my first cigarette and taking my first drag.

I must have inhaled a bit too quickly, for I began coughing and hiccuping like an asthmatic as my eyes watered under the smoke's spicy bite. I thought I was going to die and never see Aledia again. I threw down the cigarette and crushed it in a rage. My throat was dry, my tongue rough, and I kept coughing, eyes bloodshot. I suddenly remembered having read in a magazine that smoking is hazardous to your health, that tobacco causes cancer of the throat, of the tongue, of the lungs, and other crap of that sort. I didn't want to die of cancer; I got scared and my breathing became strained, and I had the impression that my bronchial tubes were covered with thick coal and that soon I was going to spit up chunks of blood mixed with black soot. Once my breathing returned to normal, I ran to wash my mouth out, I chewed ten pieces of mint chewing gum and ten pieces of licorice-flavored gum, but my breath still smelled like tobacco, a smell that would henceforth make me want to heave. It surely was not the breath Aledia expected from me, she who was all roses, incense, and Oriental essences. It was at that moment that I decided never to smoke again, a vow I have kept to this day. You could be tough without having a cigarette in your mouth.

Being a tough guy was nice and all, but it wasn't the same thing as killing Aledia's father. I remembered that if there was one place where they did a lot of killing, it was the movies. I asked my twin brothers to let me watch all their videos, they were happy to oblige, and it was with great enthusiasm, even zeal, that they began catering to me. I already told you that, despite the fact that I was born two days after them, they were always afraid of me because I was taller and tougher; what's more, their fear of me had increased tenfold since I was now an uncompromising tough guy who had stood up to Maman; compared to me, they were wimps. They got out all their videos, and I watched hours of *Rambo, Death Code: Ninja, The Terminator, Alien, Lethal Weapon, The Dirty Dozen, The Eraser*; hours of murders, killings—armed, bare-handed, with automatics, bombs, flamethrowers, chain saws, in short, everything you could imagine doing to a man—plus, as an added bonus, stereo sound that didn't spare you any bone crunching. My brothers exulted, got all excited and yelled like demons whenever somebody's neck was snapped in a fistfight or when a head was cut off with a sword in one swift blow and then rolled on the floor like a ball as gallons of hemoglobin spurted everywhere. Until that day, I didn't know that the human spirit had so much ingenuity for torture, murder, violence, so much talent for killing, mutilating, taking life. I suddenly got scared. I looked at my brothers, these cowards who could be spooked by a mosquito; they were gesticulating and living out other people's violence as if it was their own.

"Hey, cool it!" I cried angrily.

They shut up right away and cuddled together, looking at me

with fright in their eyes as if I was going to submit them to the fate they had been enjoying just now when it was inflicted upon others.

"Damn idiots, cowardly chickens!" I said as I left, violently slamming the door.

I didn't want to kill anymore. I don't want to kill. I was going to lock myself up in my room, and suddenly I began thinking about Grandfather and his kindness. I remembered what he told me when we had gone to see him in his village: "The older you get, the harder life will seem to you, difficult to get through, absurd even, and the least nuisance could push you to suicide or to wish for death. But remember, Matapari, it's only when you're my age, when you will have gotten through your life, that you'll see it was worth living after all." Under these conditions, I thought, what purpose would killing serve, even the killing of men as wicked as Aledia's father?

I immediately felt like being with Grandfather; only he understood me, only he could soothe me. He told me animal tales, about the wily hare and the silly panther, fantastic stories like the one about the beautiful Mamiwata, mother of the waters, or about sorcerers who traveled at night on strange airplanes. We would walk at night while listening to the light rustling of the grass and the palms in the wind, which sounded like the moaning of the ancestors, and, holding his hand, I trotted alongside him, trying to keep up with his great easy strides; if the moon wasn't too bright under the big top of the sky, we would see Jupiter in the east, a huge star, brighter than the flickering Sirius, and we would attempt to divine the constellations that Papa had taught us about, difficult for us to do, he had said, since we were so close to the equator that neither the boreal nor the austral charts were convenient for us; thus we would see, as we would if we were in Ouagadougou, lovely Orion encircled by its trinity of stars, but we would also see the Southern Cross, which we couldn't see in Ouagadougou. Grandfather had asked me to be there the day of his burial, but in the meantime he told me: "Learn how to read, little one, you must know how to read the books of man and the book of the universe."

So I let the memory of Aledia coil in a precious corner of my heart and plunged myself headlong into the world of knowledge. There were so many things in books! Did you know that time does not exist in outer space and vice versa and that when matter becomes infinitely dense it forms a black hole, from which even light cannot escape? Did you know that only life gives life and that its cryptic secret is in a double-helix molecule that reproduces itself identically and eternally? Did you know that numbers can be golden, real, rational, irrational, perfect, friendly, complex, imaginary, and transcendent, and that there is a mathematical theory, at first glance esoteric and without practical utility, about the decomposition of large natural whole numbers into primary factors, a theory that is the foundation of modern secret codes? Did you know that . . . But what is the use of going on? It would be useless to bore you to apoplexy by talking about the vastness of the gap between what is hidden in the book of the universe and all that is already written in the books of man.

When I was little, I thought that tunes were kept in one place and I feared that people would exhaust the stock by composing too many songs and that there wouldn't be any left for the singers of future generations. I never had that kind of fear about books. I always knew that the universe was infinite and that, books being an element in its whole, there would always exist more things to write about than there would be books. And also, I really think that, just like me, each person has a story to tell. Whatever, at the end of this twentieth century, there were more than five billion people on earth, and since no census has ever recorded a decline in the human population, we aren't about to run out of their stories, each worthy of a book.

Curiously, I learned to like books even more the day Papa taught me to doubt their absolute authority. I had read I don't know where that the logarithmic tables were invented by a Scottish preacher to quickly and accurately count the witches proliferating in his parish. When I told Papa, he laughed and cast doubt on my assertion. "But I read it in a book," I proclaimed as an absolute argument. He laughed again. "You must always read a man's book with a critical mind," he said to me, "like your mother would say, only the holy books contain absolute truths, though absolute truths aren't interesting from the point of view of knowledge, but that's another story." He was right. It didn't take me long to find that out when I realized that two books I was reading about reggae did not give the same information on a specific episode of Bob Marley's life. Yet he did not live two parallel lives. Since then, I have this passion—which, I admit, sometimes makes me waste a lot of time—for consulting different books on the same subject.

Papa, who, after ten long, conscientious years of correspondence courses reinforced by numerous internships, was the holder of two diplomas—a master's in physical science and another in the philosophy of science—after all that, Papa had admitted to me more than once that he knew nothing. But I, in my ardent desire to know that I knew something, I read biographies of Albert Einstein, Arthur Ashe, Matt Henson, George Washington Carver, and Srinivasa Ramanujan, as well as Alexander Pushkin, Rigoberta Menchú, Rabindranath Tagore, and Harriet Tubman. In the company of men and women of such inspired lives—I bet you haven't even heard of half of them—who could waste his time galloping about in the plains of the Far West, cigarette dangling from the mouth, Colt around the waist, to go massacre some Indians? Who would waste his time dreaming of being Rambo or Mad Max? No, with these men and women you could become a great scholar, a great man of science, a great sportsman, a great explorer, a great architect! There were so many choices offered to me at this particular crossroads of my life, with Aledia tucked away in my heart.

I was no longer sad; on the contrary, a smile slowly welled up from my heart to brighten my face, and I was so happy, so light that I thought for a moment my body was aflame. I felt an urge for music. For once, I wanted neither rap nor ragamuffin. I chose kora harp music, without lyrics, because I noticed that the words of men often had the ability to obscure the essence of things and sometimes even corrupt them. I closed my eyes, and I began vibrating with these bright and melancholy notes. Through them, I traversed the vast spaces of the Sahelian savanna, near Ouagadougou, where there are no forests to hide the immensity of the blue sky. Then these notes became a bit nostalgic, and I wondered if it wasn't the sound of kora harp music that had accompanied the Arab caravans coming from the North, Koran in one hand, saber in the other, wending their way toward the sea, linked by the chains and neck irons of long columns of slaves snatched from the Sudan. Oh the music of the kora harp and balaphons! Peace and serenity! The virgin possibilities of my youth! I was master of my fate, of my future.

But hardly had I begun to dream of my future of significance when I heard Maman's lament from the living room—she was almost crying—begging the Lord and all the saints for mercy. I wondered what had made her quit the market stand where she would sell things to round out the end of the month and to give us little presents. I learned soon enough: her brother, the right hand of the State and our Single Party, the man who was the worthy successor to our Supreme Revolutionary Guide and was in the process of collecting the funds that would allow us to place a huge statue of the Supreme Guide in geostationary orbit around the earth, my uncle, her brother, had been arrested for plotting against the State.

16

Glory, Papa once told me when we were talking about Uncle's unstoppable ascent in our country's politics— glory, he said, has a ballistic trajectory: there comes a point when it reaches its peak, and then, the descent is unstoppable. But I didn't think that this maxim also applied to Uncle. I didn't think that he would be threatened so soon, since he, whom we considered the presumptive heir of the true father of the nation, had yet to reach his peak, meaning he had not yet become our numero uno, our new enlightened and beloved guide. I should have heeded what Papa told me during that same conversation, when he said that in Africa the most dangerous political position is number two, since despite your pledges of loyalty, the number one will always think that everything you're doing is motivated by the goal of shoving him out the door and taking his place.

A few days earlier, a bomb had exploded at the airport, killing several people, and forty-eight hours later, another incendiary device went off in a crowded movie theater, again killing several people. These incidents could not have come about at a worse time for Uncle, who was arranging a new congress for our One Party. The country, and especially the national radio and television, peddled nothing but rumors of reactionary sellouts to imperialism, and little by little Uncle felt that he was losing control of the Party machine. He who had weighed in on every decision realized that the beloved chief of our Revolution was now going over him to give instructions to his subordinates directly. The Party's "democratic centralism and rigid discipline," the merits of which he had boasted about to Papa, were things of the past.

At the time, you understand, I was freshly orphaned from Aledia, and the wound in my heart in that spot from which she had been snatched had not yet closed. So I was completely immersed in my books when the news of Uncle's fall and his arrest on the eve of the Congress came, and it took me utterly by surprise. Only the live TV coverage made it really sink in: not only was Uncle not at his traditional place at the President's right hand but he was totally absent from the stand where all of the government dignitaries sat. In his place was a man dredged up from the depths of the Central Committee who had the good fortune to be from the President's tribe. Uncle's name, which had always been associated with that of the Chief of State, had not been mentioned even once; and in his speech the new number two went as far as to say that if the project of putting in orbit the huge portrait of our great leader was being held up, this was because of "the reactionary moles who had succeeded in infiltrating all the way to the top of our Party apparatus."

Maman couldn't stop grieving. Papa was telling her that what was happening to her brother was not surprising, for it was in the nature of totalitarian parties to devour their own offspring. Maman didn't agree. Whatever her brother's crimes, she would not let him be eaten alive; she would get him out of this bad spot. In fact, her faith was reinforced by the story she had told me that I have already recounted for you, about the embezzlement in the time of cholera. No, I think I'm mistaken, I haven't told you that story yet.

It was during the great cholera epidemic that had struck the center of the country. The international aid organizations, notably the WHO, notified about the spread of the plague, had set up an emergency operation called Knock Out. This is how millions of American dollars landed in the pockets of our country's health minister. Using diplomacy, invoking the national sovereignty and the principle of noninterference in the internal affairs of an independent state, the health minister succeeded in managing this budget directly from his office. It was inevitable: the money disappeared along with the minister. This event, which put the whole country and the entire international community in commotion, did, however, infuse the epidemic, which caused eight thousand and five hundred dead in three weeks, with an exponential vigor. Fortunately a new emergency plan, this time directly managed by a Scandinavian charity organization, succeeded in putting an end to the catastrophe.

One day this minister somehow resurfaced; he was arrested, tried, and condemned to twenty years of hard labor for crimes against humanity after a well-publicized trial broadcast on radio and television. But four months later, on the occasion of the year-end speech by the Guide of our Revolution, surprise, surprise, the name of the disgraced former health minister appeared on the list of those given amnesty by the Chief of State every new year. He was set free. Some reactionary bad mouths spread noise about that money having been embezzled with the complicity of our beloved Guide and said that the guilty one had been pardoned because he and the President were related or belonged to the same tribe. Maman knew the real reason, and she had gotten it from the mouth of the ex-minister's own sister, who was a member of her religious sorority. Well, his sister had gone to see a "prophet of God" in the capital, not a Muslim marabou or an animist fetish maker, but a prophet of God, who based his invocations on the Bible. Of course he had cowries and other ingredients used by fetish makers, but the Bible was there to neutralize any animist or heathen influence. Oh yes, she had also given him a large sum of money. Thanks to the prayers, the invocations from this prophet, and maybe also thanks to the large sum of money, the name of her brother had appeared, by a miracle of God, on the list of the fortunate pardoned. Now Maman decided to do as much for her brother. Early in the morning, after saying her prayers and putting a small Bible in her purse, she hopped in a truck to be near her brother in the capital.

I can't tell you in detail what happened to my uncle, since politics, with its secrets and entanglements, its truths that aren't so true, and its lies that sound like truths, makes my head spin. I don't know if, as they said, Uncle was at the head of the biggest plot ever organized in this country, with planes, tanks, and mercenaries waiting at the borders, while commando infiltrators carried out bombings to terrorize the population and create a climate of fear propitious to their coming into power. All I know is that he had been arrested along with many other people. Foreigners had been arrested too. Aledia's father, Mr. Hussein El Faisal Al Moustapha Husseini Morabitoune, had been cited among the accomplices but, fortunately for him, he had gotten out of the country a few hours before Uncle's arrest. He had in fact left so quickly that he had forgotten to pay back several million francs to our country's biggest bank, which went bankrupt that very day. Contradictory rumors reached us about the prisoners: some said they had been interrogated, tortured, detained in solitary confinement, while others said that the President of the Republic himself had insisted that not a hair on Uncle's head be touched to show that our country respected human rights and that Amnesty International could shut its yapper. During the fourteen months of detention—that year, I did not even notice my fourteenth birthday go by—Maman lost weight. She had come and gone incessantly between our little town and the capital. She went from priest to fetish maker, from prophetess to exorcist. Papa, for his part, said, "You'll see, they're going to put on a show trial." Papa was not mistaken: there really was a trial.

I had seen trials only on TV, meaning in movies, so it was the first time I was seeing a real trial broadcast live by our national television. I was all excited, but Papa seemed indifferent. He said to me: "Michel, a real trial is not a televised spectacle." He told me that the last trial of this kind he had attended had taken place a few years before my birth. "In one of the many successful or abortive coups that burnished the history of our country as I described it to you at the beginning of this story, the chief of the State at the time, a corporal or a commandant"—he didn't remember exactly—"was assassinated." It was a story rife with plots within plots, with Cubans and the French, a former President of the Republic, a cardinal, military men, teachers, bureaucrats, working men, craftsmen, and other anonymous civilians. So it would stick, the revolutionary court couldn't figure out anything better than to pick ten random underlings, all from the same tribe as the former President, and summarily execute them "at the break of dawn," as they say. Papa had not forgotten this, and this new trial did not bode well as far as he was concerned.

The accused were all sitting on the same bench, some with their heads shaved. I barely recognized Uncle. He had lost weight, and it seemed to me that he had more gray than black on his head. I no longer recognized the powerful member of the Political Bureau who once had so many cars at his disposal that each day he would choose one that matched the color of the suit he happened to be wearing. It seemed as though he could not believe that the chief magistrate of the revolutionary tribunal who now sat before him was a member of the Central Committee with whom he had had a very good relationship until his arrest. He seemed even more dumbfounded when he noticed that the government prosecutor, the man who was going to present and defend the charges

against them, was none other than the young man he had himself
placed at the head of the Party Youth League in the face of widespread opposition.

The trial lasted a few days, going late into the night. I taped
the most dramatic episodes on a VCR, and as I tell you this story
I'm reviewing a few scenes so that my account, even if I don't keep
to the precise chronological order, will be as faithful as possible.

After the "we have seen," the "we have heard," the "notwith-
standing," the "deliberation," the "it is evident that," the first person to go was a poor semiliterate wretch, a stone breaker by
profession. How could a stone breaker be involved in the biggest
plot ever hatched against the Revolution? That was crystal clear: a
stone breaker handles the dynamite needed to blow apart the big
blocks of rock which he then breaks up. In other words, he was an
expert in explosives! The plotters had used a device with a timer
so sophisticated that only an expert could handle it. The choice of
the revolutionary court thus fell on Bissila, the quarry dynamiter.
He advanced painfully, his head shaven. The ablutions he had
been forced to perform and the new clothes they had made him
wear weren't enough to hide the ill treatment he had suffered.
The government prosecutor then began proving that Bissila knew
Uncle, the leader of the conspiracy.

"Defendant Bissila, do you know a man by the name of Boula
Boula?"

"No, Comrade Prosecutor."

"You do not know him? We'll see about that. The photos!"

A screen was pulled down behind the chief magistrate, and on
it appeared a picture taken during the parade in honor of the fifteenth anniversary of the Revolution. There was Uncle sitting on
the stand, to the right of the Chief of the Revolution and surrounded by other dignitaries. Uncle had that bloated face characteristic of people in power. Uncle in true form, at the peak of his
glory!

"Defendant Bissila. Look at this photo. Point to the man who is Boula Boula."

Without hesitation, he pointed at Uncle.

"You are able to recognize him without hesitation in the midst of a multitude of faces, and yet you say you have never met this man!"

"Comrade Prosecutor, I know him without having seen him . . . meaning that I recognized him without knowing him . . . I mean—"

"That's right, keep on entangling yourself in your lies."

"But what I mean is that if I came across Nelson Mandela in the street I would recognize him right away and nevertheless—"

"Don't compare Nelson Mandela with this miserable plotter and swindler! Do you know a soccer team by the name of Kotoko Mfoa?"

"Yes, Comrade Prosecutor, I'm a big fan of that team."

"Were you present at the wake organized when its goalkeeper died?"

"Of course, Comrade Prosecutor, where else should I be?"

"Good. Who else was there at the wake?"

"There were many other people."

"Like Boula Boula, for instance?"

"Well . . . yes, I knew he arrived because there was a scramble when the soldiers began to crack heads to make way for his escort. You could well imagine that the arrival of our Party's general secretary could not go unnoticed."

"So there. You recognize at first sight someone you have never seen, you make it so that you happen to find yourselves together one night at a wake, and you still maintain that there isn't any interaction between you two? Keep lying. Do you know the small town of Ibibiti?"

"Yes."

"Have you ever been there?"

"Yes, I went to work there during the preparations for the celebration of our Revolution's fourteenth anniversary."

"How were you recruited?"

"Surely you remember that there was a campaign to recruit workers to build the gigantic stadium that was going to host the parade. Many of us presented ourselves, and I was picked."

"So was everyone recruited?"

"No."

"But you, by complete coincidence, you were recruited, right, out of over ten thousand candidates? How come?"

"I don't know, maybe it's just luck. Oh yes, I remember, they had told me that they needed someone who knew how to handle dynamite because they wanted to use a quarry on site."

"There we have it. . . . It has taken long enough, but there we have it. And who signed your job application, do tell?"

"I don't know."

"How can you not know? We know you went to school."

"I only got as far as the third grade."

The prosecutor went to one of his aides and asked for a document that was held out to him. He brandished it, and the camera did a close-up shot. It was the Party's decision recruiting one hundred and twenty-five people to go work on the construction site of the stadium that was to be built in Ibibiti. Bissila's name was number 95. But the shock came when we saw that the document had the signature of the Party's general secretary, the EPOVWFARCEC, none other than Uncle Boula Boula. The government prosecutor was very pleased with the case he had made.

"Let's review," he said. "You recognize at first glance an individual you have never seen. You manage to find yourself at the same time at the same wake with him. And finally, when more than ten thousand people present themselves to be hired on a construction site that had not even opened yet, you find yourself by complete coincidence among the less than one percent hired by this same individual that you do not know. We all know that coincidences happen, but aren't you inclined to think that there are a few too many coincidences here?" He concluded this question with a slight knowing nod at the chief magistrate.

The latter rolled up the sleeves of his robe and declared: "The court will consider. Continue."

"You claim to have worked on the construction site for the Revolution's fourteenth anniversary?"

"Yes, Comrade Prosecutor."

"Who did you meet there?"

Bissila, the accused, was visibly uncomfortable, as if he had been caught in a trap. He looked left and right, lifted his eyes toward the auditorium, where his wife was, lowered his eyes, and said nothing.

"Who did you meet over there?" the prosecutor intoned.

He again looked at his wife and, eyes lowered, defended himself. "She was not my mistress, Comrade Prosecutor. Since I spent my full day on the site, I asked a young Zairean woman to come by from time to time in the evening where I was housed to do the cooking, in exchange for a small salary, of course . . . Strictly professional relations, nothing more. If I said nothing to my wife, it is because I knew she is so jealous she would have thought there was something other than appropriate relations between this Zairean woman and myself. I beg her to forgive me."

The chief magistrate, the judges, the prosecutor were all perplexed since, apparently, this was not the answer they had been waiting for. This time, the chief magistrate, who until then had been content to do just two things, roll up the sleeves of his robe, which had an annoying tendency to fall back over his wrists, and let out an occasional "the court will consider," intervened in the cross-examination: "Defendant Bissila, who said anything about a Zairean woman? Do you think that this court has the time to listen to the stories of your sexual escapades? Are you toying with us? We could care less if you catch AIDS or not. I will repeat the question, answer it directly: who of importance did you meet at the place where you broke your stones?"

". . . ?"

"Let's see, I'm going to help you," the prosecutor continued. "Do you know the village teacher?"

I jumped when I heard that question. This teacher was none other than Papa, even though, ever since his correspondence courses and his new diplomas, he was no longer a simple teacher but had become a professor. I remember that he often went to the different sites, talked to the workers, openly protested against what he called the slaughter of the forest. What did they want with Papa?

"Yes," answered Bissila, "I met him several times. He often came by the quarry where I broke rocks."

"Do you know his profession?"

"You said it, schoolteacher."

"No, his area of specialization!"

". . . ?"

"He's a chemist, you understand, a chemist!"

One of the judges leaned over and whispered something in the ear of the chief magistrate. The latter nodded in agreement, rolled up the sleeves of his robe once more, and addressed himself to the government prosecutor. "I am told that he is a physicist."

"Thank you for the information, Comrade Magistrate," the prosecutor went on without skipping a beat. "This changes nothing about the heart of the matter. Chemist or physicist, they are all epigones of that bomber Alfred Nobel, dangerous handlers of explosives. That's not all. Listen to this: this professor of chemistry, this fulmanic acid-toting mad scientist is none other than . . . Boula Boula's brother-in-law! As the defendant admitted himself, this professor gave him lessons in mastering the sophisticated mechanism of an explosive device with a timing mechanism of the same kind as the ones that blew up the airport and the movie theater. Thank you, Chief Magistrate."

This time, anyone could see that he was satisfied not only with his demonstration but most of all with himself, since his lips twisted in a mischievous smile as he sat back down on his bench.

"The court will consider the evidence!" said the magistrate.

After the government prosecutor's brilliant demonstration, I was trembling for Papa, and I was convinced that he was guilty. I didn't dare look at him. I wanted us to get away before he was arrested. I wanted us to run off and hide in Boko, Grandfather's village. No one would find us there. But I was strongly mistaken: Papa was hopping mad. "Ah, bastards," he raged. "They would not let me appear at the trial because they knew I could ruin their whole damned scheme, but we cannot go on like this; this masquerade must cease!"

I had been so attentive to Papa's imprecations that when my attention returned to the TV screen, a woman was speaking. She was pretty, fit nicely in a black dress; she was sure of herself, and seemed not at all impressed by the government prosecutor, who was terrorizing everyone, including the chief magistrate of the court. I learned later that she was Counselor Julie, Bissila's lawyer. There were still people in this country who dared go against the fearsome machinery of our One Party, which Uncle had established and which was now grinding him up. I only heard her intervention midsentence: ". . . refused to cross-examine this teacher who, it seemed, has taught him within just a few days to set up this sophisticated explosive device—"

"Objection, Comrade Magistrate!" cried the prosecutor.

"Objection," the magistrate repeated.

"The defense seems to be questioning the honesty and impartiality of the investigators. You realize that you may be in contempt of court. I must simply remind everyone that after Defendant Bissila's spontaneous statement, and following accepted legal norms, it did not seem necessary to have the teacher appear. In fact, from all the information we have, it seems that this individual, in whose hands we have abandoned our children's education, is practically an anarchist, and undoubtedly you remember the embarrassment he caused us, scandal I should say, when we decided to establish Party cells in the forest near the Pygmies. Therefore, in our opinion, it seems useless to trouble the good course of this trial with the presence of uncontrollable individuals."

Ah, the Pygmy episode! Uncle and the Party had planned a great revolutionary campaign: convert all the Pygmies of the equatorial forest to Marxism-Leninism. Papa was furious when he learned this. He told Uncle Boula Boula in my presence: "We mess with them enough as it is. Can't you leave them the hell alone?" He then reached for his pen and wrote to several foreign newspapers. The scandal went international when a number of important papers published his letters. But you'll have to excuse me, I'll let you in on the details of this story that made Papa famous another time if you want, for I have to continue with the trial.

"Objection sustained!" said the magistrate. He rolled up the sleeves of his robe.

"Withdrawn," Counselor Julie replied just as quickly. "Let's move on to this confession, written and signed by my client."

She turned to Bissila and presented the document to him. "Bissila, you're the one who signed this paper, aren't you?"

"Yes, Counsel."

"What does it say?"

"I don't know. They presented it to me and told me to sign or they would go at it again."

"Go at what again?"

"Start running current through my balls."

There was an indignant "oh" from the court magistrate, the prosecutor, the judges, and the public.

The prosecutor rose without asking permission, shouting at Bissila: "You are lying. The Revolution shall not let these calum-

nies stand. Counselor Julie, suppose we wanted to arrest you and
suppose you tried running away. If a police agent clipped you and
as a result you stumbled, fell, and broke your nose, are you going
to pretend that you suffered ill treatment and bring your broken
nose as proof? Are you going to pretend that you have been tortured!"

Then, turning toward the magistrate: "Comrade Magistrate,"
the prosecutor continued, "I ask that you strike the defendant's
statement from the record, because this kind of lie—"

Bissila, who had been submissive until now, so shy that he
barely dared to look the prosecutor in the face, burst out in anger,
staring the prosecutor in the eye. "Lies, you say, but it is you who
have said nothing but lies ever since I've been here. Whatever I
say, you say that I'm lying. But what do you want from me? I'm
sick and tired! I've been beaten, hung by the feet, head upside-
down, while they ran current through my balls. I even think that
I've become impotent now. You want to see my burns?" He took
off his shirt and threw it, and began unbuttoning his pants, which
fell to his feet, and Counselor Julie stopped him right when he was
about to take off his underwear. He stopped, leaned down to grab
his pants, tears streaming down his face.

"Objection," cried the prosecutor.

The camera that was zooming in to get a close-up of the
burns on his back retreated just then, as if frightened by the prosecutor's objection.

But Bissila continued talking through his tears. "I was
writhing in pain, I was screaming and wriggling under the current.
'Sign this paper and we'll stop just like that,' they kept yelling in
my ears. I fell apart and I signed. And they say I'm telling lies—"

"Objection sustained," the magistrate concurred while rolling up his sleeves. "This entire section will be stricken from the
record."

"Very well, Your Honor," said Counselor Julie (she refused to say "Comrade"), "this part can be withdrawn, for the burns we have just seen on my client's body are only figments of our imagination."

"Watch it, Counsel, or I will hold you in contempt of court and ask that your behavior be evaluated."

"Thank you, Your Honor. Bissila, here is the letter you have written and signed. The last sentence says the following: 'P.S.: I have freely written this confession, without any physical or moral coercion.' What is your educational level?"

"Up to the third grade."

"Yes, I can actually see that the statement is peppered with crude spelling mistakes. But I'm going to ask you a simple question. Answer me truthfully. What does the abbreviation 'P.S.' mean?"

"I don't know."

"You really don't know?"

"I assure you, Counsel, that I don't know."

"Your Honor, as you can see, my client doesn't know what 'P.S.' means. I just wanted to be certain."

The magistrate, perplexed, looked to the prosecutor for help. The prosecutor was furious.

"Comrade Magistrate, our colleague needs to show more respect for this court. We have no time to waste here; neither does the Revolution. We have an authentic, devastating document, and instead of facing the evidence of her client's guilt, this lawyer is making us waste time by deciphering Latin abbreviations."

"Your Honor, I was simply wondering how my client could have written this statement when he does not know the meaning of some of the terms used."

"Comrade Magistrate," the government prosecutor continued, waving the back of his hand as if he wanted to sweep away unimportant words, "these clever but futile diversions will not divert us from what is essential. Here is a specific question for you,

Bissila: Saturday, after placing the bomb, you admitted that you immediately called Boula Boula. What did you tell him?"

"No! I did not place the bomb, I was not even here the day of the bombing. I was five hundred miles from here, squaring off big blocks of stone that I had to place on the walls of Captain Ngoma's veranda. You can check that!"

"Once more, you are lying, Bissila! It is true that you were in Punta Negra that particular week, but what you are not saying is that you had asked your employer for permission to leave for the weekend, for so-called family reasons."

"But no, Comrade Prosecutor, I had asked for three days' leave two weeks before the bombings. I took the Blue Train on Sunday, and I returned Wednesday on the express train."

"Comrade Magistrate, there is no point continuing. This man lies like he breathes, and he will never tell the truth. You have read his signed confession. He was here in the capital that day. You have also read Captain Ngoma's letter confirming that he had given him a leave of several days. The defendant undoubtedly used that time to go commit the crime and to collect his pay for these doings. Thank you, Comrade Magistrate."

"It's not true," shouted Bissila. "I was at Punta Negra when the bomb went off!"

"The defendant will be silent!" the magistrate intoned. "If you continue to demonstrate a lack of respect for this most revolutionary court, it will cost you. In any case, the court will consider your behavior."

He turned to Counselor Julie. "Counsel, do you have any further questions for the defendant?"

"Thank you, Your Honor. Bissila, you maintain that you weren't here on the day of the bombing. Can you give us the name of a witness who can confirm that you were really at Punta Negra that day?"

At this question, Bissila threw furtive glances at the magistrate and at the prosecutor, opened his mouth to talk, closed it again, and said nothing. "They . . . they . . . they told me not to mention his name."

"Oh?" Counselor Julie exclaimed, feigning surprise. "Who could have given you such an order?"

"It was when they questioned me. When I said that I had seen this person in Punta Negra and that I had run some errands for him the night of the bombing, the examiners said that if I ever repeated this name, they would not only start torturing me again—they'd send me straight to the gallows."

"And who was this person whose name was not to be mentioned?"

"Am I allowed to say it, Counselor Julie?" asked Bissila, looking as if he wanted to make sure the sky wouldn't fall on his head if he did.

"Do not be afraid," his lawyer reassured him. "You can speak without fear, we are here to determine the truth."

"I was running errands for Colonel Bikedi on the night the bomb went off in the capital."

The government prosecutor looked stunned, as if a well-hewn cobblestone had landed on his head.

"Are you sure about what you are telling us here, Bissila?"

"God knows, I'm telling the truth."

"Objection!" cried the prosecutor.

"Sustained," the magistrate replied.

"In none of his previous statements has the accused mentioned this witness," the prosecutor shot back. "He's lying. If he was telling the truth, that name would have appeared during earlier questioning because, believe me, no one can resist the tortu——uh . . . the . . . uh . . . an interrogation of several weeks."

"Most respectfully, Your Honor," Counselor Julie pleaded, "I ask that Colonel Bikedi appear before this court."

"Consider the honor of our army, Comrade Magistrate," the

prosecutor pleaded as well. "Do not embroil it in these sordid events."

Counselor Julie sat down. The prosecutor sat down. The magistrate, who was already sitting down, rolled up the sleeves of his robe, cleared his throat, and said nothing for a while. We sensed he was in trouble. After some hesitation, he cried: "This session is in recess. We will resume in an hour."

He knocked his gavel on the table and got up. The sleeves of his robe fell back over his wrists. That was the end of the broadcast.

"Gum in the works," said Papa. "He's probably going off to take his orders. We'll see who's telling the truth."

I was glad that the session was in recess, for my eyes were starting to hurt after six hours of uninterrupted TV. My brothers, who were waiting for just this moment, swooped in to watch a martial arts video borrowed from I don't know where.

It was already dark outside. Papa stood up and went out to get some fresh night air and to stretch after so many hours sitting. One curious thing, though: he seemed pleased with the hearing. Intrigued, I followed him outside. He was looking at the sky, where the stars glittered in total freedom. Just as I lifted my eyes, a shooting star burst out of the nothingness and streaked across the sky in a luminous furrow. I let out an "ah" of enchantment, and I wondered if you could catch a ray of light and what it would be like to ride it.

17

An hour later, I returned to my seat in front of the TV for the trial. My brothers were still watching their Chinese movie. I suppose that I arrived at the movie's most heart-pounding moment, what with the way they were holding on to their chairs, eyes gleaming with excitement: a sword blow to the neck, the head flew off and did somersaults on the ground while a geyser of blood spurted out of the open neck. Suddenly, a lion's roar, a fighter leaped out of a barrel that was lying around, adjusted his course in midair, and flew feet first toward the nape of—At that exact moment, without asking, I zapped the remote. Out of the corner of my eye, I watched my twin brothers, and I could guess that a great many questions probably remained unaddressed in their minds: Did the adversary's nape get pulverized by the aggressor's flying kick? Or did the man under attack instead turn around in time to shatter the adversary's skull with his blade or to slice him apart piece by piece, buckets of blood gushing? Neither of them had the courage to speak, but I was certain that, if human eyes could spit bullets, my body would have had more holes than the Chinese grater Maman used to strain her ginger. I calmly continued my zapping as if nothing had happened until, satisfied once again that I was the sole master onboard after Papa, despite their right of primogeniture, I returned to the channel broadcasting the trial. Unfortunately, the trial had not yet begun, and the channel was broadcasting Russian and Cuban revolutionary songs as if to prepare us for the lies that were going to be offered later by all these reactionaries who had plotted with Uncle against the Revolution.

"Can we watch our movie while waiting for the trial?" Banzouzi stuttered. He stopped as soon as his eyes met mine. I didn't even bother answering and pretended to be religiously attentive to these stupid revolutionary songs, which weren't worth a single verse of ragamuffin.

Finally the session resumed. Counselor Julie was sitting next to her client. The prosecutor was sitting between two of his colleagues, leafing through a thick file. The comrade magistrate hit the table with his gavel. "This court is in session!"

Papa was as tense as if he was sitting on the bench of the accused.

"An army officer has been wrongfully implicated by the accused. This implication, bordering on slander, deserves an unambiguous denial so that the people see that our Revolution has nothing to hide. That is why this high-ranking officer has spontaneously asked his superiors for the authorization to come and take the witness stand, and he ought to be commended for this. We ask that General Bikedi please come forward."

The general entered with all of his decorations. He took the witness stand.

The magistrate said, "General, you have not been accused, you are not even a witness in this trial. You are here only to clear up a point or two; it is thus unnecessary for you to take the oath." He turned to the prosecutor. "Comrade Prosecutor, any questions you'd like to ask the general?"

"Thank you, Comrade Magistrate. General Bikedi, you are in fact a general?"

The general was surprised at the question. "But of course," he answered, perplexed.

"Comrade Magistrate," continued the prosecutor, "I am simply proposing that the general not be submitted to a point-less cross-examination. You see, the defendant told us earlier that General Bikedi was a colonel, which now discredits his entire statement. When one makes a mistake about the rank of a general, one can only be wrong about everything else."

"Your Honor!"

"Yes, Counselor Julie."

"Since when is the general a general?"

"I was promoted to general last week," the person under question shot back.

"My client is not supposed to be aware of the promotion list for the thousands of soldiers who make up our army," said Counselor Julie, looking at the prosecutor.

"General Bikedi isn't just anybody. His promotion has in fact been announced on the radio and television."

"You see the satellite dishes growing like mushrooms on our roofs, and you still have not understood that no one watches your television and no one listens to your radio, both confiscated by force—"

"Counselor Julie! You will stand down," interrupted the magistrate, "and know that I do not tolerate our democratic institutions being insulted here. Though you may be a lawyer, you are liable like anybody else for contempt of court."

We could see that he was highly upset as he rolled up the sleeves of his vast robe with restrained rage. "Just as well as far as I'm concerned," he said, in a conciliatory tone. "Counselor Julie."

"Comrade Prosecutor," the magistrate continued, managing

to calm down, "proceed with your cross-examination of the general."

"Thank you, Your Honor. General, the defendant maintains that he knows you."

"Knows me, that's saying too much. He's an unskilled laborer that I have employed—"

"Laborer!" Bissila exclaimed. "You mean to say I'm not a professional? I have worked ten years with an Italian, Mr. Cascadini, and I was such a good worker that before leaving our country, he gave me a stone dresser's certificate. I bet you don't even know what a stone dresser is. Well, it's a master mason who knows how to cut a stone and arrange it like a fancy tile setter would. You say I'm just a laborer? Do you know how to install a cyclopean, polygonal, or irregular structure on a building? I didn't go to university like you, but I'm a master craftsman, I know my profession as well as you know your Kalashnikov—"

"Bissila, Defendant Bissila, don't get upset! A laborer can do good work. You maintain that you were with the general in Punta Negra when the bombing took place?"

"I do maintain it!"

"It's not true," said the general. "I didn't even see him."

"Why sure! I came across you in the morning in front of the hotel you were coming out of; you were with some Japanese. You told me you were glad to have bumped into me and you asked me to come see you that night—"

"It's not true. I have never hosted a Japanese delegation to Punta Negra. This is easy to verify, isn't it?"

"Thank you, General. It is pointless to continue importuning you with the defendant's baseless allegations. Actually, the minister of foreign affairs and the army chief of staff have confirmed that no Japanese delegation has visited our country in two years." The prosecutor sat back down.

Counselor Julie asked if she could proceed. "General, you

maintain that you have never hosted a foreign delegation in Punta Negra?"

The general hesitated, then answered: "I didn't say that. I said that I have never hosted a Japanese delegation."

"So, what delegation did you host?"

The general hesitated again and finally answered: "A North Korean delegation."

"Japanese, Korean, it's all the same to me," said Bissila. "How could I have guessed just now that he was with these Orientals? I'm not God."

"It is not your turn to speak!" the magistrate cut in.

"Could you give us the dates of your stay in this town?"

"Counselor Julie," the magistrate intervened, without rolling up his baggy sleeves this time, "I have made it clear that General Bikedi is not on trial here and is not even a witness. He has shown up simply to clarify for us several dubious aspects of Defendant Bissila's statement."

I could tell by Counselor Julie's furrowed eyebrows that she wanted to explode. She said nothing for a moment, then changed her strategy: "Thank you for the reminder, Your Honor. May I please cross-examine my client?"

"I will allow it."

"Bissila, tell me a little bit about what took place in Punta Negra that day."

"It was on the very night the bombing happened here in the capital. When I went to see him in his hotel room, he entrusted me with one of those little missions I'd often do for him. I'm not lying since he's right here. Remember, General? You told me you had an important rendezvous but you had the feeling that your thing there was a bit tired and that you were afraid of not being up for it, you know. But it was no trouble at all. I went to the native quarter, and I bought this root here we call the *kimbiolongo*, then I went to an old Central African lady who sold me her famous quick-charge powder called up-up, and I can vouch for its effectiveness—"

"This is not true," shouted the angry general. "I am still quite potent!" Drops of sweat beaded on his forehead.

"It is true! I can even give you his room number and even the name of the young la——"

"Stop these calumnies," cried the prosecutor, as embarrassed as he was angry. "Are you not going to take an officer's word over a common worker's?"

Counselor Julie wanted to speak, but the magistrate raised his hand and addressed himself to the general: "General, I see that this cross-examination has lasted long enough. I thank you for your patience and generosity. This court is adjourned!"

Counselor Julie was smiling. The general went out, his shoulders slumped and his back betraying a slouch, in sharp contrast with the praetorian airs he had displayed at the beginning of the session. Papa looked on with a smile of scorn mixed with pity. "Here's what the army of our country has become," he said to me. "An officer's word, who are you kidding!"

In fact, from that day forth, in our country an officer's word wasn't worth more than that of a taxi driver from Poto-Poto (a neighborhood in our capital), or a pushcart pusher in the Total Bacongo market (another neighborhood).

I didn't quite understand why Bissila kept insisting about this meeting with the general and why the general did not want this meeting to have happened. I asked Papa: "Why doesn't the general admit that he met Bissila in Punta Negra?"

"Their entire case would fall apart, Michel. Boom! If Bissila was in Punta Negra at the time of the bombing, he could not have been in the capital at the same time. Now, according to the charges, it was Bissila who placed those bombs. Poor fellow can't be in two places at once!"

"Maman told me that only God could be in two places at once," I said, happy to show that I also knew a thing or two.

"And quantum particles! You're forgetting quantum particles. They are the most elementary particles of subatomic physics. And so, a quantum particle of light, that is, a photon, emitted at a sheet pierced by two slits that are sufficiently close together, passes by two holes at the same time. It simultaneously passes in two places. But not Bissila! He is neither God nor a quantum particle!"

18

I won't tell you about the rest of the trial in detail; anyway, it would bore you to tears, what with the prosecutor's funny way of always going back to the same things, asking the same questions. After all, there are many other things besides this trial that I would like to tell you about. So I'm going to skip its various twists and turns and get to the last day of this great trial, to the most eagerly anticipated day, the day of Uncle's appearance.

Like I said, Uncle Boula Boula was considered the brains behind the plot. According to the charges, it was he who had recruited the mercenaries waiting at the borders, ready to invade our country at the time set for the coup. It was he who had organized the bombings, using Bissila for the dirty work and Mr. Hussein El Faisal Al Moustapha Husseini Morabitoune, Aledia's father, as the money-man. Finally, it was at his residence that they had found the roster for a provisional government, which indicated who would do what after the assassination of the beloved Guide of our Revolution, and which listed Uncle himself as the future President. But despite the seriousness of the charges, I was confident that Uncle would come out all right and would present a defense as tough as Bissila the stone dresser's.

So we were all in front of our television set, Papa, Banzouzi, and Batsimba—my ziggy-wiggy brothers who you know already—and myself. Maman was the only one missing from the roll call, but I already told you that she had set herself up in the capital, where her proximity would improve the chances of her prayers of intercession before the Lord to get her brother out of this bad patch. I was even sure that she was among the public that packed the courtroom this memorable day.

Uncle was led inside. I got all choked up. He seemed tired, and his eyes wandered, distraught before the closed faces of his inquisitors, dressed in revolutionary red, and three-fourths of whom were there thanks to help received from him when he was still number two in the government. The expression on his face indicated that he was seeing or smelling something that we ordinary citizens did not see or hear, he who held a doctorate in agitation and propaganda from the Karl Marx Hochschule of Leipzig in the German Democratic Republic, because, like Mama used to say, it takes a sorcerer to recognize another sorcerer.

He took the stand. After the usual ritual—"surname first name profession swear to tell the whole truth and nothing but the truth raise your right hand and repeat after me"—the prosecutor rose, took up his most serious tone, and began to speak.

He started by talking about Uncle, the poor devil, sometime swindler, once condemned for abuse of trust in a suspicious affair that implicated his consulting business with drugs and thrown out of the capital. "Meanwhile," he continued, "ours is not a party that cuts off people's heads, but is a generous, humane party that believes in the progress of man on his way to the socialist city on the hill, and so this Party decided to give this crook a second chance by taking him back into its bosom. And the Party's magnanimity would permit this incorrigible reactionary camouflaged in red to climb every ladder to find himself in the number-two position and thus become the most powerful man in our country after our dear beloved President. Unfortunately, just like a log won't turn into a crocodile no matter how long it might soak in the river, it wasn't long before he returned to his true nature, his dirty deals and trafficking of all sorts, from influence peddling to Oriental rugs, not to mention his embezzlement of public funds and his corruption of housewives. But all of this will be peanuts after I'm done telling you about something unpardonable, once I show you how he has betrayed the nation, betrayed the Party, betrayed the President of our Party, our Guide, protector of our sovereignty and our freedom. This gentleman allied himself with reactionaries to overthrow our Revolution!"

I was watching Uncle. Each charge seem to fall on his head like a hammer, bending his back a little bit at a time. I knew that these accusations were false, for Uncle had told me about the circumstances in which he had once left the capital. As for his consulting business, even the Americans had stolen their ideas. Uncle had embezzled nothing, neither money nor housewives; quite the contrary, he had helped several of them and a few then left behind their miserable lives to become city dwellers at a time when our Party was taking many urban initiatives. For example, I won't even cite Auntie Lolo, who oddly enough did not show up to testify on Uncle's behalf: out of a small-time bush salesgirl in old Bidié's shop, Uncle had made a president of our nation's Women's Revolutionary Union. And so, confident and reassured, I knew that though Uncle was now limp and slumped, this did not at all mean that he already felt guilty or beaten. Rather it meant that, like a crouched feline, he was ready to spring up from his silence to utterly confound all of his inquisitors. Heartened, I was no longer paying attention to the prosecutor's accusations, which to me sounded more and more like the yapping of a miserable puppy.

"In conclusion," the prosecutor said. At that point, I began to listen more attentively. "To wrap up these lengthy closing arguments, Comrade Magistrate, this individual, Boula Boula, deserves one punishment, the only one appropriate for crimes of high treason against our Revolution: the death sentence and the banishment of his name from the memory of our Party and our nation for thirty years!"

"No!" I cried.

"Bastards," Papa growled.

"They're going to kill Uncle?" Banzouzi and Batsimba asked in chorus.

Their talk irritated me. "Nobody's going to kill Uncle," I shot back. "You'll see when he rises to his defense."

As I predicted, Uncle rose. We were holding our breath. He began to speak.

"Comrade Magistrate of the Court, Comrade Prosecutor. First of all I must express my gratitude toward the President of the Republic, the Guide of our Revolution, the Man of the People, the Man of Concrete Action, the Friend of the Youth, our Leader. It is thanks to his magnanimity that I have been given the opportunity to respond to all the charges against me. He could have summarily thrown me in prison, condemned me to forced labor for life without a trial. But because he is a fair man, a man who loves the truth, he insisted that this trial take place. So as a testament to my gratitude for the Party, for the Revolution, and for the President, for the great working masses, which are the base of our Revolution, I must tell the truth.

"I admit to having betrayed the views of our Revolution. I have betrayed the Party and its President. It's true, I was in contact with foreigners, notably Lebanese capitalists who pushed me to corruption and influence peddling. I ask to be forgiven. Forgive me. I admit that several times I gave in to the tempting opiate of the masses and secretly attended Catholic masses at the behest of my sister, and I also consulted a marabou from Mali and a Pygmy fetish maker when I felt my position in the Party threatened. But I do not want to waste your time, Comrade Magistrate; the comrade prosecutor has already said it all.

"I ask for one thing only; I know that our Party, this Party that I have regrettably betrayed, knows how to forgive. I also know that the Guide of our Revolution is generous, magnanimous. I have faith in him and I implore his sense of mercy. I have learned a lot from my mistakes, and, believe me, if the Revolution gives me a second chance, I'll sacrifice myself for it, for our Guide. Long live our Revolution, long live the Supreme Guide."

He slowly headed toward his bench. That old devil Boula Boula. I knew his balls weren't well hung, but now I really think he lost them.

"It can't be," I exclaimed, "I don't recognize Uncle anymore!"

Indeed, I no longer recognized Uncle, the ex-boxer with the big pecs and biceps and all that hair on his chest, I, who wanted to be incised with the kaman to be strong just like him, my uncle. His behavior now almost made me believe a story that had been going around for a while. Some gossips claimed that one night, to amuse himself, the Guide of our Revolution scared everyone by declaring during a Party meeting that he was going to have all of the ministers and members of the Political Bureau killed to give the Revolution a fresh start. Uncle was the first one to get on his knees and beg the Comrade President to let him live. I'm sure it wasn't a true story, that's why I haven't told it to you and never will . . .

The case was closed. The television had also stopped broadcasting. It was only forty-eight hours later that we learned of the verdict: Bissila was sentenced to twenty years of hard labor; Aledia's father, Mr. Hussein El Faisal Al Moustapha Husseini Morabitoune, was sentenced to death in absentia. As for Uncle Boula Boula, he was sentenced to death, and his name would be purged from Party memory and was not to be pronounced in our country for twenty years, the space of a generation.

19

It took me a long time to fall asleep after the verdict. I had read in a magazine that to fight off insomnia you should count the sheep on the ceiling. They aren't real sheep, but the idea is that by steadily concentrating on imaginary sheep, the mind forgets all the day's troubles and, returned to serenity, will slowly doze off, like a man rocked by the back-and-forth movements of his hammock. I tried to see those sheep several times, but I managed to dream only of big elephants, then dinosaurs, and finally crocodiles chasing Uncle. I got scared, and I began thinking about his punishment.

I didn't know how they executed people sentenced to death here but, thanks to my books and the miles of videotape I had watched when I was preparing to kill Aledia's father, Mr. Hussein El Faisal Al Moustapha Husseini Morabitoune, I knew plenty of methods used internationally. I knew of the classic war movie method where they tied a man to a pole, blindfolded him, and then a volley of bullets finished him off as soon as the command-

ing officer of the platoon yelled: "Fire!" In novels, the condemned
man was always offered a last cigarette or a last glass of rum before
getting gunned down. I had also read that in Dahomey, in the
time of King Behanzin and his amazons, a dead ruler was buried
along with his living spouses and his servants. While here, during
the time of the kingdom, we buried thieves and adulterers alive
in the middle of the market and then planted a nsanda tree on
the spot. Now we mostly used the "necklace," which consisted of
putting a rubber tire around the neck of a thief caught red-handed
and setting it on fire. In Rwanda and in Burundi, they executed
people with machetes. I was told that when Papa was young, there
was an emperor in Central Africa who fed his adversaries to crocodiles. During World War II, if they didn't execute their prisoners
with swords according to samurai tradition, the Japanese managed
to kill people by simply making them gulp down huge quanti-
ties of water. I've even seen a high-tech execution in a British or
American film where a man's head exploded from the force of
high-frequency decibels pulsing through a set of simultaneous
translation headphones the poor sap happened to have on. A jab
with the point of an umbrella was all the Romanians required to
send somebody *ad patres*. I'll stop there because the methods that
human ingenuity has invented to take away life make for a long
list. Considering all this did not help me figure out how my uncle
would be executed, especially since our underdeveloped country
had called for gentlemen from several countries to set up our
security forces—countries like France, Romania, Israel, China,
Japan, and others, each with its own method of execution. But just
as I was about to sink into despair, I had a brilliant idea: I would
figure out how to save my uncle.

I began reviewing everything I knew one more time. The first
thing that came to mind was how to enable Uncle to escape from

prison. I've seen escape plans in lots of movies. First, there was the most common one: sawing through the bars of his cell. Excellent! How much could a metal saw cost? If I didn't have enough money, I'd force my brothers to cough up all their money and maybe even ask Papa to help me out. But I immediately realized that there weren't only bars, there were also guards, electronic cameras, and hidden infrared alarms. I gave up on the sawing through the bars idea. I then thought of the prisoners who tunneled beneath the walls of their prisons, but I supposed that these days all the prisons were built on top of cement or concrete, even in countries still climbing the path to development, such as ours. I quickly ran through the ways of escaping I knew about and realized that there were more ways to kill people than to save them.

I then remembered that my brothers had devoured an even greater length of videotape than I had and that there was no reason for me to be the only one racking his brain about how to save my uncle from the guillotine. I got all riled up, hopped out of bed, and approached their double bed; I violently snatched the bolster from under their heads after turning on the light. They woke up with a start, and Banzouzi choked off a snore. They rubbed their eyes, dazzled by the light. They were furious and would have strangled me if they could.

"Listen," I said to them, "we've got to save Uncle, we must get him out of jail."

"Yeah, cool!" said Batsimba, suddenly enthusiastic. "It's real simple, we have to do like Schwarzenegger did in *Terminator*: his body gets all soft like jelly, and then he goes through the bars and reconstitutes himself on the other side."

I looked at him, incredulous. Tired and powerless, I turned off the light, went back to bed, and finally managed to fall asleep without having figured out how to get Uncle out of this rotten fix. But before completely sinking into sleep, I said one last prayer:

"Goodbye, Uncle, I shall never see you again since they're going to kill you. I would like the whole world to mourn you: would that tomorrow the sun doesn't rise, may the birds chirp no more, may the bees no longer suckle the flowers to give honey to men. . . . Farewell, Uncle."

20

After slavery, colonialism, neocolonialism, and scientific socialism, democracy descended upon us one August morning, in the middle of the dry season.

I laugh today when I hear all these people come on the radio or on TV or in the newspapers and give hazy and contradictory explanations for its arrival. They sometimes say that this celebrated democracy was imposed on the African people by the French president in a speech before African chiefs of state. Naïve are those who still think that a speech could change something. If I were to piece together all the speeches I've heard ever since that illustrious August morning, it would seem that our country is much more than a democracy; it is a veritable paradise. Others say that democracy arrived here thanks to the struggle for women's rights, while others feel that democracy got here thanks to the workers and their unions. I should also mention those people who attributed our new democracy to the students, to the peasants, to God, to the collapse of the Soviet Unions, and to the end of the Cold War, and I'm skipping the better ones I've heard.

You just had to get a load of all of them gloating, puffing out their chests on TV. Everyone had always been a democrat and everyone had always fought for freedom, for the multiparty system. No one had been for the one-party state, for censorship and Communism. No one had ever adored our enlightened Guide, our beloved Comrade, whose portrait would be revolving around the earth in a geostationary orbit had Uncle not pathetically failed in his role as national broker. This reminds me of what Papa had told me Grandfather once said to him: that at the time of the Independence everybody pretended to have been an anticolonialist; everybody pretended he had been imprisoned at least once for insurrectionist activities. No one had ever collaborated with the whites, of course; no one ever dreamt of Paris. Really, I have to laugh, because I know whence came the movement that launched democracy into orbit here and who launched it. And so, I'll tell you: the movement started in our school, and the one who launched it is . . . Papa!

You must wonder how the hurricane of democratization that swept both our country and Africa could have come from a small regional school, from a village that itself was lost in the immensity of the equatorial forest. Well, I'm going to tell you.

Everything started when Maman came back home. I suppose that after her brother's conviction, she had concluded that proximity had no bearing on the efficacy of prayers, contrary to what she had first believed when she went to live near her brother. So she might as well come home. She informed Papa of her plans through a passing traveler, and since we didn't have a telephone at home, Papa went to call her at the post office to get the exact date of her return and to ask her to run a few errands.

And so we went, Papa, my two twin brothers, and I, to wait for Maman at the market, at the place where the trucks that came from the capital unloaded their goods, passengers, and luggage. We waited for a long time because the bus was late. But as Papa often told us, time was never on time here in Africa. When the brakes stopped squeaking and the dust cleared around the bus, we saw Maman get off—Papa spotted her first. I admit that I did not recognize her right away, not because it had been a long time since she left but because she no longer looked like the woman who had left us a little over three months ago. What struck me was her gaunt face and all the white strands streaking the black mass of hair she had pulled back in a severe bun. Was it the effect of the days of fasting, of all sorts of deprivation, of interminable prayers in her brother's favor? The next thing that struck me was that the only item left in her religious arsenal was a Bible sticking out of her handbag, she who I remembered last with her hands around a rosary, a cross, and a pack of candles wrapped in a poster of the Holy Virgin. She wasn't even wearing a cross. In fact, she was now holding a book entitled *Humanity's Great Myths*.

Papa warmly took her in his arms, then it was our turn. I was truly happy to see her, and I admit that in spite of my nearly fifteen years of age and the macho airs that I forced myself to maintain before my two brothers, I was choked with emotion. You always love your mother, no matter what else you may think.

She had hardly put down her luggage and handed Papa the big packages addressed to him from the capital when she found the house in disorder. She began by telling us to take our clothes, socks, and shoes, which were lying around in the living room, the dining room, and the kitchen, back to our rooms. She then asked us to sweep the house and the yard, to do the dishes and sort out our dirty laundry, because she was going to do a big wash. Then we had to chop some wood for the kitchen fire. She came and went, unflagging. And we came and went, flagging. I admit that I then somewhat regretted her return, since a mother always makes you work too much.

A door slammed, and we saw Papa leave his study, in a rush. "I'm stepping out to make some photocopies, I'll be right back," he said to everyone in general.

All preoccupied with Maman's return, we had forgotten about Papa. As soon as he had taken his packages from Maman's hands, he had disappeared into his study, only to come out now. From the jerky way he was moving, I knew that his brain was boiling furiously, just as when he would get all excited with his science or epistemology books; and I was bracing myself even, I don't really know why, expecting to see black smoke coming out of his ears to relieve the pressure of his overheating brain like fumes escaping from an internal combustion engine.

It wasn't long before he came back with a dozen copies, which he threw on the dining table that Batsimba had just cleaned. He went in his study, came back out with a marker, and began writing his name and our address at the bottom of each copy, preceded each time by the words "Please contact," which he underlined. While he was scribbling, I was surreptitiously trying to read what he had written. He noticed and said: "You can read it, Michel, it is a political tract but not a secret one."

It was not very long. I read the text twice, but I did not understand much because there were too many words whose meanings I did not get: "universal suffrage," "popular sovereignty," "constitution." There were also entire sentences I did not understand: "We no longer want a 'popular' democracy nor any other qualified democracy, we want simply democracy." He told us it was a political tract, but that couldn't be right since I did not recognize any of the words our instructors had taught us in the political courses designed for us Young Pioneers of the Revolution, future heirs of our President's great work. There was, for instance, no mention anywhere of "the hero of the people," of the "proletarian revolution," of "democratic centralism," of the "working class," and so on. And there were no quotes from our Enlightened

Guide, Hero of the People, the Man of Concrete Action, whose words supplemented every political text in our country.

"Papa," I said, while he still had about three copies left to sign, "your political tract is strange. You're not using the right vocabulary, and you don't even mention the President's name. It's not going to have any impact, if you want my opinion."

He stopped writing for a moment, raised his head to look at me, and laughed. "It is just an open letter addressed to the President of the Republic. It was written in the capital and is being circulated around the country to gather signatures. Why should we use his vocabulary? We are asking for the freedom of all political prisoners, including Uncle Boula Boula."

"But the text is too difficult, we don't understand anything. What is, 'simply democracy'?"

"We want to end the single-party system and the dictatorship. No more do we want a 'democracy' of intimidation and heads rolling. We demand that the people choose their own leaders in free elections. We demand freedom of expression, association, and free enterprise. All of this must be guaranteed by a supreme, inviolable document, a constitution. This is what we mean by *democracy.*"

"But, Papa, what use is democracy going to be?"

"To live a full life!"

"Cool. A full life. So there won't be any more nights when we have to go to sleep without dinner?"

"Uh . . . not quite. We'll be able to read the books we want, to undertake what we can. To be free, Michel, be free!"

"But what is being free, Papa?"

"Listen, Michel." I sensed a note of exasperation in his voice, maybe because I could not quite understand what seemed so obvious to him. "Once you start piling up questions, there comes a time when the questions make no sense. What is being free? How do you explain freedom plainly to a fourteen-year-old child? How can I explain to you that there are people who believe that freedom is important enough to die for? For now, let me finish my open letter. We'll talk about democracy and freedom later. In any case, what is for certain is that we'll fight until this dictator leaves power."

"You mean to say that you're going to chase our President from power?"

"What do you think?" he replied, amused.

"What do I think?" I was stunned. In my mind, the Chief of Our Revolution could never be overthrown, nor even contested. I considered him as immutable as nature, like the moon that shone at night in the sky or like our great river that had snaked across the immense equatorial forest since the dawn of time: they were simply there. You didn't ask why. It had been twenty years since he came to power. I was born under him, and I grew up under him. The radio, the television, the newspapers, and the school had taught us since the cradle—no, since before the cradle—that it was he who gave us everything, bread, milk, honey, and candy. It was in fact the candy episode that had convinced me.

This took place when I was nine or ten years old, when our village hosted the celebrations for the fourteenth anniversary of the President's (successful) coup, an event presided over by my uncle Boula Boula, now in prison. Right after the part where Uncle had refused to let Maman start the ceremony with a prayer, we, the students of the regional school, were all lined up in the big new stadium. After several ovations for the benefit of our leader (who was standing with his hand majestically extended just like in the pictures of Mao Zedong that we all had since he was one of our models, along with Ho Chi Minh, Castro, and Lenin; and surrounded by his whole political entourage, with Uncle to his right), a voice addressed us through the loudspeakers: "Children, close your eyes."

We all closed our eyes, not quite knowing what was expected from us. "And now pray, ask God to send you some candy." It was

a strange request. Even Maman, who was always praying, had
never asked us to close our eyes and ask that food fall into our
mouths. If it was that easy, we would not have been starving last
night. Since there wasn't enough to eat, Maman often managed to
make us have only one meal a day, late enough, around three in
the afternoon, which left me kind of hungry. But never mind that;
we obeyed, and our little voices rose in chorus up to God in the
great stadium, as if we were singing a fugue, with some going too
fast and others catching up behind, as if we were chasing and running from each other at the same time, each inventing a prayer in
his own way. I would have liked to say a prayer in Arabic, invoking
the holy Koran, which had presided at my birth thanks to the
presence of Imam Konaté, but I chose to take it easy by improvis-
ing on a prayer Maman often said, exuberantly crossing myself to
display the depth of my conviction: "Our Father, who art in
heaven, give us this day our daily candy . . ." So we recited, eyes
closed, for three or four minutes.

"Stop!" the voice then cried, "open your eyes!"

We opened our eyes and looked carefully at the green grass to
see if anything had fallen from the sky. But, as hard as we looked,
there was no candy to be found.

"Has God given you any candy?"

"No," we all cried out, a bit disappointed since we were hoping for some candy.

"And now close your eyes again."

Once more, we obeyed.

"Repeat after me."

And we all repeated after him: "Our Enlightened Guide, the
Supreme Leader of Our Revolution, Friend to the Youth and the
Children, show us that you love us, send us candies and cakes,"
and so on. And then, I swear to you, it was incredible, a rain, a
shower—what am I saying?—a hail of candy beat down upon us,
and when we were finally authorized to open our eyes, there lay
on the green grass not only a carpet of candy but also madeleines,

biscuits, cookies. We scattered like happy little chicks, and I dutifully stuffed my pockets. They let us enjoy our chaos for a few minutes, then the loudspeakers came back on: "Who sent you those candies? Was it God?"

"No!" we said in unison, this time without a false note.

"Who sent you those candies, then?"

Once more, cacophony. Some were crying: "Our Beloved Guide," others: "The Friend of the Youth," others: "The Hero of the People," "The Apostle of Peace," et cetera. But it didn't matter since it was the same person. Some already had candy in their mouths, others were crunching biscuits, while I had already managed to swallow two madeleines.

"Who is the Man of Concrete Action, God or our Supreme Guide?"

"Our Supreme Guide!" our little voices cried.

"Who tells the truth, God or our Supreme Guide?"

"Our Supreme Guide!"

"Who should you believe, God or our Supreme Guide?"

"Our Supreme Guide!"

This was the man that Papa was talking about overthrowing. The man whose portrait had knocked him unconscious the day I was born. The man thanks to whom, I was willing to bet, the sun rose every day. Had I not learned that the earth revolved around the sun every twenty-four hours, which is how come there were nights and days, and that these nights and days were of about the same length because we were so close to the equator? He wanted to put this man out of power? No, honestly, I wondered for a moment if Papa hadn't been smoking something strong.

"Don't wait for me to start dinner, dear . . ."

While I pondered, Papa had finished writing on the photocopies, put them in a big folder and was getting ready to leave again.

"Now where are you going?"

"It's urgent, I must put up the photocopies of this open letter and gather signatures. It would be best that after tomorrow at the latest I send the names of the signatories to the capital for publication."

"After all my prayers, all the money I spent, it won't be your photocopies of open letters that'll free my brother," said Maman, disenchanted.

"Your prayers and your money did not work because you weren't fighting for what's essential. When I think about it, it's no accident your brother is where he is. He has himself supported if not inspired plenty of show trials. As they say, 'He who lives by the sword . . .' What we are doing goes beyond him, and if we succeed, and I am sure we will, he will not be overlooked. All right, I have to go, I will try not to stay out too long."

21

A violent banging shook the doorframe of our brick house. We all had a start. Mom was in the middle of *Humanity's Great Myths*, one of the books she had brought back from the capital, and I saw her serene face turn anxious, as if the knocks foretold a fresh via dolorosa. All of us, Banzouzi, Batsimba, Maman, and I, found ourselves in front of the door all at once, and I don't even remember who was the first to push it open: Yengo, a friend of the family, was there, his shirt soaked with blood. Before he even said a word, Maman screamed: "What happened to him!?"

"They . . . they . . . arrested him," Yengo managed to stutter through his lips, which were now twice as thick.

"They arrested Papa?" cried the two twins, while I, the triplet, cried: "Let's go free him!"

We continued to press Yengo with questions and somehow managed to piece together his chopped and mangled account.

He had run into Papa, who had asked if he could help put up copies of his "open letter to the President of the Republic." They had put up the first one on the big tree at the intersection of the streets that lead to the city hall, the market, and the school; then they had slapped some on the big bulletin board in front of the school, where our unique Party put up its propaganda tracts full of pretty pictures. It was as they were thumbtacking the big board in front of city hall on which people put up their classifieds that the security agents came upon them. They began by beating on Yengo, who refused to let go of the photocopies he had, and they ripped Papa's shirt (he received a few stray blows) when he tried to come to Yengo's help. Finally they ended up at the public security station—that's what we called our police headquarters—and Yengo was freed only at the urging of Papa, who kept insisting that the poor boy had nothing to do with this and that he would not answer any questions so long as Yengo wasn't released.

While Yengo continued to explain what had happened, two other people came to bring us the same bad news, and, as I turned around to see my brothers' reaction to my proposal about going to free Papa, there were already eight more people. The news of the arrest of my papa, the principal of the regional school, had spread quicker than rumors of a coup in an African republic.

Things were moving very fast. Maman was already in battle gear: dressed in a two-piece outfit, a blouse and a boubou wraparound skirt, she had tightened the string of the skirt the way women did before a fight because there was no worse humiliation than to be stripped of your skirt by your adversary and end up in your underwear or totally naked. It was worse than being beaten. Everyone talked at once, and I think that there were now more than twenty-odd people packed into our small yard. I was pleased to notice that nearly all the teachers from Papa's school were present and even the others who taught at the high school. The procession set off toward the public security headquarters.

Maman had asked us to stay and watch the house. But since she had said it to the eldest, Banzouzi ("Banzouzi, stay and watch the house with your brothers"), I acted as if I had understood that the orders were given only to Banzouzi and then to Batsimba, who seconded him. For once, I followed the custom that held that the eldest had more responsibilities than the youngest. So I left to go free Papa.

I followed the marchers, keeping toward the back of the procession so that Maman wouldn't notice me. Funny how events reveal new aspects of the same people. Until now, I had known Maman only as the woman who made us wash ourselves, not blow our noses in our hands, brush our teeth, take turns doing the dishes, and wake up in time for school. As the woman who cooked our food and who, thanks to the income from her little market business, enabled Papa's meager teacher's salary to buy us manga comic books, videotapes, and books. But now, I saw a different person. She was firmly leading the protest, geared up like a woman prepared for battle as I have already explained, issuing instructions left and right.

I did not know how we were going to obtain Papa's freedom. As soon as we were in the street, I lifted my eyes to the sky for some reason. It was incredible. The opaque clouds of the dry season, the clouds that night after night concealed the moon, the stars, and the planets, weren't there anymore. You could see all the stars in the sky. Thanks to Papa, I knew quite a few of the constellations in our equatorial sky, but since the positions varied not only with the seasons but also with the time of observation, I wasn't sure if the reddish point shining over there was Antares or just Arcturus. Ah, if only Papa had been there! I would have asked him: Papa, do the stars shine because they're free?

But we were already in front of the public security station where Papa was being held, according to Yengo. I looked around. Were there a hundred of us? Two hundred? I couldn't tell you, but there was no doubt that people had joined us along the way. Since everybody was speaking at the same time, I didn't get what the chief sergeant said to Maman, who was questioning him. He was waving his arms, standing in front of the station, a gun at the hip.

I heard muttering from the crowd, indignant voices, then Maman's voice, seconded by others, shot through the noisy confusion: "We're going to get him out of prison," and the procession set off once again. I then understood that Papa had been transferred to the prison. So that's where we had to go.

I don't think I've told you that our town had no streetlights, so the nights were darker than the black holes in Papa's physics books. Thus people brought candles of all kinds, emergency lamps, and battery-operated flashlights to guide us in the night. And just as you would expect, it wasn't long before songs began to soar full-throated, songs interrupted only by our slogans every now and then. And so we walked, sang, and chanted our way up to the prison door.

When I say "prison," you must not think of the kinds of buildings I saw in that movie about a prison mutiny in Attica, New York (another video from my twin brothers' collection): impenetrable walls and doors surrounded with automatic alarms, watchtowers, bars and fences, long stacked-up catwalks, barbed wire, electronic sensors and cameras, dogs. And it was even less like Sing Sing. It was only a modest, stubble-roofed building with a few high, barred windows and a veranda that accommodated three or four lounging guards, one of whom was an officer, who spent their time playing cards. There wasn't an ocean around it like on Robben Island, where Nelson Mandela spent eighteen years of his life, but a wall of clay, cracked here and there from the humidity and sun, and with only one opening, a rusty metal gate, now closed. This was the gate before which Maman and the others stopped, at first unable to figure out how to set Papa free; at one point a few of the others made bold and pounded on it, but in vain. Suddenly there was a strange silence: everybody was all ears.

From far away we could hear the sound of music: violin? clarinet? organ? We couldn't say. Then we saw flickering candles in the night, then the hum of human voices along with the music reached us, and silhouettes finally appeared behind the wavering flames. They kept advancing. The music grew louder and clearer. We recognized the tune at the same time as we recognized the fellow leading the procession: it was old Bidié with his bandoneon, his Argentine accordion, playing the Internationale!

Ah, friends, I swear to you that I am not a sentimentalist, but seeing old Bidié approach and feel his way across the dark night, squeezing out the notes of the Internationale on his legendary bandoneon, supported by voices emanating from dozens, even hundreds, of silhouettes brandishing torches and moving toward us—nobody was more moved that I was! I would have cried my eyes out if I had not held myself back. Old Bidié had come out of his lair to demand my father's freedom.

Up to now, I've mentioned old Bidié in passing while telling you my stories of Auntie Lolo, who we hadn't really seen here since she left for the capital with Uncle Boula Boula; but let me tell you that old Bidié, just like Mama Kossa and Mr. Konaté, was an essential part of my childhood. Like Papa and Grandfather, he was the source of many of my reveries. We kids liked him because we knew that if we hung around his store long enough he would give us candy—sometimes even a small bottle of Coca-Cola to share—but mostly because he would tell us stories about his trips and play his strange accordion for us. Whenever we would say to him, "Play us something on your accordion, old Bidié," he would reply, "It is not just any accordion, children, it is a bandoneon."

After Auntie Lolo's departure—and after he was bankrupted by the schemes of Aledia's father, the Honorable Hussein El Faisal Al Moustapha Husseini Morabitoune—Bidié no longer traveled and hardly ever came out of his house. He grew even older, though he already seemed very old to me. His eyesight had gotten worse, to the point that he wore thick bifocals set delicately on his nose. Papa and Maman had taken a real liking to him and often sent me to bring him food and staples—salt, sugar, and soap, invariably explaining, "Here we never abandon an old man." We sometimes went to visit him with Papa, and it was during one of those visits that I was told the whole story of his youth. And that got me dreaming.

A long time ago, in the mid-sixties, when he was a young man, while his comrades dreamed of France and diplomas, he dreamt of America. He stowed away on a Panamanian ship anchored at Pointe-Noire, and after several lengthy digressions (which I will tell you about some other time if possible), in which he was thrown overboard by sailors who discovered him in the slipway where he was hiding, and in which he outswam a shark until another ship's crew could fish him out of the water, he found himself under the protection of a captain who hired him as a kitchen boy on his boat on a long route to Argentina. Then they navigated along the South American coast, which is how he got to know Rio de Janeiro, São Paulo, Montevideo, and Bahía Blanca. When the captain retired he brought Bidié to his home in Argentina, far off in the pampas in a village called Laboulaye, a name I remember because it rhymes with Abdoulaye, Mr. Konaté's truck driver's name; when the captain died, young Bidié went back to Buenos Aires, and there found work as a bouncer in a nightclub, which is where he learned to play the bandoneon. Then he joined a tango orchestra. It was Bidié who first told me about the pampas. And I dreamed of being a gaucho astride a horse on those great plains that knew no enclosures or barbed wire, a proud gaucho in his Indian poncho, lasso in hand, a free man, face beaten by the harsh winds from faraway Patagonia, galloping toward the oversized horizon . . . It was he who first told me about Patagonia, and I wondered if the Patagonians of Tierra del Fuego and Ushuaia who lived so far down in the Southern Hemisphere didn't walk upside down. And I dreamed of going to Ushuaia one day.

Then he came back home with his bandoneon that enchanted us so. He entertained us with tunes of exotic dances, unknown here, which he called java, polka, tango, lambada, bolero, valse, paso doble, and I'm forgetting the others. Sometimes, he would play our local tunes, rumbas, beguines, and others. He even

played ragamuffin and reggae just for me. But after the incident
with Uncle Boula Boula, he had sworn that his instrument would
never play the Internationale again. I have told you so much already that I can't remember if I told you about that, but all you
need to know is that he despised our One Party and, to my great
sadness, despised Uncle too.

Now here was this old fighter standing before us, belting out
the Internationale in the Party's face (and maybe even in Uncle's,
at the bottom of his cell), all for Papa's sake! It was as if he had
grabbed the other side of the stick to mete out vengeance upon
everyone who had hassled him up to now. We all straightened up
and sang at the top of our lungs.

I looked around. If perchance an angel, peeking out between
two clouds, had glanced down just then—the candles, lanterns,
flashlights—he would have thought the sky and the earth had
traded places and our lights that illuminated our freedom were the
very stars of heaven. In fact some angels had joined us already—it
was as though I could hear their wings flapping gently in time
with us and feel them brushing my face as they passed. When old
Bidié stopped playing to a thunderous ovation, I admit that I had
tears in my eyes, and all the more so when I heard the students cry
out, from the bottom of their hearts: "Free our teacher, free our
teacher!" That teacher was my papa! It was really something to be
a teacher!

The sit-in outside the prison lasted until morning. Without
the aid of a Foucault pendulum, I made sure that the earth was
still spinning on its axis by observing the movement of the stars
in the canopy of heaven until their glare disappeared, and they
were swallowed up by the dawn. That was when our local police
launched their first assault.

As we sang and chanted, we had let ourselves be surrounded
unawares by the troops the prefect had sent to disperse us. I
couldn't believe how many of them there were—fifty at least,
though the local force didn't have more than fifteen members, half

of them good potbellied family men for whom military duty wasn't a full-time daily thing, the other half consisting of one polygamous husband with three wives and two polygamous husbands with two. The prefect must have sent a dispatch to the neighboring districts. Their leader shouted a few warnings that nobody heard, and then they charged.

They must have lacked training, because they couldn't remove the pins from their tear gas canisters to throw them at us—canisters that dated from the feast marking the fourteenth anniversary of our beloved chief's coming to power, when lots of weapons had been imported for his protection. Had the canisters rusted since then, or were our police the rusty ones? Their writhing made us howl with laughter. We were openly mocking them and doubled our volley of slogans. That's when the first political slogans were heard: "Away with dictatorship," "Away with the One Party," "Long live democracy," et cetera. Finally, the police were able to unpin their canisters, which they threw at us. The explosions were deafening.

At first we retreated before the acrid smoke, and they went at us with their clubs. Then suddenly the wind turned and went their way. Just like us, they didn't have any gas masks, and now their side was in a panic. They began to sniffle and tear up, and took small steps backwards before finally turning around and running like hell. We were happy, we were laughing, we booed and chased them. I even threw a few big rocks in their direction, while others proudly showed me the clubs they had picked up as trophies and even used in the chase. We had won! Nothing could stand against the freedom fighters, right? Certainly not the prison door, which we had decided to knock down with the horns we had grown during the chase.

22

Our victory didn't last. Less than an hour later, just as we had managed to knock down the big gate (it had taken us a while to find a tree trunk tough enough to serve as a battering ram), carried away by our own momentum, we were sucked into the enclosure behind the prison walls. A real army surrounded us. The soldiers started by shooting in the air. I am not hiding the fact that this was the first time I heard gunshots from such close range, and it was really something other than what I had heard a thousand times on my brothers' videotapes. I felt the presence of death in each bullet that whistled through the air. We had all instinctively thrown ourselves to the ground. When the soldiers saw we weren't armed, they too came through the gate and started in beating. It was every man for himself. As if our panic weren't enough, every so often the soldiers let up on the beating to fire their guns overhead. If they'd meant to lock us up right away, they could have done so with no trouble—we wouldn't have offered any resistance. But they wanted to teach us a lesson first; they wanted to subdue the horde of peasants who had dared to challenge the beloved President and his Party, and they taught us good. I thought my only hope was to escape before they slaughtered us all. As I ran for the gate, I saw the butt of a shotgun come down on the back of old Bidié, who collapsed, letting go of his bandoneon, his cherished glasses flying off God knows where. At last I reached the open gate, whose supporting wall we had battered down, and just as I was trying to jump over it, I felt a boot kicking me sharply from behind. The kick was so strong that it lifted me at least a yard off the ground; I sailed and landed brutally, face first, on the ground.

My lips and my nose were bleeding. I had a big bump on my forehead. I was hurting. My vision was blurred, but I could still see the stocky silhouette of a tree with a scarlet red parasol, and I began to crawl toward it, laboring painfully. I must have passed out for a spell once I got there and leaned against its knotty trunk. When I came to, I found myself on a low hill, looking over the battlefield like a general in the countryside. What I saw wasn't pretty: gunshots; shotgun butts coming down on men, women, and children; men, women, and children trying to flee. I was enraged. I immediately thought about the boot I'd felt in my behind: imagine if I'd got it in the front, right in the family jewels! Would I ever have recovered? My anger swelled until I was furious. Why were men making other men suffer? Why were they beating on these women who they didn't even know and who had done them no harm?—these people who only wanted to express themselves and who were merely asking for Papa's release? But actually, weren't these people really asking for democracy? If I hadn't come to demand Papa's freedom, would I have taken that kick that could have turned my family jewels to mush? And suddenly I had a revelation, a moment of enlightenment: We were fighting for freedom, we were fighting for democracy. In reality, that kick in the ass made me understand the meaning of democracy.

All of a sudden, I had a start. I first noticed an uncovered military truck leaving the prison enclosure and stopping in front of an

officer who was giving orders. Right behind it was a woman—she
had sprung out of the prison walls like a jack-in-the-box. I recognized Maman! She threw herself onto the flatbed and then fell
again, pushed back brutally. My blood boiled, and I started down
the low hill. I ran like a wild man, ignoring the spot that was starting to hurt. Meanwhile Maman had gotten back up and clung
firmly to the truck, screaming and screaming. It wasn't long before I understood why: There was Papa, sitting, surrounded by
soldiers who were obviously making fun of him—pulling on his
hair, beating him, forcing a cigarette between his lips (and since he
didn't smoke, this of course burned him). In my race toward the
truck, I yelled: "Papa, Papa!" I was almost there when the truck
brusquely took off, dragging Maman a few yards before she let go.
Aiaiaiai! Good thing she had tied her wraparound skirt tight like a
woman ready for battle; otherwise she would have found herself
wearing nothing. My head was like a wayward compass needle, os-
cillating between Maman and Papa. Finally, before I ran to Maman, my mind seized one last fugitive glimpse of Papa: Papa tied
up, humiliated but sardonic under the blows and the curses, Papa
rolling off in a truck toward an uncertain destination . . . And I felt
like I was reliving the last moments of Patrice Lumumba's life,
those last moments captured on that tape we had watched two or
three times at Papa's insistence, Papa who always said that our
generation ought to know Africa's history. Lumumba, a freedom
fighter from Grandfather's era; Lumumba, handed over to his
killers by Mobutu; Lumumba beaten, tortured, humiliated; Lumumba in a truck rolling off toward his death in Katanga. Lumumba! Papa!

23

*L*andscape *After the Battle.* The title of that Polish film from Papa's video library came to mind as I looked around once the truck that took him away was out of sight.

Of course, there were no charred tanks, nor any abandoned trucks, nor any dead bodies oozing here and there, but it was just as if there were: abandoned shoes and sandals, women's wrap-around skirts and head scarves strewn about, a few sticks and clubs. And there was old Bidié's priceless bandoneon, crushed and stomped on. You even had the acrid smell of tear gas and the stench of gunpowder. As in a real battle, there were also human victims, men and women with bloodstained clothes, but I couldn't tell if their wounds were serious or not. I saw a woman with a fractured left leg, which was delicately being set in a sling made of two tree limbs and bamboo crosspieces. I saw our geography teacher with an eye swollen so badly that someone had wrapped a bandanna around his head, which made him look like a pirate. And I saw and heard human suffering: old Bidié, sitting, holding his broken eyeglasses frames in his hands, dazed and haggard, and staring far off into the distance. Maman, with scraped elbows and knees, torn skirt, and eyes turned toward the horizon where Papa had disappeared, as if she had suddenly run out of the energy with which she had defied the troops. Then there was everyone else, each wounded and suffering in his own way. And this universe of pain that surrounded me had an elusive but gripping sound track, consisting of deaf moans, funereal chants, lamentations, and groans, now and then pierced by a shattering scream as brief as lightning tearing through a dark thunderous sky.

That was the moment when I first understood what it is to die for freedom. If old Bidié had been killed by a stray bullet, or Maman, or my geography teacher, or any of us, they would have died in a struggle to free Papa—for freedom, in other words. And that would really be the truth. And it wouldn't be wrong to confer the title of hero for the cause of liberty on any of them. Still, neither old Bidié, nor Maman, nor my geography teacher, nor any of us had woken up this morning and thought: Today I'm going to get myself killed so that freedom might triumph. What counts is the deep conviction that brought them to join the others in protest, and it would have taken only the random path of a stray bullet to have transformed your regular average fate into a heroic destiny.

Cries. Groans. Sadness. A few hungry dogs wandering the gloomy landscape. I was so struck by these events that I was almost choked with emotion and speechless when, a few months later, I told Grandfather about them during our last visit to his bedside. It was he who calmed, reassured, and comforted me, saying: "Matapari, life is just little gray clouds in a big blue sky." Well, at the time, I was crossing a valley full of gray clouds.

The soldiers were gone. We returned home dragging our wounded fighters as best we could. We even managed to mobilize a pickup truck to take those who really couldn't walk and made special arrangements for old Bidié. I picked up his bandoneon, now just a heap of warped, broken pieces, and on the way home I swore that when I grew up, after my visit to Ouagadougou with

Aledia, I would go all the way to the whorehouses of Buenos Aires to nab a bandoneon out of the hands of a tango player and steal a tune, a timbre, a boisterous rhythm to bring back to the old man. Just as he did in his youth, as a tribute to him, I will get there in the most roundabout way. I will arrive in Ushuaia in Tierra del Fuego, then go through the Strait of Magellan to reach Patagonia and the Patagonians; I will then cross the rivers with names like Chubut, Río Negro, and Colorado, and I will rediscover the pampas (which I already knew about) before returning to Buenos Aires.

However, at this very moment, I was not in the suburbs of Buenos Aires but approaching the door of our tin-roofed house, with its brick walls, behind which were latrines that let out strong odors of disinfectant, the whole thing topped off by a television antenna. There were many agitated people around me, including my brothers. Oh yes, my brothers. I had almost forgotten about those two. They approached me with questioning eyes, and I realized then that I had lived through an important, perhaps historic, moment that they had not. I searched my body for some sign of my participation, a stigmata that I could display for their sake. Unfortunately, I had nothing—no bloodstains, no torn clothing. My nose and lips had stopped bleeding and returned to normal size. Truth be told, I had only gotten a kick in the butt, and to my knowledge, getting one's butt kicked never made a hero out of anyone. Obviously, I kept from telling them what had happened, and instead made up a story in which I defended the widow and the orphan, ripped the nightstick out of the hands of a roughneck soldier who was about to hit Maman, and at the same time, like a ninja in a karate movie, dodged a bayonet that was about to slice me into pieces, et cetera. Of course they believed me, wide-eyed and mouths gaping. I was certain they took me for Rambo come to life.

I can't tell you exactly what happened next because adults have the bad habit of finding ways to keep children away when they are making decisions. All I know is that I found myself a clandestine passenger in one of the trucks bringing our village delegation to participate in a mass protest planned in the capital to free all political prisoners and, as far as we were concerned, Papa above all.

It was the first time I found myself in such a throng, a crowd worthy of a World Cup final. Flags, banners. Slogans, cries. But most of all, words: the words that had been off limits to us for so long, words for which we had lost jobs or been sent straight to prison. Words that defied guns and death, words that called out the future. I didn't know that talking, crying out, saying words out loud, could have such a liberating and mobilizing effect. We felt strong pronouncing them, we felt proud. We walked and walked.

We started at Red Flag Circle, heading for Lenin Avenue. At Karl Marx Square we met up with demonstrators coming from May Day Place, and there were probably more than a hundred thousand of us when we poured into October Boulevard, which would to take us to Revolution Square, where the big demonstration was to take place.

We never made it to Revolution Square.

Today, as I'm telling you this story, I can only remember the screams, the tears, the blood of those who, trapped on Madukutsekele Bridge, drowned in the stream trying to escape the machine guns. I remember the faces of the people being trampled, the dry sound of bones breaking, the crushed rib cages in the savage stampede of a panicked crowd: Those who fell didn't have a chance. I remember the whistling bullets, the smells, the tear gas, the screams, the screams, the screams. And then at last, the firm hand of Papa's friend that caught, pulled, and dragged me to escape from this hell.

We never found out how many people died that day. We never found out how many bodies this stream had carried off into the river. Rumor had it that the presidential guard had ceased firing only because they had used up all the ammunitions in the city arsenal and that, ten days after the events, the river coughed up catches never before seen in the history of fishing.

Nightfall came down on a wounded, disgusted country where the smell of blood and gunpowder penetrated everything. No matter that you washed your mango or guava, banana or orange with soap, the insipid, heart-wrenching smell of blood still stuck. I watched the sky that night, even the moon's crescent shriveled into a red sickle cell, its light piercing through a bloody fog. Daylight never came; instead, an opaque dry season fog had taken the place of morning.

The following is a kaleidoscope with a thousand fussy fragments, a succession of messy, chaotic events that I would be unable to reassemble chronologically, so I'll just go through them quickly: Women market peddlers march in protest; three women shot dead near the presidential palace. The great hundred-year-old baobab tree that stood by the docks uprooted by a light wind, a breeze almost. Arrest of all signatories of the open letter to the President asking that a national convention vested with full authority be held immediately. Plane crash killing more than sixty of our compatriots in the Tenere Desert. Death of our neighbor Sita's dog, run over by a rickshaw. Emergency meeting of the Party Central Committee prompted by a press release regarding the formation of multiple parties. Frogs falling from the sky on Makoua, a small village located right on the equator, during a violent storm. Widespread weeklong strike by workers asking for a pay hike. National soccer championship won by the Black Demons for the first time in twenty years. Emergency meeting of the Council of Ministers, granting a general raise to all workers. A woman gives birth to seven children in a village in the Mayumbe forest, and one of them is immediately nabbed by a female gorilla. Chief of State reaffirms that the creation of a political party is still illegal and that no one will remove him from the presidency. Workers, students, schoolchildren, and women march demanding the immediate establishment of multiparty democracy, freedom of expression, and the liberation of all political prisoners. Train crashes at full speed into an elephant couple that had found no better place to copulate than railroad tracks: one hundred and twenty dead, all traveling first class. Signatories of the famous open letter are freed. Immediate rearrest of the freed prisoners, following a press release (presented by Papa) in which they affirmed that civil disobedience would continue as long as all political prisoners were not set free and as long as the date for the national constitutional convention had not been set. Rumors of grisly child murders in a neighborhood in the capital, complete with ritual removal of the heart and the testicles. More marches by students and women, more strikes. The Honorable Ambassador Dieng fires two bullets and kills his fourth wife (the youngest and most pampered) and saves the other four rounds for the woman's lover, who was none other than his chauffeur, having caught the two red-handed committing adultery. Meeting of the Party Central Committee followed by a press release proclaiming the release of all political prisoners, the end of the Party's monopoly on power, the legalization of political parties (each person had the right to create his own party), and a national convention to be held in forty-five days.

The country erupted in joy. Calm soon returned. We were all standing in front of the prison to attend the liberation of the political prisoners, including Papa and Uncle, of course. Maman was there also because she had come back. Oh, I should tell you that, in the meanwhile, she had found time to go back to our village to bring medicine and other necessities for the people who had been so sorely tried during their attempt to free Papa. Namely, she had brought a new pair of glasses for old Bidié (and I take this occasion to renew my pledge to offer the old man a bandoneon when I'm old enough to earn money) and crutches for that woman whose leg had been broken. That was just like Maman. For her, these sorely tried villagers, who had stood by her ever since that first battle and had suffered far from the spotlight, were as important as the inmates in the capital whose every statement was picked up by the international press. And so now she had returned in time to attend the liberation of her brother and her husband.

The big gate opened, and the prisoners came out. Many were in a lamentable state and there could no longer be any doubt about the conditions of their detention. But we were happy nevertheless, and made a joyful noise. We had hardly hugged Papa and Uncle when they were snatched from us to fall into other abrazos. Then we spontaneously began walking home—toward the big house Grandfather had built in the capital where we had always stayed. It was ours now.

What surprised me when we got there was how, in the blink of an eye, Uncle had somehow become the star of the demonstration, around whom all the journalists and many formerly imprisoned freedom fighters gathered. Papa had gone off somewhere while Maman arranged transportation to the hospital for the prisoners who needed urgent care. Uncle talked. He talked about how he had fought for freedom, how even in prison he had been among those who had initiated the "open letter to the President of the Republic." He explained how the urgent need for democratization that had stirred the country like a groundswell had been prompted by his arrest. The questions from journalists burst forth from all sides, while Uncle, obviously enjoying himself, smiled again and again at the photographic flashes. I'll admit, at that particular moment I was completely confused.

First, I could not understand how Papa and Uncle, whose ideas were diametrically opposed, could end up in prison for the same cause. Uncle had been one of the Party's good eggs; he had always said that the Party's direction was irreversible because it followed the course of history. He had sent people to prison and even to the execution post in order to uphold the Party and once even considered converting all the Pygmies to Marxism-Leninism. The Party's government had made him rich and famous. It had enabled him to snatch Auntie Lolo away from old Bidié. Sure, he had been wrongly condemned, not because he had fought for democracy or for the multiparty system but rather because, in the perpetual struggle for power, someone else had been slicker than he and had him ejected from his position. What had happened to him was typical of these totalitarian regimes, which had the habit of eating their own children, as Papa would say, but his behavior at the trial had been in no way exemplary.

Papa, on the other hand, had always stood against the tyranny of this party and had never missed an opportunity to speak out to Uncle and even to ridicule him. I recall the time at the food fair when Papa and I set up a stand of local produce, with insects and fruit prominently displayed. No, they had not gone to prison for the same reason, and I refuse to believe that all those who went to prison under a dictatorship at one time or another are heroes by definition. I can bear witness that it was after Papa's arrest and his transfer to the capital that the people's latent thirst for democratization was thrust into daylight. Right now he should have been here near his companions who had suffered so much with him, yet he was not here . . . ah, there he is. I see him coming, stack of newspapers in hand, eyes shining with that excitement I know so well whenever he reads something that fascinates him. Or was it the excitement, the joy, of being free after weeks of incarceration? Free to walk around with his hands in his pockets, to see the leaves of the palm tree swaying in the wind, to admire pretty girls with smiles like Aledia's? Or was it the pride of having contributed to the downfall of an iniquitous regime? All at once the journalists abandoned Uncle—the tame politician, proud holder (according to his official biography) of a doctorate in agitation and propaganda from Leipzig in the German Democratic Republic—to rush toward this little teacher, who had been unknown to the media just a few weeks ago. I was proud of Papa. All the questions came at once: What are you going to do now? Create a political party?

Coordinate the opposition? Make a bid for the presidency of the Republic? Don't you want to make a statement to the press?

"Calm down, calm down," he said, trying in vain to contain the journalists in search of a scoop. "Really, this is magnificent, this is wonderful! Do you realize I was in prison and knew nothing about it."

"About what?" a thousand voices came at him.

"Fermat's last theorem has just been proven! Do you realize this? It has taken three centuries! Three hundred years!"

"Fermat's last theorem?" they repeated in unison, intrigued, wondering if the long imprisonment had not somewhat softened the brain of this small-town teacher, who was undoubtedly a bit insane in the membrane.

24

Papa, to my great dismay, stayed no more than forty-eight hours in the capital after his liberation. I was hoping that we would stay another week so that we could splurge in town, sneak off to the movies, and go see a Black Demons game. I also wanted to go hear Mamhy Claudia, a friend of Maman's, a new rap and ragamuffin star in our country who was very successful as part of a band called the Peace Warrior Group. Then I remembered Auntie Lolo. I would have liked to see her again too, since no one in the family had known where she was since Uncle's incarceration. Anyway, she and Aledia, whose Lebanese father, the Honorable Hussein El Faisal Al Moustapha Husseini Morabitoune, I still curse, were the first women of my life. But Papa didn't see it that way; his only wish was to leave this suddenly loathsome capital as quick as possible, and so, forty-eight hours after his liberation, the whole family was already on the road, cruising at high speed on the rubber-smooth asphalt, which snaked through the savanna as far as the eye could see. Our big, comfortable all-terrain vehicle chewed up the road like a hungry lynx before spitting it out behind us. It seemed that Papa thought we should flee. But from what?

I would have liked him to stay on with his fellow dissidents, and to ask after those who had stood in the front lines to get him out of prison: old Bidié, my geography teacher, that woman who had gotten her leg broken . . . And all those who didn't know him but had risked their lives for his liberation, those people who had proven the existence of human solidarity and, what's more, had shown that one can live out one's ideas instead of just thinking them. So I felt that the least he could do was take the time to thank them. Was this struggle in which we had taken part—Maman, the twins, other unnamed people, and myself—was all this anguish, all this blood, all the dead bodies, worth so little to him that his first public statement was about some Englishman's solution to Fermat's last theorem, when the prison doors of a bloody dictator had just opened up to free so many suffering human beings? This, though no balm had yet been applied to soothe their burns and heal their wounds? Of course, I'm not denying the importance this math problem had for Papa, but was the solution to a theoretical quandary more important than human suffering? Wasn't worrying only about what mattered to you, while ignoring the world around you, the very definition of selfishness? Was Papa selfish?

No, no. To assuage my doubts, I studied his face. He was reading an article with the headline "FOR SURE THIS TIME: FERMAT'S FAMOUS THEOREM FINALLY SOLVED."

I knew about Fermat's proof from my talks with Papa. If its demonstration was difficult, the mathematical formula that described it was, on the other hand, very simple: given $x^n + y^n = z^n$ is impossible if x, y, z are whole numbers and n is greater than 2. Fermat expresses it this way: "It is impossible to write a square root as the sum of two square roots, a fourth power as the sum of two fourth powers, and so on, except for the second power." In other words, suppose I have a square rug. I can always find two other square rugs whose combined surface area will be equal to that of the first rug. On the other hand, if I have a bar of soap from Marseilles, for example, I will never find two cubes whose combined volume is equal to the volume of this first bar. It's impossible. That's Fermat's theorem. Simple enough to understand, isn't it? It's not interesting in itself, but what made it famous is the phrase that followed its exposition: "I have found a wonderful proof, but the margin of this book is too narrow for it to fit!" And this too narrow margin had not only defied the most brilliant mathematical minds for three hundred years but had also given rise to new mathematical tools, new methods of solving problems. Yes, all because of a simple question of margin! And that's probably why it fascinated Papa.

I then looked over to his wife sitting next to him, my mother. She too had taken part in the struggle for freedom. I can still see her in front of our small-town prison; still see her defying the troops, trying to snatch a shotgun from a soldier's hands; still see her being dragged for a few yards on the rough ground by the military truck she had gotten hold of after being pushed back by a violent kick in the chest. She had endured more, her flesh suffered more, than either Papa or Uncle Boula Boula. And yet no one spoke of her. Now that I think about it, she couldn't be any more different from Papa. He lived out his ideas and his passions without worrying about the consequences to others; she always stopped to make sure her actions didn't make a commotion. That wasn't all—her ideas were also very different from Papa's.

She was a believer, a Christian, while Papa, like Grandfather, was clearly a nonbeliever. Her struggle for her brother and then her fight for Papa's release had completely changed the way she lived her faith. She had become more reflective and now did without all the godly things that had decorated the house and her own person: no more pictures of the Virgin, no more beads, no more candles, no more holy water, and no more crosses. I even thought for a moment that she had converted and become a Protestant.

One day, when I asked her why she no longer wore the prominent cross that showed she was a Christian, she answered: "Faith is something between you and God, you don't have to show it off." Even her reading was no longer restricted to the narrow universe to which Father Boniface's teachings had confined her; now she was open to the world. She read works of mythology and texts about the various spiritual paths open to humanity. I saw her devour a book on the conquest of Latin America the year marking the fifth centenary of what Europeans called the discovery of America. When there were no customers, she also sometimes read at the market, where she had a stand. That's how, one day, I was most surprised to see her reading *Cosmos*, by Carl Sagan, a book in which the American astrophysicist clearly explained, in terms easily accessible to the layman, the origin and the future of the universe and of humanity in light of current scientific theories. I had wondered then how she had reconciled this with the creed of her primitive faith.

Suddenly I felt a jolt. Maman woke up with a start, Papa stopped reading, the headphones of Batsimba's Walkman came out of his ears: a bag that was poorly fastened to the luggage rack above our heads fell; the rubber-smooth asphalt had brutally given way to a road at first sandy, then rocky, upon which the vehicle was now jolting in a veil of auburn dust.

I don't know how long we drove on like this, jolting left and right in an all-terrain vehicle that had literally become a pain in the butt. We crossed the great plateau of the savanna around the capital with its stunted shrubs; we almost suffocated when we suddenly got caught in a brushfire and thick smoke filled our vehicle. Why was it that, during every dry season, we destroyed these shrubs and grasses? I couldn't tell you. Some said it was an ancestral custom and that ancestral customs were made to be kept. Others said the ashes obtained in this manner served as natural fertilizer to the new growth and thus gave new life to the soil. The only good memories I had of brushfires were of the times we children went to set traps for the wild animals that fled the flames, from great antelope to tiny savanna rats and crickets. I also have bad memories, like the time a few years ago when the wind abruptly changed direction, turning the small fires the village people had lit into one huge inferno that not only ravaged the village, killing ten people, but also killed one of my friend's little ducks. The duck's fate saddened us so much that we refused to drink Coca-Cola for three days as a sign of mourning. Ever since then, brushfires have made me shiver the way I was shivering now, as huge yellowish flames licked the windows of our truck. Finally we managed to get through.

Then we reached the forest, the real equatorial forest. The driver had stopped to take a breather and stretch his legs, and we got out to have a picnic. He gave us half an hour. We were near a small rust-colored stream that carried along the forest humus dumped into it by the brooks that fed it. The stream was clear enough for us to see its schist and sandstone bed. My brothers and I shed our clothes and jumped in the water to wash and get rid of the smoky odor that clung to us. We made the water clap by beating it like a drum; we splashed each other giddy with great sheets of water, laughing until it hurt. Never had I been so happy with my brothers. Come to think of it, they weren't so bad. They were pretty wonderful in fact. I have probably been unfair with them in this story, showing you only their annoying side, but they probably would have done the same with me if they had been the ones telling it. Deep down I loved them a lot.

Maman had prepared chicken sandwiches that we swallowed whole, and bananas—the tiny extra sweet bananas we called pig bananas because it was said that pigs loved gobbling them up. I wanted to drink some Coca-Cola but there wasn't any, so like everyone else I made do with the fresh water Maman had brought in a thermos bottle. When we were done eating, Papa told us: "We still have ten minutes or so, children, let's walk a little."

We followed him. We had hardly left the road when we found

ourselves in the kingdom of the trees. They say that Earth is shared by the water and the land, but I think a third share should be attributed to the humid tropical forest.

I had the impression I was entering a vast cathedral whose pillars were trees, whose roofing was canopy, and whose framework was the countless branches that supported this dome of greenery. It took a while for my eyes to adjust to the crepuscular light that reigned under this living vault. By chance, we had entered a part of the forest where there were giant trees with raised roots shaped like flying buttresses leaning to support them. Once they were on the ground, these stiltlike roots, reaching as high as fourteen or sixteen yards up the tree trunk, would splay out and writhe over a vast area to better distribute the enormous weight of the tree.

I struck a hanging bunch of scarlet-flowered heliconia: the movement was passed on to the boughs it touched, the boughs passed it along to their many smaller branches, and the smaller branches in their turn passed it on to the vines twining around them, and in the blink of an eye, an entire section of the forest was moving as one, as if part of a continuous matrix: I then wondered if it wasn't the flapping pearly blue wings of this butterfly that I was watching fly about over there, glinting in the evening fog that surrounded us, forcing a sulfur yellow tree snake out of its fruit palm shelter like an undulating living vine that slid along the rugged trunk—if it wasn't the movement of this snake that had provoked the howling of that tribe of leaping monkeys that fled from one branch to another; if it wasn't those monkeys who in turn had caused two squawking hornbills to take flight, thus shaking the small branches that finally communicated their movement to the scarlet-flowered heliconia bunch that had in fact struck me.

I was delighted, bewitched, swept up in the magic of a wondrous and unpredictable world where everything seemed supernatural. I don't think I would have been any more filled with wonder had I landed on an unknown planet in another galaxy. It was at that very moment that I truly understood why Christopher

Columbus, when he first encountered the tropical rain forest, realized that he had not reached the Indies in his journey toward the
west but was convinced that he had landed in the Garden of Eden.

We felt so small! No one spoke, not even my brothers, who
could not go anywhere without their Walkman, humming ragamuffin or rap songs; we were all mute, listening to the forest. Are
trees alive? Of course I know that they're not conscious, but could
we swear that the forest did not in its own way know about the existence of man?

The loud electric noise of a car horn reached us. It was the
driver calling his passengers. It was time to get back on the road.

We kept driving. This was turning into a very long trip, and I
dozed off. As for my two brothers, they were completely asleep:
Batsimba had his mouth open and his headphones still on; Banzouzi's hands were folded on one of the many comic books from
his library of Japanese mangas. Papa had long ago stopped reading
because the jouncing of the vehicle made it impossible. He was
watching the trees go by from the window. I noticed that the
driver often indulged in a strange maneuver. He sped up every
time an animal crossed the road. This was paying off, since he succeeded in killing two boars and a hedgehog, which he quickly
loaded in the back.

We kept driving. I grew tired, since we weren't driving on the
road for the most part but on routes the loggers had cleared for
their trucks. I didn't like these loggers much because they didn't
hesitate to cut down even hundred-year-old trees. All I have to do
is recall what I had seen during the construction of the great stadium in our small town during the festivities for the fourteenth
anniversary of the reign of the one we called our Supreme Guide
before the coming of democracy, a time when Uncle was still rising through the hierarchy of the Single Party. I remember Papa's
invitation to the pupils of the school: "Children, come attend the
massacre."

Suddenly, the sky darkened. I had forgotten that we were at the end of the dry season and that the first rains could fall at any time. In this season you could not trust the bright white of the tufts of cumulus that sprinkled the blue sky with their soft silk because these nice-weather clouds could, at the slightest puff of wind, turn into a powerful mass dark with cumulonimbus, omens of a storm. The first rains are usually terrible. They are often torrential, and their violence always catches one by surprise. The sky was now very dark, as if night had fallen and there were no stars. Then I saw the first lightning bolt, heard thunder, and suddenly there was a deluge.

We could no longer see through the windows because the rain was so thick that we were surrounded by a veritable fog. The driver had to stop. All the passengers had woken up and were listening with apprehension to the heavy crackling of raindrops on the metallic shell of the truck. To the lightning and the thunder. Tropical floods! Maman had told me a story from the Bible in which, in the days of a man by the name of Noah, men had sinned so much that God had gotten real upset and, to punish them for their iniquities, made rain come down for more than forty days and forty nights. The whole world was under water. Only Noah's little ark, swaying here and there, stayed afloat. In it, Noah had gathered all the living species that were later to repopulate the earth. Papa, who was listening to this, told me as soon as Maman had finished that the legend of the great flood was the most common legend among all the peoples of the world. It wasn't just a story from the Bible. You could already find it in prebiblical texts like the Sumerian and Akkadian legends narrated in the Epic of Gilgamesh. I had right away taken a liking to the word Gilgamesh, just as I had to words like Ouagadougou, Patagonia, Titicaca, and Uttar Pradesh. In any case, I was hoping we wouldn't stay stuck there for forty days or even forty hours, even if we looked like the heroes of a new lost ark in the middle of this hurricane with our women and children, our men, two boars, one hedgehog, and that's without counting my two brothers, who were a species of their own.

We could not leave the truck, what with the raging buckets of rain falling on the road. Fascinated by the devastating force that accompanied the liquid mass engulfing the truck, that fragile shelter in which my father, my mother, and my two twin brothers huddled together, I began thinking about water, about everything I had read and learned about it in school. First of all, it was a small molecule with a simple formula, H_2O, two hydrogen atoms joined to a central atom of oxygen at an angle of 109 degrees 5 minutes. It was a liquid with abnormal properties. And it is this abnormality, stemming from those celebrated hydrogen bonds, that had shaped life as we know it, because without water, life would have never occurred on our little planet Earth, which would have been as sterile as Venus or the moon. It was the most abundant element on Earth. Not only was it our planet's natural air conditioner, thanks to its oceans, but it was also used to transport the nutrients inside our cells. There could be no rain forest without it. It was so precious that plants had come up with the most ingenious strategies for storing it—the strangest strategy being that of the baobab, which had come up with a trunk-bottle, an enormous trunk that could be as wide as the tree was tall, giving it a ridiculous shape but an efficient reservoir to stock up the water fetched by its spiralling roots from deep in the ground, thus enabling it to survive through long months of drought. On the other hand, wherever there was no liquid water because the ground was frozen most of the time, the best strategy was not to lose the little water one had. This was the way of the pines of the boreal forest, the world's largest forest, which had resin-filled pine needles to protect themselves from being freeze-dried. Finally, for the plants of the desert, the challenge of retaining water was evaporation, so they were driven to equip themselves with rough and rugged leaves, which were sometimes purely and simply thorns. As for us humans, we

are the most unfortunate of all because we don't have any strategies to stock up on water as we do with energy, thanks to our fat
cells and the sugar reserves in our muscles, so though it is possible
for us to fast for an entire month without great risk, it is impossible for us to go without water for more than forty-eight hours
without endangering our health.

But it was also true that water wasn't merely benevolent. It
could also be violent and destructive, bursting dikes, provoking
tidal waves and mud slides. And when it wasn't violent, it behaved
deceptively: it flowed, dripped, seeped into this, pressed against
that, crushing, eroding, grinding, dissolving anything in its path . . .

Tired of the monotonous sound of water falling on our truck,
Batsimba turned his Walkman back on, Banzouzi went back to
reading his comic book, Maman returned to her account book to
do the numbers for her small business after weeks of interruption.
Papa, by contrast, had not gone back to his reading but seemed to
be reflecting on who knows what problem. Having nothing to do,
I took out my electronic calculator and tried to figure out how far
away the lightning was. In physics, I had learned that light moved
at 186,000 miles a second, while the rate of sound passing through
the air was about 1,100 feet a second at room temperature. Thus,
as soon as I saw a burst of lightning, I noted the seconds or frac-
tions of seconds that it took for me to hear the thunder. All I had
to do then was multiply that number by 340 to know the distance.
This was so absorbing that I soon forgot about everything else and
I didn't sense the time go by.

Finally the rain stopped. Not gradually, but all of a sudden, as
abruptly as it had begun. The sun reappeared just as suddenly in a
great blue sky. It was wonderful and unbelievable at the same
time. Had it not been for the tumult of muddy water that continued to roll down the sloping road, carrying off the grass, branches,
and small stones, I could have sworn that there hadn't been a
storm moments ago. We rushed to open the windows misted up
by our breath, which had transformed the cabin into a sauna, and

we eagerly gulped the fresh air that carried smells of the soil and the forest, whose fragrance I had discovered earlier that day. We stayed in the truck a good thirty minutes before the muddy flow turned into a harmless trickle of water. Then we went down to inspect the road. Things didn't look so good. We were stuck: there was an uprooted tree blocking the road in front of us, and behind us part of the embankment had been swept away and piled up on the road. With much huffing and puffing on everyone's part, we succeeded in removing the tree, and then, as if that wasn't enough trouble, the truck refused to move when the driver stepped on the accelerator; the wheels had gotten stuck in the mud. We had to get down once more, dig our heels into the dirt, put rocks and branches under the wheels, and push and push before we, poor shipwrecked folk, could get going again. I understand now why Mr. Konaté's trucks took this road only during the dry season. We were about to go through this ritual ten, twenty more times. The incident that caused us the most distress was when a little bridge over a stream collapsed just after our two back wheels had crossed it.

Then night fell, our two headlights piercing though the darkness on a road worthy of the Bandama Rally. Despite all these problems, however, the driver had still managed to add a gazelle and an antelope to his game bag.

We arrived in our village the next morning, exhausted, dirty, and muddy as yams. I think I slept twelve hours straight, because when Maman woke me, it was already the morning after our arrival.

25

Well, let me tell you, politics isn't always such a sad affair! Especially the liberal pluralist democracy that descended upon the country with all that new business they call an electoral campaign.

But before I explain what an electoral campaign is, let me first tell you about the National Convention, a homemade invention.

We were told that just as an astronaut could not go from the high pressure of his cabin to the low pressure of space without first going through a decompression air lock, so we could not go from single-party rule to a liberal, pluralist democracy without passing through a sort of political air lock, meaning a national convention. This convention was a decontamination zone (just as astronauts were put in quarantine when they came back from the moon), without which we risked transplanting the totalitarian virus onto the new democratic soil that lay just over the horizon. It enabled all the sons and daughters of the nation to learn from a past unworthy of a civilized land, from all these years of blood and tears lived under the thumb of the Single Party. We would then commit to never let it happen again, to never lie again, never steal again, never kill again, never covet our neighbor's wife. Finally we would part with an embrace in the spirit of brotherly love.

All of this was fine, but where could we find representatives for this convention, representatives of political parties and of civil society in a country that, ever since I was put in this world, had known only one party and no independent associations?

If you think the situation was hopeless, then you don't know the first thing about our country, small in size, but rich in resources. Within a week our nation's native enterprising spirit, long held captive by the Party's shackles, exploded into seventy-seven political parties. The number reached seventy-eight when Uncle Boula Boula founded one of his own. I found out about it because he sent a letter and some membership forms to Papa, who called Maman and showed them to her, saying: "My incomparable brother-in-law has found a new vein to tap."

With my usual curiosity, I read the letter. It was a kind of circulating memorandum in which he announced the formation of his political party. He drew attention to the fact that the struggle for freedom had always been his own; that he had always been a man of courage, as demonstrated by his imprisonment for having publicly expressed his disagreement with the Chief of the Revolution when he had come to realize that the government he helped lead could not be reformed from inside. He had chosen to face the horrors of the dungeon rather than to keep getting rich off the people's backs. Meanwhile, while still in prison, he had inspired the famous open letter that had led to the fall of this iniquitous totalitarian government as well as its ultimate disintegration. Today, he was ready to put his experience at the service of the people, the people without whom he was nothing. He was going to serve the people and not just help himself. Hence the creation of his new party, different from all the rest, the Independent Party of the United Front for the Institutionalization of Liberty, or IPUFIL. "IPUFIL, the party with pep and pow!" was the slogan. He then signed his letter "Boula Boula, Political Leader, President, and Founder of IPUFIL."

He had handwritten a few words at the end of the letter, a personal note to Papa, which read:

> *Dear brother-in-law, I nominate you as president of your local IPUFIL section. Enclosed you'll find several membership forms. If you run out of them, do not hesitate to make photocopies. I would also like to inform you that I have chosen you as a party delegate for the next National Convention. Don't worry about the dough, I'll find a way to pay you for the time you'll be away from your family. Besides, I know how difficult the end of the month can be for a teacher. Give my regards to everyone.*

Not only did Papa not reply to Uncle's invitation but he simply threw it in the wastebasket.

The day of the convention arrived. They were more than four hundred representatives, seventy-eight political parties, and who knows how many organizations. It was a show aired on both radio and television, the likes of which we had never seen since Uncle's trial, only this time the result wouldn't be known ahead of time.

I was curious to see what would be done by the representatives of a people long gagged whose gag was suddenly removed. I wanted to see how one rebuilt a new world atop the ruins of a dictatorial regime, a new world in which there would be no more torture, rape, theft, or political murder. I wanted to understand what freedom and justice meant.

So, glued to the screen, I saw the first doings of the representatives of a long-gagged people whose gag had been suddenly removed: they were granting themselves privileges! Yes, the first decision of the representatives was to grant themselves a per diem equal to a teacher's monthly salary, explaining to the gentle public (us, that is) that these self-proclaimed representatives of the people deserved to be sheltered from the temptations of corruption.

They then began their speeches. I heard each one of them stress all the big words I cited a little earlier, but there was one thing I could not understand very well: Why were all these people pretending that all the wrong that had been done to this country, the chaos, the political murders, the economic crimes, the divorces, and poor harvests, had been the fault of one man alone, our current President, whom no one considered the Enlightened Guide of Our Revolution anymore? He was now evil incarnate. Apparently, he had seized power and then ruled for close to twenty years all by himself, and none of them had contributed to keeping the system in place. More surprising still, no one had ever really belonged to the Party, or if they had, they now claimed, it was only to allay suspicion.

Meanwhile I recognized among the speakers some of those men who, through radio and television, had taught me since the cradle that our nation owed everything to the Guide—roads, good harvests, vaccinations, births, and good grades in school. Together we had celebrated his birthdays as national holidays. You do understand, as I told you, that I'd been born fourteen years earlier, and I had known only one president, the very one we were now spitting on. And it was thanks to them that I had learned to love him, to respect him, and to want to be like him when I grew up. I began to suspect that he wasn't a very good person only after Papa's arrest and the business outside our small-town prison. So how could they suddenly see things so differently? I had been told that adults hardly ever changed their convictions, so what triggered their about-face—what was the kick in their ass that now propelled us into democracy? I really had no idea.

Just as I was about to lose hope, I remembered Uncle. If you've followed my story since the beginning, you must know that I was always very close to Uncle, especially when I was little. We even had secrets that we swore never to tell, like the one when he caught me under the bed while he was playing at scaring me with Auntie Lolo. If there was anyone who could enlighten me about what was actually going on, it was him. So I impatiently waited for the moment he took the podium.

Unfortunately, Uncle only got me more confused. He took the podium and solemnly declared that he too had never believed in the Single Party. He who had wanted to convert all the Pygmies of our equatorial forest to Marxism-Leninism! I really love my uncle, but at that moment, I almost called him a liar—almost, since an uncle is still an uncle—when I heard him say that during all the years he had been a member of the Political Bureau, he had been the only one that dared look the Supreme Guide in the eye and speak his mind when necessary. It annoys me to have to diminish Uncle in your eyes, but at this point I must tell you a story I have left out until now, so you'll understand why Uncle Boula Boula's declarations before this session of the National Convention weren't exactly in strict accordance with the truth.

This happened while Uncle was already a member of the Political Bureau of the Party and number two in the government, during the period when he was preparing the celebration of the fifteenth anniversary of our Revolution, the Revolution we now called a coup d'état. One night ten days before the festivities, no one understood what was going on in the President's head as he rushed to his second home some thirty miles outside the capital. At the stroke of midnight, he sent his presidential guards on an armed raid of the homes of all the ministers in his government and all the members of the Political Bureau, with express instructions to bring them before him unharmed. The guards quickly carried out his orders, spreading like mosquitoes through the town, and in less than an hour they had harvested everyone they had been seeking, including those who thought they had found secluded retreats and were peacefully cuddling up with their mistresses. They had forgotten that our President had a security and intelligence network so effective that not one leaf on a tree could move without him knowing about it. Uncle was evidently among those caught, and, lucky for him, he slept in pajamas, which prevented him from being brought back in long underwear like the defense minister, or with only a towel around his waist like the health minister caught in his secret love nest with a newly recruited nurse.

The captain of the presidential guard stuffed this smart set into a minibus that took off like a bat out of hell in the direction of the presidential residence. As soon as they arrived, they were shoved into a room, lined up, and made to face a red curtain, backs against the wall. There they stood, puzzled, gnashing their teeth, legs atremble, and not just from the cold. The soldiers guarding them got a kick out of making sure every once in a while that their firing pins still worked by cocking them loudly, which startled the prisoners every time. How long did they wait there? They would be unable to say because they had all been stripped of their watches, which made the anxiety of passing time unbearable. To be honest, I must say that I have known something about time-related anxiety ever since the time I missed the rendezvous with Aledia, which I had set up on my own (in fact, I set it up all by myself in my head since, thanks to Auntie Lolo's carelessness, I knew that Aledia was to come to their store at 11:30 on the dot) and then missed it because my math class let out four minutes late. First I was mentally pushing the hands of the clock so that they would speed up, and afterwards I was imagining a little gnome hanging on the hands to stop them from moving forward. Ah, the anxiety of passing time!

Suddenly, the red curtain was quietly spread apart in a smooth and automatic motion: the Supreme Chief appeared, sitting in his command chair, dressed in a simple, carelessly tied nightgown and some cheap plastic sandals that were sold in the markets of working-class neighborhoods. But don't they say that a chief remains a chief even in his underwear? Anyway, at his side were six guards armed like the guards of any self-respecting chief. Behind him, there was the famous "wall of mirrors" that Uncle had once installed. The Chief did not speak. He stared at them one by one with the unbearable glare of a wild animal tamer; then, with a movement of his index finger, he asked them to come forward. They all rushed, to avoid running the risk of being the last one to obey, and clustered respectfully a few feet away from the glowering Chief, who finally bellowed: "I'm going to have all of you shot!"

The government dignitaries looked at one another, taken aback. Two of them, with weak bladders, wet their pants. One fainted dead away on the marble floor. The others kept on looking around them, panicked, as if searching for a way out. Before them were only the President and his very best soldiers; beyond them, just the wall of mirrors, a checkerboard of little glassy pieces, concave or convex, that shattered the image of your body into a myriad of loose puzzle pieces so that you lost your grip on things, as in the incoherent world of Escher, whose books we owned. They then began moaning all at once: "You are our father, Comrade President, you can't kill your children—what have we done? We have done nothing, we ask to be forgiven even for what we have not done," et cetera, et cetera.

"You bunch of hypocrites!" the Supreme Guide raged. "At the count of ten, I will give the order to fire!"

He lifted his pinkie. In a metallic chorus, the guards cocked their weapons. ". . . four . . . five . . ."

It was no longer beads of sweat running down their foreheads, it was the Amazon. They were no longer just shaking by shivers, they were practically doing the twist.

". . . seven . . . eight . . ."

The witnesses are unanimous in their accounts that Uncle Boula Boula was the first to fall to his knees to beg the Supreme Chief to spare his life. The others did it only after seeing the number two melting in tears, meaning they were simply going with the flow. The spiteful smile of the Supreme Guide turned into a condescending and magnanimous grimace. He lifted a finger. The soldiers lowered their weapons and uncocked them with a flourish.

"Take them back to their homes."

The curtains closed. The Chief was gone. That was all.

The lamentations ceased. The government dignitaries got back up from their groveling position, confused, embarrassed in front of each other. They were wondering if what had just happened to them wasn't a multimedia exhibit of virtual reality pirated from an Internet Web site when the harsh voice of the captain of the presidential guard brought them back to the reality of the living room in which they had almost been gunned down a moment ago. Did anyone still have any doubt who was boss? Beyond that, who could now believe a word of Uncle's bragging?

So I truly hoped he would stop his parade float before people started booing. But to my surprise, he was being applauded! I was perplexed, quite lost. Go figure human nature!

The convention went on like this for three months—with people who were obviously lying, with young people full of passion and sincerity, with others wanting revenge, reform, utopia, or a job at the end of the convention. One representative got carried away by his enthusiasm and started singing cha-cha tunes. What promises! What words! I may be too young to know, but I wonder if in the end every new order didn't begin with a speech. Simply with words. Besides, Maman had told me that it was written somewhere in the Bible that "in the beginning there was the Word," even though Papa immediately added, "except for the instant before the Big Bang, when there was nothing, neither silence nor speech, neither space nor time."

26

If, as scientific studies have shown, Africa is the cradle of the human race, then I tell you that Africa is also the cradle of democracy!" the chairman of the convention proclaimed from his podium.

"And if Africa was west of the Atlantic Ocean," grumbled Papa, "we would call it America, and it would have been the first country to have sent a man to the moon."

"And so, on that note," continued the president, "we are going to invent a new democracy, an African democracy!" He practically shouted the last two words. "Yes, my brothers and sisters, this African democratic renaissance, embodied in this room by the representatives from our political parties and our modern society, must not forget that it also digs its roots into our age-old traditions as deeply as the acacia of the Sahara or the baobab digs for water. Therefore, in recognition, the presiding chairs of this assembly have unanimously decided to place our closing ceremony in the hands of our ancestors, by way of the representatives

of traditional Africa. And who else represents the African tradition
if not its wise men and fetish makers?"

"Behold, my brothers, Africa has just invented a new kind of
democracy, a democracy of fetish makers," launched Papa, as if
the television receiver was a transmitter.

Unlike Papa, I was happy about the news, because for once I
was going to get to see actual fetish makers.

I know that Africa is said to be the continent of sorcerers and
fetish makers. They were everywhere and so governed people's
lives that an African would rather sacrifice a chicken to ease a fever
than take an aspirin. I read an awful lot of foolish things about
these people, but as Papa told me once, one must always read any
book written by man with a critical eye. I say foolish because, believe me, I've spent my whole life in Africa and have never seen a
single sorcerer. I have never seen a single fetish maker. The first
time I ever saw a traditional warrior with bow and arrows was during the ceremony for the fourteenth anniversary of our Revolution, when that guy Etumba expressed the desire to have a fistfight
with imperialism. That said, I can tell you right now that I no
longer trust the performance of the fetish makers ever since that
time they gave a bad name to African soccer.

It was during the 1974 World Cup in Germany. Like most of
the stories that took place before my birth, this one I got from my
uncle. At that time Zaire had a president who had delusions of
grandeur, and since he had not been the first African president to
send his subjects to the moon, he wanted to be the first to engrave
the name of his country on the World Cup winners' list. He felt
that the skills of the players and of the European coach who had
been paid his weight in gold would not be enough to make his
dream come true; he also had to call on Africa's traditional genius.
He organized a nationwide contest to recruit the nine best fetish
makers. Why nine I couldn't tell you and neither could Uncle, but
it seems that it had something to do with the number of seats
available on the special plane the President had chartered.

The testimony of the players on the team that served as a guinea pig to test the prowess of the chosen fetish makers left room for no doubt. A goalkeeper claimed that the ball would either burst into flames or grow spikes before his very eyes, depending on whether it was a penalty or a corner kick. A defender said that the ball became invisible each time it penetrated the penalty zone. Another goalkeeper swore that each time he lunged at a well-kicked ball, he saw a little monkey appear out of nowhere, grab the ball away, and throw it into the net. Was there any doubt that the World Cup would be ours? But listen to what happened: During the first game against Yugoslavia, the national team had nine goals scored against them in the first half alone. The funding was cut off right there and then, the national team was quickly brought home, and the nine fetish makers were immediately thrown in jail. So don't you talk to me about fetish makers!

Yet here they were, standing before the representatives of the National Convention as guests of honor. I was fascinated by the camera close-up of them: faces painted with white kaolin clay and red tukula powder, an assortment of bird feathers, feline claws, and palm-wine gourds. Then each one of the four hundred representatives, accompanied by the incantations of these famous sorcerers, washed his hands in a big basin of water, which in our culture meant that everything that happened in the past has been forgiven, or so I've heard. After a while this became so absurd that I went to pee three times and was almost tempted to go join my brothers and watch *Goldeneye*, the latest James Bond in their possession. I nevertheless returned in time for the end of the ceremony. All's well that ends well, the convention chair concluded; now nothing could stop the birth of republican democracy in our country, a democracy that would flourish like a healthy palm tree.

We were ready for the electoral campaign.

27

W hat is an electoral campaign anyway? I'll tell you—
not the theory of it, since you could read that in any
book, but the practice, as we lived it daily.

Papa had explained to me that a democracy stood for freedom
of expression and association, free enterprise, and the right to free
and fair elections, since that is how the will of a sovereign people
is expressed. Perhaps you don't know what I mean by "free and
fair elections"? If I had to explain every new term democracy
brought with it, I'd never finish my story. But I'll try anyway. I can
understand that you might have a hard time understanding since
you've grown accustomed to the elections that were held up until
now by the Single Party.

With the Party, it was quite simple: the Party President called
a congress. The Party President was nominated as the only candidate, and this lone candidate instantly and unanimously won the
ballot, with a long standing ovation from the voters. My uncle told
me once that a secretary of the Political Bureau who was in charge
of organizing the congress had been arrested and thrown in jail

because the Party President had been elected with only 99.98 percent of the votes instead of the expected 100 percent. They wanted to make him give up the names of the 0.02 percent who had not voted for the Chief, since they were undoubtedly enemies who had infiltrated the Party leadership.

Now, in the days of free elections, whoever was of age to vote—which unfortunately was not yet the case for me—could be a candidate for his party or even run as an independent candidate, and everyone was free to choose whomever he wanted. But how did one choose among several candidates when one did not know them? The electoral campaign was the answer to that dilemma.

We had choices. Too many choices. Thirty-three candidates from seventy-eight parties. Maybe our country was small, with limited means in terms of industrial development, financial resources, sanitary equipment, or anything else of that sort, but it contained a wealth of exceptional political men capable of getting it out of the rut of underdevelopment. Each proposed a solution to turn the country into a prosperous little Western European country. The only mystery for me was that I could not explain why we were still living in such poverty when so many people obviously had so many miraculous solutions.

The campaign? I followed it closely on television and in village and town meetings, and let me tell you right now that I had it figured out so well that I knew the day I reached the legal age to become a candidate I would be an absolute political tiger. The process was simple: it involved, on the one hand, seducing the voters by convincing them that you were the man or woman who was needed in the right place and, on the other, knocking down all the other candidates by calling them incompetent, lying bastards, dirty rotten scoundrels unworthy of holding the fate of the nation in their hands. Obviously, you mustn't forget to pepper your speech with the most fantastic of promises and, from time to time, distribute a little money, or maybe a lot.

Of all the candidates who entered the fray, the first one to really draw my attention was Professor Pentium-75. I'm sure you realize Pentium-75 wasn't his real name, but that nickname we gave him stuck because the day he presented himself on television was also the day a commercial first aired for the new computers with Pentium-75 microprocessors, which apparently operated twice as fast as the old computers with 486 DX processors. The nickname stuck with the professor even though today we can find Pentium microprocessors that run still faster, at 90, 100, or even 133 megahertz.

I was blown away by Professor Pentium-75's curriculum vitae, I who was so fascinated by science. With his round alchemist's glasses, he appeared before the cameras in a white lab coat, implying that he had felt compelled to interrupt (against his will) a scientific experiment of national importance, while the other candidates vainly paraded about in suit and tie. On that same occasion, he dealt a hard blow to all those who thought that Africans lived only on drumbeats and feelings, meaning they were incapable of such rigorous intellectual activity as science. Yet make no mistake, Africa's future lay in science, and Professor Pentium-75 was without a shadow of a doubt the genius this continent was waiting for.

"Indeed," he would say, "disproving what the rest of the researchers in quantum physics have thought, I have demonstrated that we could break isolated quarks and observe them individually. The article I have sent to the *Zeitschrift für Physik* on that subject has not yet been published because the editors are still looking for an outside reader competent enough to understand it. Indeed, I made a lot of money in Japan developing sugarcane that could grow on the steep and volcanic tuff slopes of Fujiyama. Why is that important? Because (1) it shows that I have not come to help myself but to help you, to put the wealth I acquired over there at the disposition of this poor country of yours, and (2) if I can grow sugarcane on pumice stone, nothing will stop me from growing tomatoes on our most arid lateritic soil, be it as infertile as concrete. Indeed, I led the FAO team that managed the green revolution in the state of Andhra Pradesh in India. If I am elected president of the Republic, I won't fail to find a variety of manioc that does not contain cyanic acid, for surely you know that it is the cyanic acid in those manioc tubers that causes goiter and cretinism in many Africans. Indeed, to answer my country's desperate call, I have refused the offers of two American universities, which, upon seeing that my name was mentioned for the Nobel Prize, wanted to lure me over there for a premium. In fact, when you interrupted me, I was adding the final touches to a device I've invented, a device able to stop the transmission of AIDS; for I have discovered a new equation: drugs + AIDS = civil war! As in Rwanda, as in Liberia. Thus, the device I invented is able to detect an adulteress, and when one speaks of adulteresses one is really talking about casual sex, and when one speaks of casual sex one is obviously talking about AIDS!" What genius! What a brain! Here was the internationally renowned man we needed to lead this country, long live Pentium-75! Too bad Papa wasn't there to see the broadcast, for I was sure that he would have given Pentium-75 his vote.

Our little country was beset with political geniuses, each one with a simple and original solution—"we just have to do X in order for us to catch up to Japan quicker than Japan caught up to Europe during the Meiji era." So you won't be surprised when I tell you that no sooner had the potentially multi-Nobel Prize–winning Professor Pentium-75 (whom we now just called Professor P-75 for short) scientifically and technologically disappeared from our screens than there appeared the one man who, in a campaign full of amusing candidates, would become as fearsome a champion as the late Khomeini. Naturally, the population nicknamed him Tata Ayatollah, then, more informally, Tata Tollah.

Tata Tollah did not make science his daily bread. He drew his legitimacy straight from the founding fathers. His genealogical tree went as far back as 1482, when the Portuguese explorer Diogo Cão discovered the mouth of the great Congo River for the

Europeans. History had it that Diogo Cão was received by the Congolese King Nzinga Nkuwu. After much feasting and gulping down of calabashes of palm wine, a drink unknown to the Portuguese navigator, the latter made unambiguous advances toward the king's niece. The girl turned around, bent over, lifted her wraparound skirt, and showed her naked buttocks to the explorer. This manner of cursing, which is still practiced today by the women here, was supposedly the first act of resistance to colonization. Diogo Cão took the meaning of this gesture for granted and became aroused. He had an erection, which, because of the curse, turned into a painful hard-on that went limp only forty-eight hours later, and not because of the prayers in Latin sung by all the members of his crew before a cross brought over from Portugal, but thanks to a mansunsu leaf poultice, a leaf also known as *Ocimum basilicum*, applied by the best fetish maker of the kingdom, Nganga Lukeni. (The story ends quite well for Diogo, since ultimately Nzinga Nkuwu converted to the faith of the Roman Church.) All of this is to tell you that Tata Tollah claimed his descent from that woman, the first resister in the kingdom, first to show that even buttocks could be used as weapons. And so he considered himself the natural heir to the game bag that held the mystical instruments of power. And thus true heir to the ancestors. But that wasn't all.

Tata Tollah was also a Christian, and part of his power came from that. In a dream, he had seen the Son of God or else the Archangel Gabriel—I don't remember which—showing him a shining crown with his name etched in golden letters: this meant that he would be president of the Republic and that no earthly thing could stop him.

Dressed in candid probity and in a big, white traditional robe, he wanted to be the prototype for the modern African deeply embedded in his ancestral roots. "No," he would say to the journalists, "don't listen to those idiots who say that I don't have any degrees. I was always head of my class in elementary school, and so I was skipped ahead from the third to the fifth grade. I also have done important scholarly work; most notably I have authored a four-hundred-fifty-page manuscript about the resistance movements against colonization in our country, and I also have a work in progress, entitled 'God, the Ancestors, and the Path to Democracy.' I don't need to boast about all of this because a true leader does not measure his worth in education. As you all know, science without morals ruins the soul. We must refuse the development imposed on us by the West. What I would like to build here is a family-based society in which solidarity is the rule. Africa will be saved only if we go back to our roots." Long live Tata Tollah, the savior!

Of course there were other candidates. For example, there was a former IMF official who wanted to save the country through well-structured reforms. His plan was to progressively reduce the salaries of state employees so that, within five years, we would live in a country without government wages, since, as everyone knew, these were the principal obstacle to foreign investment in our country. There was a former intern from the German Commerzbank who proposed to rent out the country to the Germans for ten years so they might develop it with Prussian efficiency. There was also a former champion one-hundred-meter sprinter whose program was to reduce the number of widows and single women in this country by sending all men who were under fifty-five years of age to run laps in stadiums. Practicing a sport, he thought, lowered the chances of hypertension in men and would thus reduce their mortality rate and the number of widows. There were so many other proposals! I won't mention them all, since they had all been eliminated in the first round of voting, leaving only Professor Pentium-75 and Tata Tollah for the runoff.

Had the rest of the campaign been limited to the televised debate between the two candidates—we copied what was done in America and France, since the people of those two countries were already practicing democracy before my birth—I would have ended my story here, because it was not a very interesting debate. Each one just repeated what he had said before. But there were these last two town meetings held in our good old town by both of the candidates.

I will end up believing that our town was blessed by the gods because, within the space of a few years, three of our nation's major events were held there. The first was my tumultuous birth; the second, if you recall, was the celebration of the fourteenth anniversary of our ex-revolution; I say ex-revolution since our democratically correct language now considered what had for twenty years been called a revolution a vulgar coup. The third was this last event, the final two campaign stops.

We found out soon enough that the campaign was to wind down in our town. In fact, ever since the ceremonies that Uncle Boula Boula had organized in his capacity as the FARCE, the name of our good old town had acquired a certain nostalgic and mythic resonance. The closest other example I could give you would be Timbuktu: of its past glory, there was nothing except a city cooking in the furnace of the Sahel sun, hardly accessible by the quicksand trails winding through the knolls and dunes. Yet mention Timbuktu and you will inevitably evoke such famous travelers as Leon the African or Ibn Battuta; and its medieval university that offered scholars from all over the world its knowledge of astrology, law, history; and its camel caravans with their loads of salt, spices, silk, copper, and pewter; and of course, alas, its columns of slaves by the boatload coming from the south.

Such was the case with our town as well, except that we were located smack-dab in the middle of the equatorial forest. Of its glorious stadium where a hail of candy and madeleines had once descended on us, all that was left were damaged bleachers, dislocated by the tentacle roots of the fig trees, as if the arms of an octopus had infiltrated every crack, breaking up the stone into loose blocks like the ones you saw in pictures of the Angkor Wat temple in Cambodia. The lawn had disappeared under weeds and brush. Obviously, we couldn't hold a campaign event there. But just mention our town, and memories of a place that had known the glory of receiving delegations from all over the world instantly came to mind. What's more, our town was above all considered the starting point of the democratic movement that swept away the unjust and dictatorial single-party regime. It had acquired historic status.

History is made in such a way that, often, some events are associated with certain places even though these events may have a more distant, more complex origin. Therefore, just as the Boston Tea Party was considered the starting point of the American Revolution, and the storming of the Bastille that of the French Revolution, and the assassination in Sarajevo as the start of the First World War, our town was considered as the place where the revolution began. Why not, after all? Was it not the place where I got the kick in the rear that would transform me into a die-hard democrat?

28

I f you wanted a show, then this was a show all right! You
wanted science and technology? You got science and technology!

When the announcer shouted, "And now, the Professor," instead of a drumroll there was an explosion of synthesizers accompanied by a profusion of fleeting montages flickering on a white
sheet behind the platform that had been built under the covered
market where we were standing: mathematical images of strange
computer-generated spirals, their coiling controlled by equations
straight out of chaos theory; then, multicolored psychedelic Man-
delbrot fractals; and finally, in the eye of the last spiraling coil that
had contracted into a small luminous dot in the middle of the
screen, there appeared a map of Africa that soon expanded to fill
the entire sheet. In the heart of this Africa our country came into
view, and at last, from the heart of our country emerged the can-
didate-professor against the backdrop of a star-filled sky.

Papa once told me that when he was a boy, he often followed
the televised news of a neighboring country; it always started with

a title sequence showing the face of the Beloved Founding President slowly descending from the sky through the translucent clouds, like the Messiah from heaven. I didn't really know much about those times since I was yet to be born, but that was the effect this little video had on me. Our professor's face appeared in a cluster of stars, and then the film stopped all at once, the platform filled with white smoke pierced by thin laser beams as in nightclubs. In the midst of all the smoke, the lasers, and the sound of techno music, the curtain suddenly opened to a drumroll and . . . Professor P-75 appeared in the flesh! A thunderous standing ovation. My brothers, who had also come with Papa, were ecstatic. They saw in the professor a living character from their Japanese manga cartoons, Goldorak or maybe Dragon Ball Z. The crowd went nuts, completely enthralled. Was it magic? Was it science? Was there even a difference between the two for the thousands of peasants attending the show? A man who could do that could only accomplish miracles for his country.

He sat onstage with his lieutenants and his bodyguards standing behind him. He raised his hands in false modesty; the applause doubled instead. He had without any doubt won this round.

At last, he began speaking: "First of all, before I even greet you and thank you for your warm welcome, I must tell you right now that, since my studies have shown that your area is the biggest pineapple producer of the region, I have decided to set up a factory here whose goal will be the transformation of pineapple juice into fuel! The oil produced in this manner will be used for the peasants' lanterns until the completion of the hydroelectric dam I will build once elected president. The rest of the fuel will be used for airplanes, and I am even looking into building a runway big enough for cargo planes to export the rest of this fuel."

The crowd went wild. Papa, who was a physicist and knew chemistry as well, asked me: "Did he say turn pineapple juice into oil?"

"Yes," I quickly answered.

"With a bit of jazz and palm wine, I hope," he continued.

I did not answer because I did not want to miss the rest.

The professor raised his hand. "But I'm not done. What else do you produce here?"

"Beans," the crowd replied in one voice.

"That's what I thought. That is why I have also decided to set up a pork and beans canning plant here. The engineers are already here," he said, pointing behind us.

We all turned around, and I saw a big diesel MAN truck I had not noticed until now. And for the benefit of the crowd, men in blue work suits held up their yardsticks, theodolites, and other land-surveying equipment. The professor wasn't kidding around.

"I will import pigs from South Africa or Namibia, until we have our own local hog farms, because there's no pork and beans without pork."

He paused for a moment and then added: "I am going to create the world's greatest hog farm, and we will use the hog bristles to make toothbrushes and thereby become the world's leading exporter of toothbrushes."

He paused again under the applause. He was proud of himself. No hot air, only concrete things.

"Now that I have given you concrete plans," he resumed, "I can begin my speech."

He spoke for a long time. As I recall, he said that Africa's future was in science, technology, and management, and in nothing else. He wasn't one to linger, to cling to the past with no ambitious international agenda in sight; he wasn't about to carry on as one oblivious to the fact that we were at the dawn of the third millenium. On the contrary, thanks to his solid international connections, money was going to rain upon the country the very day of his election into office. As a result, he did not need money from international organizations such as the IMF and the World Bank, so not one state employee would have to be fired. Once he built the dam, the country would be flooded with so much light that this region of black Africa, when seen from space, would serve as the exception to Olbers's paradox stipulating that night is black. Finally, looking up as if inspired and peering toward the hill where the last houses of our town stood, he said: "Development also means sports. What beautiful mountains you have around here! Don't you think it would attract tourism if we could create a ski resort here? I see your incredulous smiles. Skiing in the tropics! Know that nothing is impossible with science. It isn't necessary to import snow from Europe; we can use technology to make snow fall in this tropical country, and I will work on that as soon as I am elected . . . Thus, with its snow, electric lights, roads, canning plant, and toothbrush factory, in less than one term of office, our country could become a little Switzerland."

The crowd went nuts.

I must admit I was amazed. If I were of voting age, I would most certainly have voted for Professor P-75. I agreed with his program in every way except for turning our country into a little Switzerland. Why? Because, from what I read in the newspapers, after the fall of Duvalier's son Baby Doc in Haiti, after Moussa Traore's fall in Mali, after Marcos's fall in the Philippines, and after all I had been told about Mobutu in Zaire, Switzerland seemed like one big safety deposit box into which all these princes stuffed their money; and it was on this mattress of money made off our backs that the Swiss bankers slept peacefully and made the fortunes that they threw back in our faces with all the arrogance of these so-called rich nations. Also, in a book that Papa was reading about this country, a book I didn't read because it was too boring, the author quoted Voltaire, who once wrote that if you ever see a Swiss banker jump out of a window, follow him, for there must certainly be some profit in it. So, another Switzerland? No thank you, not for me. On the other hand, I was all for turning pineapple juice into oil; and I was all for turning our little hill into a tropical ski resort, since I had never seen snow before; all for more light, because then even the gorillas in the forest would be able to spot their food at night under the canopy; all for the pork and beans plant; and yes, I was all for making our country into the leading exporter of hog-bristle toothbrushes. This is where the power of technology and science has brought us. And a man who could make snow technologically, and who had already invented a device that scientifically detected loose women to stop the spread of AIDS, would work nothing but miracles in his country.

I thought that Papa would be enthusiastic about having a fellow scientist to vote for, but to my surprise, he was not impressed at all. What was the matter? Was it the thought of a canning plant, when together we had once led a campaign against the canned goods of the Honorable Hussein El Faisal Al Moustapha Husseini Morabitoune, Aledia's father? He laughed when I posed that question to him while we were heading back to the house through the enthusiastic crowd.

"Listen to this story about a sandwich shop in New York," he said to me. "The owner had challenged all of his clients: 'If we don't have the sandwich you want, we'll write you a check for a hundred dollars.' A Congolese man who missed his native land happened to drop by and asked, without trying to be mean, for an elephant meat sandwich. 'Yeah, sure,' said the owner, and disappeared into the kitchen right away. He came back ten minutes later, disappointed, with a hundred-dollar check. 'Sorry, sir,' he said to the Congolese customer, 'we don't have any more bread.' "

I laughed my head off, even though I didn't quite understand what he was trying to say.

I'll tell you right away that Tata Tollah didn't fail to amaze us either. And I had really been afraid he would make a fool of himself after Professor P-75's extraordinary show.

You can think whatever you want about me, but I was in the crowd that went to the airport to wait for Tata Tollah. Even though we were told that his event would be held at the marketplace, we all knew that he would arrive by air, and one could arrive by air only via the airport. Still, I just couldn't see how an airplane, even a small one, could land on our old airfield, which had gone to seed ever since the celebration of the fourteenth anniversary of our ex-revolution. The runways had as many potholes as a telescope picture of the visible side of the moon. Even a bicycle couldn't navigate them. I thought for a minute that "arriving by air" was only a figure of speech and that Tata Tollah was going to do the Air Makana trick instead, a story that made a lot of noise here and that we still talk about today, some ten years later. Let me tell you all about it.

Not far from our country's capital, there are two neighboring villages, and since here we don't like to waste our energy naming things, we just called them Makana I and Makana II. These two villages were famous for the quality of their rattan and bamboo crafts. One September morning some customs officers at Charles de Gaulle Airport in Paris who were accompanying a group of immigrants on their way to deportation stopped two older individuals who wanted to get through customs: they had neither passports nor identification papers, nor any visas, evidently. The funny thing was that no plane had landed. The customs agents and the French policemen were perplexed. Since the French did not speak our language and since these two did not speak French, communication was difficult. Despite this, they were able to identify them and found out that they had come from an African village called Makana II. Unfortunately, this village did not figure in any atlas or in any CD-ROM files the police had, so they called on several African embassies in Paris, and, in the end, our embassy recognized these individuals as its citizens. What happened next was simple. The two old men explained that they had made their overnight trip by Air Makana, a mysterious airplane they had built in their village, Makana II. They had come to get their nephew who lived and worked in France, and who had enriched himself while forgetting them in their misery. Unfortunately, dawn had surprised them. Since this mysterious airplane could fly only at night, it took off at the crack of dawn and left them there. Needless to say, the authorities were incredulous. A fax was sent immediately to our country's government, which soon organized an investigative commission composed of the French ambassador and military attaché, as well as our minister of foreign affairs, national security director, and minister of the interior. The members of the commission went to Makana II, and I can't adequately convey to you their surprise when they saw the little bamboo airplane exactly where the two illegal passengers had told them it would be, well fastened in the branches of a safoutier tree. Who could still doubt that Africa had its mysteries?

So when I saw in what shape the runway was, I thought that Tata was going to do the Air Makana trick with his bamboo airplane. But not at all; he had us right where he wanted us. While we were waiting at the airport and looking at the place where planes were supposed to land, a helicopter appeared and headed toward the marketplace. With a great deal of playful jostling, we all ran there. When we arrived, the helicopter had not yet landed. It was suspended in the air above us, held aloft by the rotation of its blades like a great dragonfly. We pictured Tata Tòllah sitting up there, slowly coming down from the sky like a god, for only gods came down from the sky. But when the machine was low enough, it disappeared in a cloud of ocher dust that settled only when the blades stopped spinning.

Then he appeared.

The crowd was delirious. We chanted tirelessly and rhythmically: "Tata, Tata, Tata!" Dressed in a long white tunic, onto which a discreet yet noticeable little cross was curiously fastened, he came out of the machine while shaking a black wooden scepter (made of ebony?), symbol of traditional authority. Framed by his protocol officers, he attempted to head for the platform under the shed but was quickly picked up and planted in a litter that we call *tipoye* and on which blacks had transported whites during colonialism. I found it quite ironic that the man who had come to save us found nothing better to do than be carried around in a *tipoye*. Tata was pleased and couldn't stop shaking his scepter. Many people wore robes with his likeness. The litter bearers stopped a few feet away from the platform. They helped the leader down, and he reached the platform by walking over the robes that activists had spread out on the ground: a leader was not supposed to get his feet dusty. Thousands of people then raised their voices to sing his praise.

He finally arrived at the seat that had been prepared for him, a rattan armchair with an imposing back. I wondered if this armchair had not been crafted by the basket weavers of Makana II. He stood beside the chair as he was being dressed in traditional raffia. A calabash of palm wine was held out to him, he poured a few drops to quench the thirst of ancestors, took a swig amidst applause, and finally sat down. The opening rites completed, the event could begin.

His project was simple. There were as many "all we need to do's" as with Professor P-75. Unemployment? He was going to reduce it within six months by transforming our society into a vast network of relatives, a large and typically African extended family. We would no longer need diplomas to hold government office, for as everyone knew, there were no such things as silly jobs, only silly people. These foolish people were the ones who thought that a cart pusher could not become a prime minister. To deny, for example, that a palm wine maker could become a deputy was to do wrong to these brave gatherers of the palm wine so essential to all of our ancestral ceremonies. "And so, to make our country a country that is truly administered by its people, we'll keep away those pretentious intellectuals and replace them with palm wine makers as deputies and senators. We will include peasants in the ministry of agriculture, mothers who are market vendors in the ministry of commerce, and why not, yes, why not, fetish makers in university hospitals. We must love God and the ancestors. No later than yes-

terday, our great freedom fighter Moutsompa came to me in a
dream and said: 'Tata, you're on the right track, continue the
fight, nothing can stop you on the road to the presidency.' I was
reassured. Each time I feel stuck, I disappear for a while, get on
my knees before my candle to pray, and it isn't long before God
almighty gives me the solutions in my sleep."

He paused to let the weight of his words settle in our minds.
Then he went on: "Now let's send a message of peace and brotherly love to the world."

He turned around, and I saw a white dove come out of a
skimpy little cage that had been covered with a heavy cloth up until now. He took the bird, held it up for everyone to see, and
shouted: "In the name of God and the ancestors, go forth, dove,
and carry my message of peace to the world."

He let the creature go . . . and it hit the ground with a thud.
An *oh* of disbelief came from the crowd, which had been psycho-
logically prepared to applaud the bird's flight. A bad sign for Tata,
I thought. Will they now start to doubt him after this first failure?
But he had already picked up the animal, brought it against his
chest, and was discreetly massaging its wings and feet like you
would massage an athlete's muscles before a competition. But no
one was paying attention to his hands, since all of the crowd's attention was on his mouth and his words pulling us like matter into
a cosmic black hole: "Yes, I understood the message. God and the
ancestors have refused the message of peace I have sent to the
world because they feel that this country must make the solemn
commitment of electing the man they have already chosen, the
only one who can bring peace, prosperity, and happiness to this
country. This man is—"

He didn't get a chance to finish his sentence. Like an explosion from the very depths of the heart, a single cry came from the
thousands of men and women present there, including mine of
course: "Tata, Tata, Tata Tollah!"

"So," he went on, still discreetly massaging the bird, "again, who's the one who's going to save this country and the man you'll be voting for?"

"Tata, Tata, Tata Tollah!"

The applause went on and on. He had won the battle. He took the dove in his two hands, shook it a little as if judging its weight, and when it started beating its wings, he let it go: it flew off.

The crowd went wild. I was looking at Papa. "Clever, very clever," he said to me, but I didn't understand what he meant.

"Before I go," Tata declared to the roaring mass, "we're going to ask God and the ancestors to bless our beautiful country. Let us pray silently!"

This took a few seconds, but I assure you that there was total silence. It was truly amazing to see this sea of people standing in a silence so complete that not even a baby dared break it with its cries. It might have been silent like this before the creation of the world. Slowly, still without a word, Tata Tollah raised a lit candle. Then, in the crowd, thousands of lit candles were immediately held up to the dusky sky. When had the crowd brought them, when had they been lit? Until now, I hadn't noticed anything. Then Tata began stomping on the ground with his right foot. Thousands of right feet followed. Imagine this: thousands of candles held to the dusky sky, thousands of feet stomping the ground. Slowly swelling, bursting, growing, a deafening roar arose from the depths of the earth and the earth began vibrating in its turn under our stomping. I swear to you, I felt the vibrations going up my spine and felt myself plunged into a state of indescribable bliss.

Reverberation upon reverberation, the vibration reached the mountains and the surrounding trees, and from echo to echo, amplifying still, the roar seemed to be coming from the whole universe around us. It was like the distant rolling of thunder, or the sound of a horde of stampeding elephants, or like the crashing of dozens of old trees falling at the same time, struck by lightning, or like the roaring of a mud slide crashing down the mountainside af-

ter a violent tropical storm: it was probably the response from the
ancestors. I was in a trance. I no longer knew where I was, nor
who I was if not but one particle among the bodies and souls of
this huge mass stomping on the ground around me, with me,
drowning in the dust and bathing in the candle circles of light,
now singing songs of praise to the man in the long white tunic
standing on stage, raffia cloth around his shoulders. Along with
everybody else, I felt ready to do anything I would have been
asked to do. The last vision that appeared to me was of a helicopter emerging from a cloud of dust, rising slowly to disappear in
the clouds while hundreds of people ran and jumped to try to
touch the machine in which the messiah was going up into the sky.
After all, didn't all saviors ascend into the sky? I'll tell you: if I
were of voting age, I would probably have voted for this Moses
who had come down unto us from a helicopter. A guy who could
go off, have a chat with God, and come back, could only do miracles for his country.

When this was all over, I felt as if I had not quite been myself
because I couldn't really recall what happened. It was as if I had
been in a state of intoxication. Papa, whom I had forgotten during
this massive trance, was staring at me with an amused air, as if
mocking my excitement. It was just the two of us walking home
through this crowd, which was now noisily scattering. This was
one of those moments I very much appreciated, being alone with
Papa without my brothers. It was on these occasions that he would
speak to me as he would to one of his peers. Frightened in retro-
spect by this huge crowd calling for a savior, I took his hand and
suddenly felt reassured. He squeezed my hand into his as if he had
read my mind and sensed, through our skin contact, the fragility
of a son. He stopped and looked at me. "You know, Michel, a German writer that I like very much once wrote: 'No good will come
to a people that needs a savior.' "

And we kept walking.

29

I have spoken so much about the effervescence that politics had brought to our country that you might think normal life no longer existed. Far from it.

I kept going to school. Ever since the day they decided I was a precocious child, they started making me skip grades, and so today, at fifteen, I found myself in the eleventh grade while my two brothers were still in ninth grade like everyone else. I was even told that I would be subjected to tests at the end of the first semester and, if the results were satisfactory, I would pass my baccalaureate this year instead of waiting for next year. If I got my diploma and got into the university, Papa had promised to make one of my greatest dreams come true: he would sacrifice several months' salary to buy me a multimedia PC; this would let me connect to the Internet through the university. Papa's promise and the thought of becoming an Internet user surfing at will in the universe of cyberspace had gotten me so excited that, near the end of the first semester, I had slipped from being head of the class (just once) because of a silly, careless error figuring a square root during a math exam.

I had chosen to major in the sciences, just like Papa. I had a passion for science. But science was so vast and so interesting with all its various fields that I didn't yet know which branch I would specialize in.

I liked mathematics because of Fermat and his too narrow margin, but also and mostly because of Srinivasa Ramanujan, whose biography I had read in a single night. Ramanujan was a bit like me. He was born in a small village in India near Madras, a no-name village just like ours. His story was the only one like it in the history of science. Without any formal education in mathematics, this boy who had been forced to abandon his studies in secondary school had succeeded in his short life span in discovering previously unknown theorems of numbers theory. His genius has been recognized by all mathematicians since. So you can see why this man fascinated me, and I didn't see why I, too, coming from a little no-name village in equatorial Africa, couldn't become the Ramanujan of my country and why I couldn't claim a Fields Medal before reaching forty.

I also liked physics because of Papa and because of the Nobel Prize–winning Pakistani physicist Abdus Salam. I had met him when he had presided at Papa's graduation ceremony. As a little kid poking my head between the legs of doctors and Ph.D.'s, I listened entranced, as if face to face with a character who had left the pages of a novel to come to life right before me, like in the movie *Who Framed Roger Rabbit*, where the cartoon characters played with live actors. I hope you can understand how after such an encounter I wanted to become the Abdus Salam of my country, and why not win the Nobel Prize after getting the Fields Medal?

I won't go into my passion for biology, for all the life sciences, ever since the day our botany teacher introduced us to the abundance of life in the tropical rain forest. I would not want to bore you any longer because I don't know if you're as passionate about

science as I am. But at least try to understand why it was so difficult for me to make a choice. As Maman would often say to me,
Living a life is like driving down the road: you always find yourself
at an intersection. You have to choose your path carefully if you
want to keep going. In my case, I want to keep going, I want to
make progress. So I will have to choose, sooner rather than later,
which highway of science I want to commit to.

But life wasn't all election campaigns and intersections to negotiate, it was also full of sad things that came upon you without
warning. And so, while we were waiting for the results of the first
round of the presidential vote that had been going on for five
days, we received a telegram saying that Grandfather was gravely
ill. His situation was so serious that the worst could happen at any
time.

Maman started crying as soon as she heard the news, and
when I saw her cry, I started crying too. She wanted to be near
Grandfather at once. Between our little village and Grandfather's
place, there was a 125-mile rail line, and there was usually one
train a day. If she hurried, she could catch the next train, which
was due to leave in a little more than an hour, and to be sure she
would have a seat, she would have to buy a first-class ticket. Our
village was some 30 miles from the nearest station, so we had to
hurry. Papa wouldn't be leaving until the afternoon, since he had
some important purchases to make; one had to be ready for anything in times like these. Maman had also called Uncle Boula
Boula. Uncle told us that he too would hit the road to meet us as
soon as the election results—to be announced any minute now—
were heard.

We were dropped off at the train station, well ahead of the
train, since it happened to be late as usual. If everything went according to plan during the trip—and in Africa every trip was an
adventure—our diesel locomotive would make the 125 miles in a

little less than five hours. It was no TGV, or the Japanese Shinkansen. And if the bus that was to bring us from the train station to Grandfather's village was there, it would be possible for us to be by his side before nightfall.

Luck was with us. We had just entered the dry season, which meant that there wouldn't be any rock slides or felled trees on the tracks. Since we were in first class, we had no difficulties finding two window seats facing each other, while the second-class cars were overcrowded.

In our country, train rides were always slow. In the beginning, I was entertained by the variety of the landscape that challenged the train with its steep hills, deep valleys, and long, winding turns around hostile topography. I also took note of the diverse vegetation, alternating from dense forest to wooded savanna. In the end, I dozed off, and it was in a state of semisleep that I began thinking about Grandfather and for the first time realized that he could die.

To me, until now, Grandfather was one of those things that was simply there, unchanging, eternal, without any need for explanation or justification. How could I say this? I could conceive that a star in the sky could use up its nuclear fuel and die, disappear, but how could it be that we could wake up one morning to find our great Congo River no longer there? Grandfather was for me like our great river, that inexhaustible sum of everything that existed in our primal forests. Grandfather was our source, his village was the village of our origins, his life the seed of our lives, his views and convictions the fire of our ideas and of our actions. You understand, don't you?

Come to think of it, I believe that I am what I am more because of him than because of Papa. He had been the first one to tell me when I was but eight years old that, after eating, dancing, and making love, a man should use the rest of his time to try to unravel what was behind the appearance of things, since the rambling universe wore a mask. "You must know how to read both the books of man and the book of the universe," he had told me.

Didn't my passion for science come from those words? How had I
come to know about Ushuaia, Ouagadougou, Patagonia, Andhra
Pradesh if it wasn't through an old map hung up on the wall of his
study, in which the world was a multicolor patchwork of colonial
empires? Come to think of it, I was closer to him than to Papa.
What would I do without him now?

Tears began running from my closed eyes long before I even
realized it. I wiped them with the sleeves of my shirt as I sniffled
and opened my eyes: Maman was looking at me. "Are you crying
because of Grandfather?"

"Yes."

"He isn't dead yet, you know," she attempted with a smile,
slightly forced all the same.

"I love Grandfather a lot. I don't want him to die."

"We can't do anything about death, you know that very well.
Even stars die."

"But, Maman, don't we pray to save people? Let's pray to save
Grandfather."

"Prayer isn't meant to avoid death. It is more of a consolation
for the people left behind after someone passes."

"Maman, what is death exactly?"

"Ah! That I don't know, Matapari. It depends on what you believe. When all I knew was Christian spirituality, I would have told
you that death was release from original sin and that it was only a
road to heaven. A Muslim will tell you pretty much the same
thing—that life here is fleeting, that only heaven counts and we
reach it after death. In our traditional religions, on the other hand,
death isn't a state, it is only a journey to reach the land of the ancestors. The Kongos call this land Pemba, and it is also the place
where the sun goes at night when it disappears from the sky. What
I mean is that the dead aren't ever really dead. In Buddhism, every
being dies only to be reborn in another body, which will suffer and
die in its turn to be again reborn, and so on, a cycle of the reincarnation governed by the karma from our good and bad actions. In

Judaism, death renews the ties with God which the first man, Adam, had broken. So you see, there isn't just one answer."

All of this was new to me. I didn't know that there were so many roads to spiritual salvation. On the other hand, I knew that, in physics, there were several ways to reach a certain state. Nature always chose the path of least resistance. Shouldn't it be the same for the path that leads to God, to salvation?

"Maman, after everything you've told me, what is the best path to God?"

Again she smiled that smile that was sweet and sad at the same time. "Those who think there is only one path are those who know only one path. The best way is the one with which we feel at ease, by conviction or by tradition. What is important is to respect the faith of others."

"I feel at ease in science. Can I find the path to God through that?"

She smiled at me again, her eyes filled with affection. A childish question, she must have thought. Still, she replied. "Trying to back up religion with science is a mistake. Some say that the believer needs to keep up with new scientific discoveries not only to reaffirm his faith but also to revise and update it periodically. This way, never again will people excommunicate a Galileo. I think this is a mistake, since that would be making faith a human construct. God would then only occupy the dark spaces not yet illuminated by science, and the range of his presence would keep shrinking as man's knowledge keeps growing. In this game, religion always loses, or rather, science would always win."

"But why would science always win?"

"Because we must not put religion on the same level as human reason. It will always lose and seem ridiculous. Look, religion once said that the earth and, later, the sun, were at the center of the universe; astronomy then forced it to change that position. According to the Bible, the earth and humanity are less than six thousand years old. But geology and paleontology have come up with many irrefutable proofs showing that the earth is several billion years old. Once more, religion had to give. When the theory of gravity showed that the planets did not move because they were being pushed by little invisible angels, religion had to yield once again."

She was quiet. I was still looking at her, but I had the feeling that she wasn't so much talking to me as thinking out loud.

"All the popular science books I have read up to now, at least the ones I think I understood, agree that if the conditions of conservation of energy are met, a particle could begin moving spontaneously without the need for a supreme regulator to give it that first push. I also understand that the theory of evolution clearly explains how a structure as complex as a clock could emerge from a simple structure without the need for a clockmaker."

After these words, she fell silent. I thought she was through asking herself questions, but by the twinkle in her eyes, which weren't looking at anything in particular, I didn't dare ask the question I had in mind. I did well, for she began talking again.

"No, God is omnipresent! He is within and beyond physics. So we have to place him above everything possible to humanity, above everything that human beings can comprehend. It is the only way to preserve the mystery of faith. Thus, even if we were able to make life in a test tube or to detect it on another planet or another galaxy, this would have no kind of impact on our faith."

She paused again, then went on as if to conclude: "Science and faith are not in competition; they aren't the same thing. That's why many men and women of science still feel the need for faith."

She said nothing else. I closed my eyes again and continued to think about Grandfather. I don't know why, but I felt comforted. I now felt certain that Grandfather would wait for me before he died.

Our trip went smoothly. The train didn't break down. There weren't any rock slides, and the bus that traveled the great distance between the train station and the village was waiting for us when we got there. We arrived late that afternoon, and Maman and I were immediately driven to Grandfather's.

I had not seen him in several years, and he had clearly gotten older and was weakened by the illness. He was lying in his big bed on a paspalum. What reassured me was that he wasn't in a coma; he was clearheaded. He could talk, albeit in a rather weak voice. There were lots of medicine bottles on the nightstand, but someone had also brought in many of his familiar things: his old encyclopedias, his big old catalogs, his statuettes, and his carved masks, which had always attracted and scared me at the same time, as if he wanted to say goodbye to all these things that had accompanied him all through his life.

Maman leaned over and kissed him. He spoke her name and smiled. She sat on a chair near the bed.

"Where is your husband?"

"He will arrive tonight with the other two children."

I too leaned over and kissed him. He motioned for me to come and sit by his side.

"Matapari," he said, "I had asked you to be here the day of my funeral, remember? So here you are."

"Yes, Grandfather," I said.

I remembered it perfectly like it was yesterday, though this happened quite a long time ago, when I was hardly eight years old.

"How old are you now?"

"Fifteen. No, in two months, I'll be sixteen!" I said proudly for some reason.

He paused for a moment. Maybe to catch his breath. The silence was very heavy.

"I hear you are very smart, the brightest of all my grandchildren, maybe even something of a prodigy. You are truly worthy of your ancestors."

A wave of warmth—pride, modesty, and affection—came over me. I said nothing. He was quiet again, more to gather his thoughts this time than to catch his breath.

"I was told that you helped your father when he was arrested. Is that true?"

I wasn't sure why he asked me this question. But then I knew. This was a man who had fought for freedom his whole life. He had not hesitated to give a priest an uppercut to save the separation between church and school, since this was a principle that guaranteed liberty. He had stood up to a colonial governor and even to powerful military men. And now, on his deathbed, he was still talking about freedom! Here was a man who was going to die free. Grandfather, I, like you, now make the pledge to die a free man.

"Tell me, Matapari, what did you see, what happened on the battlefield of liberty? What did you do when the soldiers, armed to the teeth and ready to wage war, came at you?"

I told him. Everything, without leaving out the kick in the butt. Every detail came back to me with surprising clarity. I could hear the gunshots; I smelled the gunpowder and the tear gas. I saw Papa being arrested, roughed up, and Maman throwing herself at the army truck. I started shaking with emotion and began to cry for I knew this story comforted him somehow. I don't know how long I went on.

When I finally fell silent, my face awash with tears, I noticed that he had managed to lift his hand and place it on my knee. His face was calm, beaming with a happy serenity I had not expected. "Don't you cry, Matapari. You know life is lots of little gray clouds in a great blue sky."

His hand left my knee to fall back on the mattress, and he closed his eyes. Alarmed, Maman quickly got up to lean over him. No, Grandfather wasn't dead, he was breathing peacefully.

30

Papa and my two brothers arrived a few hours after we did, at night. They must have driven very fast despite the state of our roads, which often looked more like an obstacle course than a state route. Their clothes and their hair were covered with that irritating red dust characteristic of lateritic soil in dry season. They must have been exhausted.

We went to meet them. When I saw my two brothers getting out of the car, I ran toward them, and the three of us embraced, overcome, as if it had been aeons since we left each other. I know, I have told you so many things about them that you must think that I didn't love them and that they have always passively submitted themselves to my rule; but today, before my dying grandfather, I admit that I have hidden from you those times when it was I who yielded to them. The most humiliating case for me was the day they ridiculed me in front of the bathroom.

Our bathroom was a hole in the ground twenty yards from the house, its frame consisting of geometrically questionable steel and protected from the sun and the rain by a roof made of palm leaves.

We periodically sprinkled it with cresol to kill the unwanted odors that often came out of it. One day, while I was squatting atop the hole in dire need (diarrhea), I felt something on my thigh. When I looked, I saw a big cockroach with its ash gray back slowly creeping up my body. I screamed in horror and tried to flee from the hole. In my haste, I had forgotten to pull up my pants, which were still around my ankles, so my feet got caught in them and I fell out of the shelter. Just as I was about to get up to pull my pants back on (and thank heaven that nobody witnessed what had just happened), guess who showed up? Banzouzi, laughing and calling for Batsimba. And then the two of them were just standing there, cracking up, bent in two. There I was on the ground, butt naked, pants dirty and wet. I finally managed to get up. I started yelling at them in a voice intended to be threatening: "Get lost now, you don't want to mess with me!" But the voice they heard was trembling with anger, indignation, and shame all at once, and that's when they really started laughing their heads off. They practically had tears in their eyes. I made as if I was about to go after them, hoping that would make them go away. I was wrong, because Banzouzi gave me a nasty kick instead. I realized that if I didn't watch it, they might beat the crap out of me, so . . . I made tracks, their insolent laughter trailing my getaway. Since that incident, I was kind of careful not to provoke them too much.

We stopped hugging to follow Papa, who, as soon as he got out of the car, had hurried to Grandfather's bedside. I kissed him on his sweat-drenched forehead.

Grandfather opened his eyes, recognized his son, and a smile lit up his ailing face. "Finally, you're here," he said. "It is you I was waiting for. Now I can go."

The twins approached too.

"Banzouzi and Batsimba. How you have grown! Thank you for coming."

We were then all asked to leave, so as not to tire Grandfather out. Only Papa stayed with him.

Uncle Boula Boula arrived early the next morning. We were all surprised when we noticed a Japanese SUV driving down the little hill that led to the village because we weren't expecting anyone else. It was only when the car stopped and the dust settled that I recalled that Uncle Boula Boula had promised to join us here after the election results were announced. The announcement must have been made. I think I told you that he had created a political party called IPUFIL, in which he had enlisted all of us, except Papa, from the get-go. Uncle always told me that, even in politics, one had to count on his family first and then on his tribe, which was nothing more than an extended family. He believed he was prominent enough to run for president. I don't suppose he had any illusions about going against Tata Tollah and Professor P-75. I think his objective was to get enough of the vote so he could negotiate with the winner of the second round, and thus find a future political career for himself. Good old Uncle, he always knew how to bounce back.

But the real surprise for me was the passenger next to Uncle Boula Boula, who was none other than Auntie Lolo. As we would later learn from Uncle Boula Boula, when she heard about Grandfather being in critical condition, she did not waste a second before she went to see Uncle to ask, to beg him, to bring her with him to help "one of my best friends and a family to which I always felt close." Despite the grudge he had against her—he considered her a coward and an opportunist ever since his trial because she had abandoned him on the very day of his arrest—he ended up saying yes. This was why they were together in this SUV that had stopped in front of the house.

After the many fond embraces with Papa, Maman, and the other members of the family, she saw me as they were heading toward Grandfather's bedside. She came to me and took me in her arms. "Matapari, how you have grown! Be brave," she concluded, as she went on to join the others.

Auntie Lolo! The woman of my childhood, my glamour girl,

the one I had long considered the most beautiful woman in the world. How many times had I dreamt of her before falling for Aledia?

But, sad to say, this was no longer the same Auntie Lolo. She had lost her looks prematurely because the skin-lightening products—products with hormones smuggled from pharmacies, alkaline soaps with mercury salts imported from Nigeria or Zaire, peeling creams—had ravaged her face. Black blotches stained her thin, yellowish skin, so thin that you could see blue veins through it. Strange acne pimples burgeoned on her pigmentless face, and, more strangely, a few black hairs grew on her chin. It didn't make me love her any less. She was a woman with a heart of gold. Contrary to what Uncle thought, she was no flake. Here was the proof she hadn't forgotten us, from the time she used to give us candy and let us drink Coca-Cola for free out of old Bidié's store up to this day. And now, in a spontaneous gesture, she had dropped everything to come help us when she heard of our misfortune.

While my brothers were devouring the manga comic books they had brought along with them, the trip, the wake, the anxiety, everything suddenly made me feel faint. I lay down on a mat, right on the ground underneath the veranda. I must have slept for a long time, because when I woke up it was nearly five in the afternoon and the sun was getting ready to plunge into the other side of the earth. Papa and Uncle were sitting next to each other and were talking politics, as if they wanted to release some of the tension hanging over us because of Grandfather's condition. They must have started their discussion some time ago, because as soon as I started listening to them, Papa began to nag Uncle: "Can't be true! You got 0.1 percent of the vote? You mean to tell me that you got about thousand votes out of a million?"

"Yeah. The people are ungrateful. I sincerely thought I would get more after all I've done for democracy in this country."

"Incredible, Boula Boula! You managed to convince a thousand bozos to vote for you? Honestly, you really amaze me."

Uncle got up, annoyed.

"Don't get upset, Boula Boula," said Papa, "you're not the first or last fellow to put on a campaign suit. Tell me, out of the two super candidates left, who are you going to support? Will it be the super Professor or the new Moses?"

"If I knew, I would have done it already. I'm waiting to see how things evolve, and then I'll support the one with the best chance to win."

"Good old Boula Boula, neither faith nor principles! You'll never change."

"But you're the naïve one. When someone like me knows he has the makings of a cabinet minister, he's got to help fate along by giving himself a little push. What about you, who have you voted for?"

"Most certainly not for you!"

"It's people like you that are killing this country. You have no family spirit. Do you know that each one of the candidates got all the votes from the members of his tribe? But you, you can't even vote for your own brother-in-law. Anyway, I know who you're going to vote for in the second round. I'm sure it will be for Professor P-75. Men of science unite, right?"

"Ha." Papa laughed. "The man who promised to invent the machine that will detect the adulteresses to prevent AIDS? For once, leave the women out of this. I will vote for him when he's invented a machine that will detect cuckolds instead, because, believe me, there are as many cuckolds as there are adulteresses."

"Stop playing with me. So you're going to vote for Tata then?"

"Both of them are all talk. Our country needs only a man who is normal, honest, a good manager and a good citizen, and whom the nation could hold accountable, that's all. Not a genius, not a superman. Right now, one candidate fetishizes science and the other one wants to turn fetishism into state science. Obviously, it worked for both of them. Our poor country!"

"Let's wait and see who wins. In any case, the atmosphere was tense when I left the capital. The voters were aligning themselves by tribe, and the two candidates have hyped their partisans with all their heated debates so much that any spark could set the capital or even the whole country ablaze. But then these are the growing pains of democracy, right?"

"This isn't the democracy we fought and went to prison for," said Papa sadly. "We didn't call for change so we could have politicians like you, Boula Boula."

Uncle did not react to this last remark, and both of them fell silent, as if realizing that this occasion wasn't really appropriate for a prolonged political discussion. Papa rose from his chair and said to me: "Michel, go to Grandfather and tell Maman that I'm going to take over her shift now. I'm going to relieve myself first."

He headed for the back of the house. I got up and went to the room where Grandfather lay. Maman was with Auntie Lolo. Indeed, Papa felt that the presence of too many people would tire Grandfather and that at most only two people at a time should be with him. I informed Maman that Papa would be here in a few minutes. She thanked me and left with Auntie Lolo, leaving me to wait for Papa.

31

I was alone with Grandfather. I watched him sleep for a long time and then let my eyes wander around the room. The first thing I noticed was his glasses, resting on one of his huge and dusty encyclopedias, as if he had just put them down after his usual reading. I thought about what these works meant to this old teacher. For him they were masterpieces holding the sum of human knowledge of his age. He who had wanted so much to understand our universe, which, he would say, often went wearing a mask. Suddenly I realized that I, a fifteen-year-old boy, knew of things that Grandfather and his encyclopedias didn't: the answer to Fermat's last theorem, cybernetics, the existence of planets orbiting around stars other than the sun, genetic engineering . . . And I also understood that in a few years, when I too became an old man on my deathbed, another fifteen-year-old boy, my grandson perhaps, would be sitting there, at the very same place I was sitting now, a boy who would know things that neither I nor my CD-ROM encyclopedias could have dreamed of. The highway of human knowledge goes on and on. In fact, wasn't it Grandfather himself who had told me: "Learn, keep learning what the wise men know"?

Then I saw the statuettes and the carved masks. It's strange. I had the impression that these objects were looking back at me and were watching over Grandfather just as I was. There was one I liked right away: a seated woman, bonnet on her head, a cowrie necklace with a leopard tooth around her neck, bracelets around wrists and ankles. Her naked wooden body bore tribal scars on the chest, where her two breasts stood erect; there was a child feeding from one of them. The other statuette, in contrast, was strange, and it had frightened me ever since I first saw it when I was still eight years old: it was spiked with nails all over except for the middle of the stomach, where there was a mirror; its fist was raised in the air, clutching a knife. The rest of the body was covered with pigments and occasional cowries, pearls, and claws (or long teeth, I couldn't be sure) from felines. The open mouth made it look even more terrifying. But since on this occassion I felt myself under Grandfather's protection, I decided to no longer be afraid: I took courage, reached out, and grabbed it.

At that very instant, Grandfather let out a sigh as if I had touched him when I touched the statuette. I was startled and turned to him. His eyes were open, and he was looking at me. "The first statuette symbolizes the ancestors. It is a representation of the basic idea of the founding ancestors, of the origins and perpetuation of the clan. You see, this is the fertile first woman, and the child she is carrying is our clan. And this child is also you, Matapari, feeding from our life source."

It was so painful for him to speak. I saw that he was suffering, and I also felt that he was trying to tell me a few essential things about our origins that I did not know. After catching his breath, he went on. "You see that oval box? Open it . . . Inside there's a red powder we call tukula. It is extracted from a plant, but it can also be made from ocher powder mixed with palm oil . . . Touch it . . . put some on your forehead . . . there, that's good . . . now put some on mine . . . there . . . thank you. When I was a child, we used this powder in all of our ceremonies; it offered protection against evil spirits."

He looked at the red stain on my forehead and I looked at his. "Matapari, both of us are protected now . . ."

He fell silent. His breathing became heavier and heavier. I wanted Papa to come, but I also wanted to be alone with Grandfather a while longer because deep inside of my being I felt that an intimate, powerful secret bond now linked us. I knew that he knew he would leave us forever, and so it meant a lot to him that his favorite grandchild learn these essential things about our origins from his very own mouth. I had leaned toward him so that I wouldn't miss anything he said, and now he managed to put his hand on my shoulder. The red tukula powder, applied by my two fingers, formed two parallel lines on my forehead.

He resumed speaking, with difficulty still. "The figure with the nails that you just touched isn't meant for passive protection. No. People call them fetishes, but that's not right. Our parents never worshipped them, they never attributed beneficial powers to them. They are *nkondi*, neutral figurines, which, once charged with a magical substance we call *nkissi*—this can be blood, nails, pulp, hair—the *nkondi* then becomes a *nkissi nkondi*; only then does it become an object that can do things . . . The mirror in the middle of her stomach enables her to see all, to foresee everything . . . Take it, she's yours."

His hand went from my shoulder to the nape of my lowered neck. "This *nkissi nkondi* will hunt down your enemies both in heaven and in hell, both in the living world and in the world beyond. Take it, Matapari, I'm passing it down to you."

He fell silent. His hand fell back on the sheet. I raised my head and quickly grabbed the spiked figure with both hands. Grandfather began panting loudly.

"Papa," I cried.

In the blink of an eye, they were all here—Papa, Maman, Uncle Boula Boula, Auntie Lolo, my twin brothers, everyone. Papa stopped short when he saw the red tukula on Grandfather's forehead and on mine, but he said nothing. For a brief moment, I thought about my birthday, when an entire delegation had gathered around my crib to verify the reality of my birth. We were all here, helpless, looking at Grandfather struggling to breathe. Papa held his hand as if to let him know that we hadn't abandoned him in his agony. After a while his short breaths seemed to stop, and then with wide open eyes trying to take in all of us at once, he heaved his chest a little and said: "Thank you . . . thank you."

Then he fell back on the mattress. He was no longer breathing.

"It's over," Papa said, closing Grandfather's eyes.

At once, everyone started crying. The women cried out, shouting in pain. Silent tears rolled down Papa's cheeks, while Uncle Boula Boula fixed the covers. I saw Maman quickly make the sign of the cross over herself. In this moment of deep pain, she had instinctively returned to the gestures of her primitive faith, the faith in which she had been raised and baptized. But then didn't she tell me that the best way was the one with which we felt most comfortable, whether by culture or tradition?

As for me, I was still sitting, my forehead red with tukula like Grandfather's, the *nkissi nkondi* in my hands. I was floating in a world of fog and haze, through which I could hear the cries and lamentations. Then a ball rose from deep within my stomach and exploded as it reached my eyes in an unstoppable flood of tears, and hiccups too. I could no longer stand being in this room, before this bed where Grandfather lay without moving. I fled outside.

32

I ran, still hiccuping with tears; then I slowed to a walk. The sun had just plunged into the other side of the planet, abandoning the scraps of dark clouds in the red-orange sky, scraps floating like the loose remnants of a sunken ship. I sat against a palm tree, the *nkissi nkondi* on my knees, watching the night spread the veil of its empire as the day died, just as my grandfather and the sun were leaving for the land of the ancestors. It happened during this moment of transition between the end of day and the beginning of night, when things thicken with mystery and aren't quite what they are, this moment when we see solid mountains move like clouds and when a breeze blows through the grass and the blades shiver like breath caressing the things of this world in a final farewell.

I lay on my back against the ground, on the grass under my palm tree, and I closed my eyes still misty from tears that had mourned Grandfather. How long was I there? Can't say. I can only tell you that I woke up under a sky that was exceptionally clear for the season. I could see there in the west, past the moon, bright

Venus going to bed as well, and right above her, a weak, luminous point, the planet Saturn. Right above my head, next to Sirius, the brightest star in the sky, I saw the glorious design of Orion. It wasn't easy, but right underneath the trio of stars that formed his belt I was able to find Orion's Great Nebula, which I had only seen in the beautiful pictures taken from the telescope at the Pic du Midi Observatory in France.

I knew the stars quite well—their origin, their lives, their demise—and I knew that Orion's Great Nebula was a veritable caldron of hydrogen molecules and dust out of which stars were born. In their relatively cold areas, these clouds of dust and very dense gases that made up the nebulas could collapse upon themselves under the force of their own gravity and form extremely dense, egg-shaped gaseous globules. Those eggs, made denser and denser and thus hotter and hotter by the pressure of the overheating gases around them, will end up starting thermonuclear reactions that will make them hatch into stars.

In the latest edition of Papa's *Sky & Telescope*, I saw a spectacular image of these star nurseries taken by the Hubble Space Telescope: huge columns of brown phantomlike dust, floating seven thousand light-years away from Earth, inside which we could see these eggs, these star embryos, as well as already hatched stars, searing and massive, shining happily.

I closed my eyes under my tree, snuggling on my little planet Earth, and I felt like I was carried away once more into this misty, drifting world. I was the Crab Nebula, I was the Dentelle Nebula. My body was light as a veil of diaphanous plasma playing on interstellar space winds, my spirit blown into a thousand psychedelic visions, and then I found myself in the middle of a star nursery, and then in the middle of a cataclysmic explosion of supernovas bright like ten thousand suns. I was a part of the dance of the universe, part of the great twirling spiral of cosmic energy.

In the evolution of the universe, the explosion of a supernova means the end of a star's life, but its debris spreads to sow stellar life elsewhere. And I was like this debris, this shock wave cruising at twelve thousand miles per second, scattering synthesized matter into the cosmic bosom: the carbon of diamonds and pencils, the iron of my *nkissi nkondi*'s nails and my red blood, the gold of our jewelry and the calcium of our bones, the nitrogen in our urine and the phosphorus in our muscles; because, just as we are men and women, we are all star dust. All of us, inasmuch as we exist: Maman, Papa, my two twin brothers, Uncle Boula Boula, Auntie Lolo, and Grandfather. Just as I too, a tiny being lying under a palm tree, crying over his grandfather on a little blue planet lost in the immensity of the universe. Because little boys come from stars too.

Brazzaville–Ouagadougou–Dolisie, 1993–1996